Prologue...

"**Is** it finished?"

"Look Manny, I told you last night, the software is sound and the app is ready... but there is this line of code that I can't delete. I don't know what it does and dude, if this glitches, I think you get that all of our butts are on the line!"

"Our butts are on the line now! Get it set up and ready for upload to the corporate server. I'll make the call."

"Manny..."

"Dude! Get it done! Do you not get what this thing does and will do to US if we don't give them what they want and right now? They have technical specialists on payroll who can delete the code, they gave us a deadline man... and I mean DEAD LINE, you get me?"

"This is people's minds and lives we're talking about man..."

"Not my problem."

"Manny dude that's cold..."

"NOT my freaking problem, man... now load it up, I'm dialing now. And if you feel bad about this, pray to whatever God you worship these days cause with this kind of tech out there, all hell is literally about to break loose."

"Dude... not your problem? This is everybody's problem. I can't..."

"You will. Look behind you. See this gun I got trained on you? It's you or me, man; if you're having an attack of conscience that's not my problem either."

"Aw hell! Our Father, who art in heaven..."

"Dude, are you really praying? Seriously? Never mind just load it up!"

"It's loading now! Hallowed... uh, holy... uh... well, I don't remember the rest but please, if you're out there and you hear me; deliver us from evil. Please God. Amen. Dude, it's loaded."

"Making the call. And get ahold of some serious sunblock man... cause hell's about to come to earth - literally. And there ain't nothing that we can do to stop it."

Chapter One

"**Do** you believe in mind control Ms. Baltimore?"

"Pardon?"

"Mind control; not like the weird, religious sycophant people that sell flowers in the airport or anything – that's brain washing I think. But the real spooky CIA, FBI, you know, government kind of mind control."

I'm not sure what I was more relieved for at this moment; that Mandy isn't facing me so that she can see my mouth hanging open, or that she continued to speak as if she really didn't expect an answer. Which was a good thing, especially since I didn't actually have one.

"This new program that my folks have Anabella enrolled in is why I asked. It's just plain creepy."

"What do you find creepy about it Mandy? Anabella's been showing drastic improvements in both comprehension and rote learning skills. I'm delighted and really surprised about the progress she's making according to her teachers. You don't think the new program is helping?"

Anabella Same, a 13-year-old autistic patient that I'm currently treating under court order was a fairly remarkable child. Though learning disabled from birth, Anabella had a very sweet and endearing personality – something one can't describe with words such as a "twinkle in her eye" or some other trite saying. Her charm went deeper than physical description. She somehow managed to package joy and effervescence into a smile that she freely delivered to all she came into contact with. She stood no taller than 5 feet with a solid build. Not chubby exactly, but a healthy kid that would never be considered small or slender. Her white blond curls were pretty but not remarkable and her light brown eyes were standard for what brown eyes were supposed to be.

Honestly? It was her smile. The child could walk into my office and no matter what went on that day prior to her visit, I always felt lighter… freer, more able to do whatever I needed to get done after her departure.

Secretly one of my favorite patients, Anabella was also my motivation for staying in my field as a Licensed Clinical Social Worker. So naturally, it was disturbing to hear that Mandy felt something untoward was going on where Anabella is concerned.

"It's just weird you know? Like, these people from that company that are supposed to be studying her – they gave mom some kind of software program- it has an app for her smart phone even. Mom can actually select something that says, "Reset" on her phone that will make Anabella drowsy and put her to sleep if she gets upset or has an episode. Isn't THAT kinda… you know… creepy?"

Remembering to close my mouth this time just in case Mandy decided to change her pose, which has her lying on the couch against the wall on my right and facing the door, I also tried to exhale quietly.

My practice was a small one. I only worked with a few guardian ad-litem's and provided services for three small companies (including state and city government organizations that have employee assistance programs). Thus my office, a small little nook over The Temple Banquet Center in downtown Alton, IL, really wasn't much to look at. Four walls and a desk, a couch, table and a chair; it was the size of a small bedroom really with a master bathroom (which was kind of a bonus).

I felt the small office shrinking and getting tinier. The walls were closing in on me. I closed my eyes, took a breath and counted. *Remember to breathe and count.* Because there was no such thing as an app for a smart phone that could do such a thing. Right? Nope... *Breathe... count...*

"My folks love this thing so much that they are trying to get me into it. Against my will mind you! How messed up is THAT?"

Breathe...

"Mandy, while you are still a minor in the care of your parents, at 16 you're pretty smart. You're also extremely centered for your age group. Why would your parents do that if you don't need it?"

No response. Hmmm. I tried a different approach.

"You're a good kid. Occasionally you're a goof, but I don't hold that against you." I grinned then continued. "Seriously though, I find it hard to believe that your parents would want to put you in a program for behavior modification. Is there something that I should know? Has something happened for your parents to believe that such a program would be necessary for you?"

While I couldn't see Mandy's face, I could see her hands. They were clasped in a dovetail behind her head and were so tense that her knuckles were turning white. Seconds tick by and after a full minute, I was ready to do away with this disturbing line of question.

"I..."

BUZZZZZZZZZ.

That was my mini alarm clock. I reached over and picked it up to turn off the end of session indicator and placed it back on my desk.

"Let's save it for the next session kiddo. I have to wrap things up a little early today and get home to my gremlin. You know how she gets when it's movie, popcorn and peanut butter night."

Mandy hadn't moved and her knuckles were still white. So I paused. I was almost afraid to hear what she wanted to say, but then again, that's what I was here for right? To provide court-mandated counseling to her and Anabella? To monitor and assess the backlash of the abuse that they'd suffered? For the first time ever where Mandy was concerned, I found it hard to do my job. And I really didn't know why that was– which terrified me.

"Yeah. It's movie, popcorn and peanut butter night... yay."

I think it was the flat, toneless way that she'd said it, but a chill raced up my spine. This really wasn't like her. Today she seemed off, as in *way* off.

I made a mental note to contact her parents as I closed my small laptop so we could walk out together.

Mandy ab-curled up and reached for her book bag on the floor. She still didn't face me, just took what looked like carefully moderated steps to the door.

Now this wasn't Mandy... at all. She wasn't the "happy-happy-joy-joy" kind of person that Anabella was, but she had opened up for me remarkably over the last 2 months of counseling. In that time, I'd never seen her move that way.

Watching her, the chill that raced up my spine got even colder.

Her hand on the doorknob, I couldn't let her go – these kids meant too much to me, more than they should to someone in my profession. It was dangerous to develop that kind of connection with a client. But these were kids. I couldn't let her leave like this.

"Mandy, you don't have to go kiddo... whatever it is, you can tell me. It won't leave this office."

Mandy's shoulders dropped, otherwise she didn't move. It seemed like an hour passed with her standing there so still, but it was actually only a couple of minutes. I'd just reached over to turn off my little desk lamp when she exploded into action. She turned and in 4 quick strides reached my desk while digging into her bag.

A journal dropped onto my desk with a loud thunk – so loud in the quiet room that yes, I actually jumped in surprise. It looked to be a 5 x 8 sized journal with a bright and reflective cover - a rainbow of colors and patterns that reflected and moved with the light filtering through the blinds. I looked up, eyes wide and mouth gaped.

"Mandy…"

"Read it. I need you to read it and believe it. And then you'll want to hear the rest of what I have to say. Remember that day when we talked about The Matrix? If you read this for me, I can show you how deep the rabbit hole goes."

Mandy had always been good at dramatic exits. Swinging her bag over her shoulder along with her blondish brown streaked ponytail, she bounced out of my front door before I could respond. She gave me no time to say," thank you," or the more likely response, "please no rabbit holes for me, thanks anyway."

Exhaling and shaking my head I reached for the journal. My fingers, as if under their own control, curled into themselves until my right fist hovered over it - as if in protest.

My life wasn't the best life and it wasn't the worst … it was just a life. I went to work (as a Hospice Social Worker), I had my own small practice as a side gig, and then I went home to my eleven-year-old dynamo – my world, Samantha. I didn't ask for much. I didn't want much. I went to church, obeyed traffic laws and I paid my taxes.

Despite the drama that I could do without from a manipulative ex-husband, one that needed to flaunt his latest (and not so greatest pick of the week every once in a while) my life was pretty much just the way I liked it. I was comfortable. Content, even.

But right at this moment: I knew; my *hand* knew, that the second I picked up that book, whatever it was and whatever it related to – It was going to completely and utterly flip my world on its ear. And I was *SO* not okay with that.

At least, that is what the little man says in my head – my little editor guy. He's the guy that stood at the printing press of my brain right before words came out of my mouth. I pictured him wearing a little visor cap and smoking on a huge cigar. He was a crusty, short, balding miniature guy with piercing eyes.

His job was simple; keep the "stupid" that inhabited my brain from flowing freely out of my mouth. Occasionally he kept my mouth as well as my body from embracing anything that could serve as a channel of stupidity; thus my hand automatically recoiling and my hesitation.

On the other hand, there was something deeper. Something that pushed me to do what I didn't want to do. I really didn't want to yield to that "something" (or more to the point, SOMEONE) right now. But He urged me to do what I was meant to do, even when everything in me – including the little editor- squealed in protest.

I finally deep sighed in acceptance as the little editor jumped up and down in aggravation. He'd attempted to stomp out that deeper urge apparently. Too bad he'd failed.

Buck up Girly! No more hesitating.

I groaned through gritted teeth and did what I should have done the moment she'd dropped it on my desk. I picked up the book, silently cursing every rabbit and their stinking rabbit holes in existence: from thumper and bugs bunny to the little chronically late, rude one that misled sweet little girls into making foolish decisions.

I've always been too curious to leave the rabbit hole alone. Silly me. Next time, I should *kill the wabbit* and ignore the stupid hole.

Because Alice, with her incessant curiosity, really wasn't the best role model was she?

I glanced at my desk clock and remembered exactly why that rabbit guy had been so rude... I was late *again*.

Oy!

It wasn't a normal thing for me to be clumsy.

That said, there must have been some type of curse or evil juju that haunted me, always when I was in a rush. It's normal for me to drop my keys once or twice as I fiddled with my difficult-to-lock office door.

But knocking my office phone off of the desk (mental note: I really need to replace that thing, it had a rotary dial for goodness sakes) and then the lamp?

Yeah, that was just TOO much. And who could leave the broken pieces of said lamp just SCATTERED all over the place without cleaning it up? *Not m*e, that's who!

So I'd lost another 15 minutes of my time there, which put my commute home (a mere 10 minutes away) at a near 20-minute drive due to school buses and rush hour. What was the point of moving to Alton, IL to get AWAY from the stinky annoyance that is driving in rush hour only to have to deal with small town street-to-street versions of the same thing?

It was like I exchanged crazy truck drivers and their smaller cohorts (crazy SUV drivers) with school buses and senior commuters that had NOTHING better to do than make my life miserable by being on the road when I was, impeding my progress!

Because it's all about you Celine. The world revolves around you, right?

I growled as my mother's voice echoed in my ears. Shaking my head to dislodge that little bit of craziness (since my mom was FAR from dead so I didn't know WHAT that was about) I jogged-slash-ran full tilt for my car.

Well, maybe I did – know what that was about I mean. It had been my mother's litany to me constantly when I was growing up. However, to me, her sarcasm was unfounded; because it *WAS* all about me dadnabbit!! As it rightfully should have been: in my own little world where rabbit holes didn't exist and rush hour traffic bent helplessly to my will. *MUA-HA-HAAAA!*

I snickered and pulled out my keys.

And there they go falling… again.

Gravity, thou art a heartless wench!

Swooping up the keys at mach ten speed, I unlocked the car door and scrambled inside. I threw my jacket, purse and laptop bag across the seat, hitting the passenger door of my adorable Honda Fit hatch-back. It didn't really help me move any faster but I definitely felt better.

Until my stupid cell rang. Because now I had to find the thing.

Reaching over to where my purse had fallen in protest of my rough treatment, I swiftly unsnapped the front pocket and dug out my ringing and vibrating phone.

"Celine Baltimore," I answered.

Hmmm… dead silence.

Great, a hang up call with an unidentified number – something else I didn't have time for. Ending the call in disgust, I tossed my phone into the empty slot in my dash and started the car, checked my mirrors then pulled out of my spot.

I hated being late. So my irritation just kept on growing, despite my attempt to calm the heck down. It was more than obvious that I needed to get home STAT to my popcorn and peanut butter before I killed someone in traffic or worse, got a speeding ticket.

I snickered again at that thought. My priorities definitely needed reshaping; at least, that's what Maggie would say.

Maggie is my older sister by a year. My parents weren't satisfied with the awesomeness that was their first born according to my dear sister, thus the beauty and sheer awesomeness that is the both of us – born on the same day exactly one year apart. How often did THAT happen?

What's stranger is that we were absolutely nothing alike but totally got along. Just like peanut butter and popcorn. Heh.

A treat Maggie hated, by the way. Of course I had to tease her about it every single time we talked. Who knows? She may be pleasantly surprised, right?

Her response?

"Ewww," (gasp and shudder), and then, *"the look"*.

I hate the look. She'd inherited it from our Mom and it always managed to stop me in my tracks. I've tried it a few times on Sammie myself. Usually when she'd get an attitude in the grocery store or wouldn't go to bed (and boy did my kid hate going to bed).

But Sammie would just purse her lips... then laugh... hard.

Weirdo.

Apparently my mom and sister's look incited fear. Mine incited the kind of humor that made kids pee their pants laughing. Oh the hilarity.

It's my fault though, really. I learned to be goofy for my patients so that they could enjoy our sessions; which definitely had its drawbacks.

Anyway, as I was saying, Mags and I are exact opposites. While she was petite but shapely, a brunette with warm brown eyes that took completely after our mom; I'm a tall (far from willowy) strawberry-blond Amazon with blue eyes and a strong jaw. I looked exactly how our dad would look if he were slightly more feminine... and wore a wig.

Maggie's husband Max calls us "the book ends that make no sense." I guess that's because, while we always hang out and consider each other best friends, we have absolutely NOTHING in common except our parents and a weird fascination for slapstick comedy.

Most people loved to laugh, but Mags and I, we *excelled* at it. If any humor can be found in a situation, we would find it. Heck, even if humor COULDN'T be found, we'd still find something to laugh at.

Okay, and believe me... this is a totally true story: It had happened again, just last year when we'd attended old Mr. Bellamy's funeral. He was our parent's neighbor in Chesterfield Valley. For as long as we could remember, Mr. Bellamy had been the crustiest and crabbiest old man there ever was.

And laid out in his casket of butter cream silk interior with an external mahogany finish, he looked like he always had in life – disapproving and constipated. As we'd paid our respects and walked past the casket, Mags stage whispered the words, "Butter cream baby... *Butter cream.*"

Her head had been down but her shoulders were shaking so bad she nearly lost her balance... twice! It was obvious that she'd tried her hardest to control her inappropriate burst of humor (not really).

What was more unfortunate? The fact that I knew exactly what she'd been referring to.

Mags had quoted a line from one of our favorite movies of all time, *Rush Hour 2.* It was the scene where Chris Tucker and Jackie Chan were shopping for something to wear to a casino opening. The Versace sales guy (played by Jeremy Piven - an actor I absolutely *adore*) in an effeminate fashion tells Chris Tucker that he wants to slap a dead animal on him. Specifically crock skin – brown – to go with a butter cream shirt.

Of course it was the WAY he'd chanted, "butter cream, butter cream," hand-shaping Chris Tucker's body in the process... *butter cream, butter cream* – it was frikken hilarious!

I guess you had to be there.

Like I said, it was unfortunate that I knew all of this. Why? Because the movie reel had started rolling in my mind's eye, repeatedly.

Only, it wasn't Chris Tucker standing in front of Jeremy this time around, but Old Mr. Bellamy. With his lips pursed in half disapproval/half snarl and his little gnarled hands slapping away at Jeremy's attempts to dress him in crock skin and – dare I say it again - *butter cream*.

Suffice it to say that, when we'd arrived at the pew to pay our respects to the family members in passing, tears had been streaming down my cheeks with my jaws clenched tight, the effort to hold in the guffaws both painful and obvious to anyone who knew me. My little editor is still teed off at Mags for that one.

What was fortunate (not really) was the fact that my tears of hysterical laughter were mistaken for actual tears of sadness by the family, which *would* have been appropriate. The family was genuinely moved by my display of heartfelt grief. So moved in fact; that I'd been invited to their home after the funeral to speak on how knowing Mr. Bellamy had sincerely touched my life.

To this day I tried to remember what my gigantic goofy streak cost me that night. It fueled my effort to assist my little editor as much as I could. One way I help him do his job is I keep us both away from Mags at any event where outbursts of laughter would be frowned upon.

What can I say? It's still a work in progress. It's kind of difficult to do that when the person you are attempting to avoid happens to be your best friend in the world.

And your sister. See what I mean?

The blowing horn (of an impatient scooter pilot no less) snatched my wandering mind back into the present and OY!

I found myself gripping my steering wheel with such force I heard the leather squeak. Navigating through the traffic in Downtown Alton wouldn't be such a problem if it weren't for the cobble stones... and the multiple stop signs... and the really slow drivers.

And it wasn't just me! It's not like I hated driving or anything.

Well, I did actually. But that was any human on the planet! It was something about rush hour that made all of the alarms in my head blare constantly. I dealt with those alarms in the only way I knew – prayer. And just a little bit of profanity. But I only THOUGHT it... See? Self control AND an iron will (heh).

But really, today I had no time to invest in the several minutes of worry that resulted in my mantra of self-control... which *then* lapses into prayer... followed by mild curses (in my head – not really) as I got through my first hurdle of back street traffic.

No time, no time, no time.

And there goes that stupid little white rabbit popping into my head again... bringing to mind thoughts of Ana's journal.

Which I forgot...

I shook my head at myself and tried not to take my frustration out on the sweet, elderly flock of nuns crossing the street. Really Nuns? Right now???

It had been the stupid lamps fault anyway! At least, that's what I told myself as I lost it and blew my horn at the pedestrian trying to walk against a "no walk sign". After I'd been so patient with the Nuns, even! What was this, New York?

Squawking through the light I made yet another mental note to stop by Target tomorrow and buy a new lamp. And then I resolved to worry about all that other junk later, including the journal, it's white rabbit and his stupid hole, instead, I focused on getting home.

And the fact that I stopped praying to focus may or *may not* have resulted in my screaming at the driver of the Jeep in front of me that was driving at Fred Flinstone's pace...

Move it along! Crazy Hippy! Who Tie-Dye's their Jeep anyway?

Chapter Two

"**Hey** Ms. Baltimore."

"Hey Brittany, how'd Sammie do today?"

"She did good. Her homework is on the kitchen table for you to look over. Oh, the popcorn is popped and on the kitchen counter. And as usual her room is still a total mess."

I tried not to frown as I hung my jacket on the coat rack near the front door. And I tried not to stomp as I rounded the corner into my spacious, recently re-decorated foyer.

The fact that she had her feet up on my newly purchased Victorian settee while texting and listening to headphones didn't bother me as much as the fact that her crud covered tennis shoes and book bag were strewn out on my beautiful Aubusson rug, which was kicked up, creased over and askew - again.

I wondered if taking the money for my monthly carpet-cleaning bill out of her paycheck would be considered a bit extreme. I wasn't a big interior design fanatic, but when I did something as lofty as redecorate my old restored Victorian home, I kind of went all out.

Going all out meant I hired someone because interior design just wasn't my forte. Cleaning and organization however was exactly my forte.

Which is probably why the shoes and book bag really bothered me. Not their crustiness per se, but their placement. It was all just lying there, in the middle of my rug and taunting me with an IN YOUR FACE attitude that inanimate objects should *not* have.

Ah, the little editor is on his job. Instead of verbalizing any of the madness swirling through my brain attempting to land on the tip of my tongue, desperate to be spoken, I said...

"Alrighty then. I guess you must be about to head out since you're hanging out in here. In the foyer. Do you need me to grab anything for you while you put your shoes on and uh... gather up those papers hanging out of your bag?"

I wasn't sure if she was smirking at me or if that was just her "thinking" face.

It had better be her thinking face.

"Yep, I just texted Jeff so he's on his way to pick me up. I gathered everything up already and just need to put on my shoes when he pulls up. It's okay Ms. B, I plan to sweep the rug and straighten it out before I leave this time, promise."

Which boyfriend is Jeff? The blond artist that looks like a vampire? Or that sulky jock with the weird birthmark on his face? Hmmm.

Shaking my head and rubbing my hands down my skirt I sealed my lips tight.

Because if I didn't have anything good to say...

"Okay."

With my keys on the hook by the coat rack and my scarf, gloves and hat on their respective hooks, I had no reason at all to hover there in the hallway.

But she wasn't grabbing a broom or anything! She was just sitting there, swinging her foot that's dangling from the end of my nearly new settee!

Maybe I needed a new babysitter? Sammie adored Brittany. But I didn't.

Well, not now – not after the repeated "carpet abuse" incidents anyway.

The little editor was working overtime to keep my snark from flying. And it was so cute how he'd tried to command my legs to move away. Because, if I couldn't let the snark fly, there really wasn't any reason for me to continue standing in the middle of my hallway. In stocking-ed feet. Holding my own shoes in unappreciated respect for my abused Aubusson rug.

That was when the doorbell rang to save my little editor from a work related injury. (Poor guy, all of that straining could sprain something if he isn't careful.)

"Can you get that Ms. B, I still need to put on my shoes."

My little editor had to be dehydrated by now. He looked faint. I didn't blame him. The effort to keep me from wringing Brittany's cheerleader neck was taking a lot out of him.

It was also probably not a good sign that I was picturing her face as I choked her; turning red and apoplectic- which would be such a terrible look with her pale blond hair. That couldn't be making things any easier for him.

I opened my door to what must have been a new boyfriend. I hadn't seen this guy before. Tall, a very young George Clooney with what looked like enough muscles to lift me (and that would be an accomplishment trust me) he looked me up and down for a full minute before he spoke.

"Here for Brit."

And there went the cuteness factor. Despite the fact that he was way too young for me to even consider appreciating his attractiveness, his inability to speak in complete sentences reminded me of how glad I was to be an 80's kid; this generation's dating pool? Yeah, NOT inspiring.

What was it about this next generation of kids that they struggled with the English language – not old English mind you, but plain, rudimentary, every day English? It must be the texting... maybe that constant finger movement short-circuited the brain, which somehow affected human speech.

Apparently my little editor agreed. He probably wanted me to try texting more in order to make his job a bit easier.

Slacker.

Hopefully my smile wasn't as stiff as it seemed as I invited the new, not so sulky, jock boy toy in to wait for Brittany by the door.

Leaving him there, I headed back through the foyer to the stairwell that lead up to Sammie's and my bedrooms. Because I still hadn't caught a glimpse of Sammie yet. And since I'm sure she'd heard me come in since the house had no soundproofing whatsoever, that meant only one thing... my kid was definitely up to no good.

And the sooner I found out what that "no good" was the easier it would be for me to neutralize the threat.

I guess Brittany should have mentioned to Jack, or was it Jim? The fact that our old Victorian lacked the insulation needed for sound not to carry through every wall. I thought this as I reached the top level of the stairs and headed toward Sammie's bedroom. Because that was when I heard something that made me long to scrub my brain clean.

"Dang Brit, your Boss Lady is a hottie."

I'm guessing that she was irritated by that remark. Brittany must have forgotten that I could hear every word through the paper thin walls since she responded with, "Ew, she's like super old Jeff. That's gross. Plus she's fat. Since when are you into fat chicks; is that like, a college thing or something?"

Yep, she was so fired. Maybe Bethany from next door needed babysitting money.

"My scholarship doesn't allow me time to scout the campus for chicks little cuz. Besides, I don't need to because they come to me. You high school kids don't know what's hot and what's not until we tell you."

Brittany snickered. The voices were fading as they approached the front door but I could still hear them clearly. I should have kept walking but morbid curiosity froze me like a statue.

"And you know what they say about mom's right? She might be old but she's still good looking. Plus, she's not fat by a long shot. It's called curves– you'll learn about those when you finally get some. Give me five minutes in a room with your boss kid and she'd leave a happy woman."

Wow... that was extremely inappropriate. Too shocked to take anything that he said as a compliment, not to mention, too disgusted by it; I wondered if it was just me? Or is it okay for a male college student relative to say such disturbing things to his younger female cousin?

Well, at least *he was* her cousin. That was way better than being just some cute guy picking her up (and by cute I mean how he'd been *before* he'd opened his mouth). It was probably a good idea for him not to talk that much. Because when he'd started I'd so wanted him to stop.

And then I contemplated the five minutes he'd mentioned. Really? Five WHOLE minutes?

There was my inappropriate humor rearing its ugly head again.

Just the thought any man thinking that any woman would be happy with an interlude attached to a five minute buzzer signaling the end of the game – had me choking on my own laughter.

And by that I mean, I was actually choking... out and out wheezing; coughing – hacking even... kind of like that time I swallowed that small chicken bone by mistake.

Don't judge me. I was hungry, the grizzle on the end of the bone *is* edible and how was I supposed to know that when I inhaled to sneeze at exactly the wrong moment the entire bone would fly down my throat? Like I said, don't judge.

Brittany's muffled response was lost to me, possibly because they were already out the door and down the front steps. Or it could be because I was lying in the middle of my hallway up the stairs, rolling back and forth, trying desperately to breathe. I'd tried to stifle my uncontrollable spout of giggles. But it was just not working.

Which was probably why my little editor was shaking his head in obvious disgust. But he was also off duty as of now so, what do I care?

***

"Mom, come look!!! They just said your name! You won, you won!!!!"

I glanced up from the kitchen table of scattered notes from my case file. Hating the fact that popcorn and peanut butter night just got interrupted by two hang up calls and a call from Mandy's parents, I got up to see what Sammie was so excited about. I watched as she rewound the DVR and pushed play.

"Oh Lance, we are so excited to announce the first EVER winners of the Brain Waiver Contest. We reviewed thousands of entries and decided to start at the beginning of the alphabet with winners from an A, town... so Alton, Illinois... here are your winners..."

I could feel my mouth hanging open – again. The phrase "jaw jacking" was taking on a whole other meaning for me. My jaw was definitely starting to feel overworked.

I couldn't move or speak as Delilah Robinson on the Obsessed Hollywood show repeated my name.

Okay. First off, I never win. Anything. I've never won a scratch off, a trivia game, not even the drawing at the employee picnic. So when I say that, I mean I never win anything AT ALL – no exaggeration what so ever.

Except for contests I never entered to begin with apparently... you know... like now.

"So Delilah, recap the contest to me and our viewer's here. What exactly did the first group of lucky leapers in Alton, Illinois win?"

Despite my shocked and numbed brain, I still caught the almost imperceptible tightening of Delilah's jaw. A Marilyn Monroe slash Lady Gaga wannabe, Delilah Robinson was THE DIVA of Diva's on the Eye Network. Her back was straight; her eyes were cornflower blue and her hair was a platinum blond so shiny it was almost transparent. The long tendrils that curled smoothly all the way down to her behind were *so* not from perm out of the box. That hair spoke of fancy salons, a cultured upbringing, money and more money.

But her clenched jaw and flashing eyes told a different story. They always gave her away. This chick had attitude that didn't come from private tutors or "the better life". Not so with Lance however. He had a privileged, high society look; like he just stepped off of the set of a Skull and Bones remake. And Lance not only knew it, but also used it to work Delilah's last nerve. Often.

"As you well know, *Lance,* the winners of the contest get to experience both wining and dining from our sponsor and network owner, Cypher-Louis, Incorporated. They will receive exclusive invitations to the Happy New Year Gala, which will take place on New Year's Eve at the Argosy casino right there in Downtown Alton!

At the Gala these final contestants will be entered into a drawing where 20 very lucky individuals will win the opportunity to be the first ever BRAINWAIVER implants! Talk about your lucky ducks there Lance, I am so excited!"

Sammie was spinning in circles and screaming, "YAY YAY YAY," at the top of her lungs.

And I felt like the room was spinning right along with her. I'd never experienced Vertigo out of nowhere just standing still before. Today was definitely a day of firsts for me.

But I hadn't fallen yet, which was a good thing. Though the nausea I was feeling was definitely a bad sign that a collapse was imminent.

What in the name of all that's funky and green was BRAINWAIVER? Was my next thought, followed by another more disturbing one:

And it's to be implanted? *In me?*

Nope. And nope again.

This had to be a mistake. I saw the little editor nodding vigorously at my assessment since:

A. I haven't entered any contests so how could I possibly win what I didn't enter and

B. If I had entered a contest, I wouldn't win anyway. Luck was never on my side (which was probably why God was a big part of my life – my philosophy? Why bet the odds when you can put everything down on the SURE thing?).

I could thank my luck for a lot of things though; like if I rolled through a stop sign, I'd get caught. If I littered or even thought about not using a waste can in the park, I'd get caught. If a crowd of 20,000 people were entering a bank and attempted to rob it with me, I'd be the one that got caught.

Luck was not my friend. The little editor embraced this logic whole heartedly to help me calm down.

My mind racing, I almost missed the commercial. It was a scene set with the textbook sports illustrated model type frolicking along a coast of white sandy beaches in a stunning, white bikini. Her joy was infectious as Mr. Right (my assumption since the guy was tall, dark and handsome with amazing teeth and sparkling amethyst eyes) embraced her and swung her around before collapsing. It was a scene that made me want to smile, despite my numbed – thus dulled, intellect. Until the picture flashed. Rebecca Grayling, 27 years old last year (according to the information listed at the bottom of the screen) had a complexion riddled with acne and an extra fifty pounds easy, sat before the camera in a room resembling interrogation rooms on those cop shows. In tears. Poor kid.

You could tell that she was a beautiful person underneath all of that, despite her choice of that hideous sweater she wore. I almost felt her sorrow as she gripped crumpled tissues in one hand while completing a form with the other. The voice over explaining the transition of the scenes made the hair on my arms stand on end. As well it should have.

It isn't every day that the poor heartbroken creature filling out those forms while she struggled not to break down in another bout of tears could be seen a year later as the gorgeous swan the commercial opened with.

But the voice over begged to differ. It lamented at being that heart-broken, complexion scarred and overweight young woman. Its voice wavered as it detailed how dreary and awful life had been before...

My heart sped up and my grip on the table turned my knuckles white as I realized what this was. I wanted to do too many things at once: turn off the television, shoo Sammie to her room, call the 1-800 number on the bottom of the screen to ask questions and cry out to God for help (because the sad truth is still true: anything that seems too good to be true usually is).

Her claims that Brainwaiver was responsible for the butterfly leaving its hideous sweater covered cocoon weren't unbelievable. They were frightening.

A shiver coursed through me in such a way that I could feel it reverberate off of my spine. More because I could see why this thing was so appealing... could feel myself drawn to it even. But the very fact that I didn't want it, didn't ask for it and definitely didn't enter a contest to win it only increased my doubt that it was legitimately the miracle worker it seemed. A mind was a terrible thing to waste on false claims. Especially mine. My poor overladen brain was already struggling with enough challenges as it was!

There had to be a reasonable explanation right? You simply cannot win a contest you never entered. I'd call them, point out the mix-up and get removed from the list. Easy peasy! Right?

So why did Shirley Jackson's, "The Lottery," keep jumping to the forefront of my mind? The little editor censured me for my dramatics – this wasn't a stoning (yet), thus Shirley Jackson's early rendition of The Hunger Games wouldn't apply right?

Bringing my mind back to dealing in the present was a struggle. But I did it. As a solution oriented person I had to focus on the now. Which meant explaining the truth to Sammie before her fit of excited jumping and twirling caused our newly tiled floors to collapse.

"It's got to be a mistake munchkin, I never entered any contests."

"But Mommy... you won!"

Dang it. Moments like this made me wish I could punch something. Or reach for a bottle of something 80 proof. The problem with that was simple though: I'm not that girl. I don't use controlled substances to manage my setbacks in life. Which did not mean that there weren't moments when I wished I could. Like now.

Yep, now would be good. I deep sighed and adopted my "stern mama," expression.

"Bed time munch, we'll talk more about this tomorrow kay?"

Tomorrow would be a better day to disappoint the kid. It flat out hurt, when I wanted to give her the world but couldn't – it hurt even more when mistakes like this –mistakes that could have been avoided by proper fact checking – forced me into damage control mode.

It was difficult to walk a straight line; eye's closed while rubbing my temples as if they'd caught fire. But somehow I managed not to run into anything (or trip over my rug, thus having to straighten it out – again).

What's more, the effort to reach my steps without fainting, falling or any such tale tell sign that today was in the running for one of the worst days of my life, nearly sucked me dry.

My bed must have decided to meet me half way; it rushing up to meet my face at break neck speed and all. Or maybe I'd collapsed on it. I've heard it both ways.

Exhausted, I promised my little editor that I'd get to the bottom of this tomorrow (because he needed those assurances from time to time) while I prepared for the onslaught of sleep.

Usually I could feel sleep creeping up on me in stealth mode, beginning with the graying of all images. I should have known that something was wrong when darkness hit me so powerfully that I felt like I'd crashed into something... or through it... like down a dark hole... as would a rabbit, one might say.

That was it!

I'm never watching *Alice in Wonderland* or *The Matrix* ever again.

Chapter Three

"**Just** accept the prize and go for crying out loud! Honey, you need a life, any life. You should go for the sole reason of breaking up the monotony that *is* your life, who's by the way, only highlight is the most boring invitation ever – a blind date with an accountant."

Subtlety. *So* not my sister's middle name (or any part of her name for that matter).

It had been two days since the "announcement". Despite several phone calls to Cypher Lewis Inc. and at least two of the subsidiary sponsors that claimed to have received my scanned and emailed contest entry, I've made absolutely no headway in finding out how this could have happened.

I'd even asked for the manager at Gateway National Credit Union (a sponsor of the contest and also my bank). The manager's excitement for my so called "lucky break" and urgings to not be embarrassed that everyone in the country knew I'd entered and won such a contest only increased my determination to fix this – her exact words being,

"Oh Sweetie, its okay that you're 34 and still enter contests like this! I mean, I thought that only teenagers and tweens would be enticed by such a gizmo but hey, no one's judging you!"

I thought it wasn't possible to feel any more embarrassed than I'd felt when Cypher Lewis' legal consultant snottily advised that all winnings were non-negotiable and non-transferrable, that my entering the contest was the same as entering a legally binding contract and how I would be remiss in my responsibility to fulfill such a contract just because I was having second thoughts due to my apparent "mid-life crisis" of momentary madness that caused me to enter the contest in the first place *yada, yada, yada.* (And yes, she said ALL of that without taking a single breath.)

But I was mistaken. Being singled out in a lobby full of bank customers snickering behind their hands at that "no one's judging you," remark was so much more mortifying.

And now here I sat, per Mags and my usual Saturday night excursion at Fast Eddie's. I had ordered my favorite; a basket of fries and the hugest butterfly shrimp you ever saw. Sadly, it was losing its appeal as I listened to my sister harp on how boring and uneventful my life was.

And she wasn't anywhere close to being done apparently.

"… what happened with that accountant anyway? I thought you guys were going out after 'The Jerk with no name' came over Friday to pick up Sammie?"

Heh. My sister still disliked Derek, my ex-husband. More than I did. In fact, I didn't really dislike him at all. Some of us take a while to grow up and become the adults we need to become to make the world a better place. But Derek had apparently adopted Peter Pan as his role-model. It was too bad that, just like most lost boys that refuse to grow up and accept responsibility, he'd turned into that "skanky old dude" that hangs out in shoe stores at the mall leering at young women as they bent over.

Creepy was too good of a word for that. *Any* word was too good of a word for that.

"I cancelled… again. "

"It's called a blind date Cece, not an imaginary one. You need to poop or get off the pit Missy!"

"Um. It's POT and no, no I don't. In fact, I don't feel that discussing poop or pots, for that matter, are appropriate dinner conversation so let's talk about something else."

"Okay Ms. Poopie-pants —since using the pot analogy seems abhorrent to you, let's get back on the subject of you and this contest that you've won. But refuse to accept the prize for... which is kick-butt and awesome by the way... yeah, lets talk about that."

"Poopie-pants? Quit being gross. And I told you, I didn't enter..."

"I know, I know... but here's the thing. Sis, seriously. This may be what you need to break the cycle of the prison gray dullness that is your life. You have always been so much more than you settle for. Maybe this contest is God's way of telling you the truth that you refuse to hear; you are more than what you've become."

"Why do I hear the musical nuances of *The Lion King* in the background as you speak?"

"Fine! Get with the program Simba! You're better than this and you need to get your OCD LCSW behind off the pot and onto the road that should be your life. You are settling babe. Case in point? Exhibit A: you should have been a Clinical Psychologist but you settled for Licensed Clinical Social Worker instead. Exhibit B: you should have dated that guy on the football team that had the hugest crush on you. But no, you turned him down. Why? Because you felt you weren't popular enough! Instead you settled for that Art Fart, Derek. You never pursued any of your dreams because you were so busy trying to help him fulfill his."

I shook my head and choked back a guffaw because I'd nearly lost it on that one.

It was a game we played often, my sis and I: To see who could make the other laugh first while talking about serious issues. I shouldn't let her know she'd gotten to me but I couldn't let that one go... I just couldn't!

"Really? Art Fart?"

"That's what dad calls him... Remember how Mom used to say that he was artsy fartsy? Yeah well, Dad turned it into his nickname, then shortened it for easier application and there you go. And "really" right back at you! Out of what I just said, "Art Fart" was your take away?"

"No Rafiki - it wasn't. By the way, your big pink baboon butt is showing!"

Ha! She tried to hide the smirk but I saw it!

"That's it, no more Disney cartoons for you! Sammie can only watch BBC from now on. Or CNN. It's important that she knows what to do when her father goes to prison once they outlaw perpetual stupidity."

Unfortunately, that last was said as I was downing some of my Diet Pepsi.

I have to say that what happened next is my sister's fault. She knew better than to say something that hilarious when I'm in the midst of downing a drink – just as my parents, old basketball coach and several now ex-boyfriends knew. You say something funny while I'm downing a drink and you *will* end up wearing said drink.

True to tradition, Pepsi flew right out of my nose and christened Mags' beautiful pearl cashmere sweater.

Hmph, what a shame. Too bad I couldn't afford to feel bad about her future dry cleaning bill. I was too busy fanning my burning nose. Though I have to say, the choking fit I was having didn't distract me from how funny she looked. And it didn't help that she'd just fallen off of her stool, giggling hilariously at the dribbles of soda and snot pouring out of my nose.

Which I just realized was happening. *EWWWWW*!

Mortification wasn't a good look for me. But I probably needed to get used to it since the half of the restaurant was laughing right along with Mags.

"What does a woman need to do to get some napkins in this joint?"

I muttered that loudly through my cupped hands, sending my sister into another fit of giggles as she collapsed back onto her stool.

Goofy Heathen!

I guess my mutter had an echo since the couple next to us (the one looking as if they were taking pity on me) had reached over to hand me some napkins. Something I wish I'd seen before I opened my big mouth since at my exclamation they (as in both of them) bent over laughing so hard that those precious napkins had fallen in a scatter to the dirty floor, DANG IT!

Stomping away from the table may have been a bit dramatic but it was well deserved. Especially since I had a strong suspicion that my sister wasn't laughing WITH me, but AT me. My first clue being that I wasn't laughing... at all!

So I needed an exit with attitude because I had a point to prove. Too bad I wasn't watching where I was going.

WHHHAAAMMMM!!!!!

"DANG IT! OW!" Only through my crushed nose that sounded more like, "mmnnggg did, mowwww!"

"That had to hurt. You okay?"

Way too angry at the black comedy that was my life to pay much attention at the moment, I jerked my elbow away from the guy helping me up.

I'm a pretty big chick so, suffice it to say, I was flabbergasted that I'd run into a brick wall (not really) only to bounce off and fall hard right onto my generous behind. It's probably impolite to mention that I was sincerely grateful for the padding I have back there. If it wasn't for that cushion my landing would have been much more painful.

Gripping my twice injured nose (because acidic soft drinks plus previous face-planting into a hard-as-stone chest equaled twice the pain) I glanced up through teary eyes into the most gorgeous green eyes I'd ever seen. Claude Have Mercy!

Green eyes, with lashes that were too long to belong to a man but did, blinked back at me before narrowing then crinkling a bit at the edges.

Okay, first you have to understand my fascination here.

A person who once dabbled in art, I know for a fact that green is not a primary color on the color wheel. It was a secondary color because it was created by mixing the two primary colors - blue and yellow- together.

That said, looking into this man's eyes, despite what I knew about art and the color wheel, I would have argued that green was indeed a primary color. The clarity pouring from them could not possibly be considered a second rate thing. They were pure and uncut, like the clearest most beautiful emerald.

"Miss? You alright?"

He just spoke right? I looked to the little editor for confirmation that those were indeed words I'd heard. I also needed the translation since I pretty much didn't catch any of it. But my little guy must have been knocked out when I'd fallen because I got absolutely no help from that quarter.

"Uhh. Yeah."

Aren't I poetic? But could you blame me? If it were just the man's eyes that were gorgeous then I could communicate with some composure that all was well, no harm done.

But those eyes bore the honor of gracing a strong, rugged face; golden in tone and dusted with dark (and might I say, well groomed) facial hair. It wasn't a mustache exactly... nor was it really a goatee... more of a stunning shadow of both. Yowza!

Attached to all of that was a full, dark head of hair with just a few silvers blended in. The kind of hair that didn't need styling, it fell haphazardly into a masculine hand-combed state. Most likely (without much effort on his part) it had settled in a way that so suited him you could swear he walked right out of the pages of a magazine.

Seeing all of that, I really did try to ignore his lips. Sadly, I failed. They were full and kind of cocked to the side a bit as he considered me, wondering I bet, if I were injured or just a little slow on the uptake. Oy!

"I'm fine, really, thanks for helping me up."

I'd spoken so breathlessly that I'm pretty sure he had a hard time catching what I'd said. Not to mention my hands still covered my nose.

More embarrassed than I've ever been (totally topping my previous embarrassment of oh, 5 minutes ago), I tried to step around him and hurry into the bathroom.

But, quicker than I have ever seen a guy move, he stepped directly into my path, blocking me. He bent forward a bit (yikes this guy was tall), probably trying to get a better look at my injury in the dim lighting.

"You sure? Let me see..."

And that deep baritone to go with. Stereotype much? I should have told him he'd come to the wrong place. The man of my dreams contest was usually held somewhere else, anywhere else – most definitely not in my vicinity.

Luckily I was forced out of my "Good gracious what a voice," daze when he reached for me. Snatching away from someone that good looking had to be a mortal sin. But at this point I was too embarrassed to care.

I shook him off and suddenly became very interested in the view around his ankles. Why didn't he just move already? Maybe he needed to know I was really okay...

"No really. I'm good, excuse me."

This time as I spoke I didn't give him an opportunity to block me. With a little body fake to my right, I adjusted and swept past him on *his* right (hey, you can take the girl off of the basketball court but you can't get the basketball training out of the girl) and hurried into the ladies room.

I tried to calm down as I grabbed gobs and gobs of tissue out of the stall to clean my face. But my heart was beating nonstop. And my head was spinning like I'd been slipped a mickey or something.

Breathing a bit slower I used hard cold facts to bring myself back to reality. Like the fact that guys like that really didn't look at women like me. It's not that I'm not attractive by any means. It was... I was... well; I'm tall. And big.

I'm not saying I'm huge or anything. But the truth is I've never been small, trim or petite. I'm built more like a Zena instead of a Gabrielle – amazon warrior verses dainty pixie-like princess. Alpha males like him tended to go for the dainty princess variety.

And that was all I needed... another crush on an unattainable guy. If this week got any worse I might just go looking for that stupid rabbit hole and jump into it on purpose.

Chapter Four

Since it took an extra moment or two to reapply my makeup, I couldn't help but reminisce a little – crashing into unattainable guys does that to me sometimes.

Mags wasn't exaggerating about the jock in high school. His name was Anthony. And the guy had been stacked. Big bulky muscles, gorgeous eyes and the cutest little grin, it was a shy kind of smile that was so out of place on his hulking form. But it was all him and it was sincere. He'd been the nicest guy. I crushed on Ant for three years which was most of my high school career.

And finally (miracle of miracles), our junior year, he'd asked me out. And I'd said no. I never told Mags about that. She would have killed me if I'd told her; not because I'd said no but *why* I did.

It was because Tricia had been standing there. Tricia was the beautiful cheerleader/girl next door type that all girls secretly wanted to be like. She was popular, sweet and despite the character of most of the "in crowd," she was also a sincerely nice person.

And she had also crushed on Ant since the beginning of time. We knew that about each other too. It was a totally unspoken knowledge – a sisterhood of unfulfilled longing; me, that girl jock basketball playing artist type, her- the popular cheerleading and club type, had a bond.

So when Ant asked me out right in front of her, instead of feeling elated and beautiful and "in your face" excited that he liked me, I looked right at Tricia and saw myself. I saw how my heart would have exploded right there in my chest if I were in her shoes and she were in mine. I saw my narrow little world end in heartache and go up in smoldering flames while Tricia linked arms with the handsome boy of my dreams and walked off into the sunset, leaving me drowning in my own hopelessness.

I just couldn't do it. Instead I did what I wouldn't have thought I'd do in a million years. I turned him down. I told him that I was dating someone already (feeling my heart splinter into billions of pieces in my chest as I lied).

What's weird is, to this day I don't know if I regret more that I never gave me and Anthony a shot... or that Tricia and I hadn't become better friends. The bond of sisterhood that day had grown increasingly strong. Though Tricia and I weren't in the same crowd, we somehow always managed to look out for one another behind the scenes. I don't know if Anthony and I would have worked out to be more than just another high school boyfriend/ girlfriend phase or something more. But I did know in my heart of hearts that, to this day, were I to call on Tricia Matthews for any reason that I could count on her to have my back one hundred percent. Somehow I felt, for that reason alone, I'd made the right choice.

Face cleaned and make up lightly re-applied, I took a steadying breath and headed to the door. Upon my exit, I was prepared to do two things; pop my sister upside the head for the umpteenth time and gather up my things to head home. Thinking about the past had me feeling maudlin plus I still had no answers about how to get out of this stupid contest. The best place to be was home where I could think things through.

"I have never known a woman to fix herself up that quickly. If they ever decide to make that an Olympic event, my vote would be on you."

OY FREAKING VEY!

Tall dark and barrel-chested must not have been clued in.

It was extremely creepy to lurk outside the doors of the ladies room unless a woman knows you're waiting for her. And, just to say, if she doesn't know you're waiting for her; it's called stalking!

Gloves off Celine, time to send Prince Charming packing!

"Alright Guy, don't know you – not sure I want to know you. And FYI, your waiting out here for me to get done when I told you I was fine is beyond creepy."

Uh oh.

In the midst of my diatribe he'd uncrossed his arms and straightened to his full height. Um... whoa...

The man had to be around six foot five inches since I stood at a solid six feet. I backed up a step and bit my lip. In doing so, I caught a good look at the winner of my future shoulda, woulda, coulda fantasy. Stacked didn't begin to describe him.

It was no wonder I'd bounced off this guy. I was lucky I didn't get whiplash!

Lost in my wowza daze, I continued to drool (just a little) over the total package. Though he was dressed in a way that would have you assuming he's an average Joe, there was something about the way he stood that screamed he was so much more than that.

It wasn't his height either. I didn't know what it was exactly. His presence, maybe?

I didn't believe in auras and I wasn't at all superstitious. Despite that, I would still say that he had an air about him. His stance was casual with hands dug deep into the pockets of his faded black jeans. He somehow managed to perfect that rugged outdoors look while mixing it up with a clean-cut appearance. He wore a quilted jacket vest and scuffed brown work boots that spoke of a man that wasn't afraid of hard work. Far from just a pretty face, he somehow consumed every bit of my senses, like he'd expanded to take over every single iota of the small hallway.

Yet, with all of that going on, it was still the expression on his face that arrested me more than anything else.

It was more than intense. He was looking at me like there was no one else in the world, in the universe even; that could possibly hold his attention right now, except for me.

Giving my head a quick shake I tried to clear my thoughts. But those eyes just kept reeling me in. In them was a look so effective a woman *had* to have taught him that. Because there was one thing most women longed for from their men, and that was to be the sole beneficiary of his attention and desire. When a man could make a woman feel like she was, put simply, his everything? Make her feel like he was totally fixated on her – that no one else would do (or even had a chance)? A woman would give *that* man just about anything.

Heck, I'd known the guy for what? Four minutes? And here I was, desperately wishing I had my virginity back so I could hand it to him on a platter. With a side of fries. And a drink.

It was sad really, how one minute I'm calling him creepy and in the next, I wanted to whisk him away (or be whisked away by him) to spend hours eating chocolate covered strawberries off of his chest and abs. The same chest that had sent me flying earlier.

I wanted all of that in complete disregard of my own personal standard. I wanted it without even knowing his name, let alone the requisite "I Do" in front of God and everybody (preferably in a lavish and gorgeously decorated ceremony).

Shameless hussy, my little editor projected.

He was shaking his head at me in abject disappointment. I guess he was back from his unscheduled break. Hmph. I should've revoked all of my previous compliments on his hard work. But that didn't seem wise since I might need his help with Mr. Supermodel here.

Another head shake helped me fight my attraction, as did his voice. I say that because he'd been speaking to me and I'd missed at least half what he'd just said (yes, yes... *again!*).

"... interested? So. Are you going to tell me?"

Hmmm. Dang it.

"Tell you what?" Did wide eyes and raised eyebrows equal an expression of total innocence? I guess not. His furrowed brow and slight frown answered *that* question.

"Your name. Were you listening to anything I said?"

Truth time. He was already teed off so...

"Uh. No? Hey, don't blame me if you're prettier than you are interesting."

Oops.

The snark flew past my lips before the little editor could stop it.

As if on cue, I saw the man's jaw tighten which meant he was probably gritting his teeth. *So* not what I was shooting for.

Normally, that reaction wouldn't have concerned me (in fact, most times it was exactly the response I'd work for).

But when his eyes narrowed into little slits that made his irises nearly disappear, I figured it might be a good idea to get out of that very dark secluded hallway. The one that I was standing in with a very large man I didn't know. A man I'd made all squinty eyed.

The little editor nodded vigorously in agreement as I ducked past with a mumbled, "Sorry, excuse me, I have to go."

I exhaled slowly once I'd passed him. It was the shaking of my hands that had me confused. It's not like I was afraid of the guy. I mean, it was obvious that he wasn't happy but I didn't feel threatened, exactly.

I didn't want to examine it too closely because suddenly I felt drained. Getting back to the table wasn't very difficult even though the crowd had more than doubled since I'd gone to the restroom.

Mags was holding her cell phone up to her mouth practically yelling into the thing. I couldn't quite catch what she was saying, but if history is repeating itself (and it usually did every single time we went out) she was probably reassuring her husband Greg that we weren't causing the kind of trouble that would have him bailing us out come Monday morning.

Greg's perfect timing and Mags' distraction gave me just enough time to compose myself as I hoped to avoid her twenty thousand and one questions about Barrel Chest Guy. No, tortures. Twenty thousand tortures that began and ended with my sister's nose way too far into my business. Truly, if she could package her interrogation skills and sell them, every prosecuting attorney or CIA operative in the world would buy her out and coast for the rest of their careers.

A quick glance at my watch told me that it was just after ten. Almost bed time. My beauty sleep was almost sacred to me. It was something that I held onto faithfully with no deviation from the schedule. What. So. Ever. Sleep was my friend. And from the moment I'd left my mother's womb, there had not been an event tragic enough or traumatic enough (earthquake, fire or tornado) that had the power to keep me from it. Not even my dear, sweet, spastic sister.

"Let's go Mags – you have exactly two minutes or I'm leaving you here."

She waved me away like I was some annoying gnat trying to lounge in her ear.

This was the reason that I drove when we went out. After that last incident my senior year where I'd made good on my promise to strand her across the river at a karaoke place, my sister knew how serious I was about my sleep. When I said I'm ready to go, I meant exactly that.

So she probably wasn't surprised when I grabbed my jacket and purse and headed toward the exit not caring if she followed. Greg would pick her up anyway; I'd just have to hear both of their mouths for the next year about it.

What could I say? My sleep was worth paying that price.

Just as I was reaching for the door I felt a trill race down my spine. I turned expecting to see my sister racing to catch me. But it wasn't her. In fact, no one was standing directly behind me. In a crowded bar. How bizarre was that?

 Instead Mr. Barrel Chest was standing about 20 feet from me, the milling crowd giving him and me a pretty wide berth. I wondered if I should feel more disturbed that he was watching me leave, or by the fact that I could actually feel him doing it. I should have been freaking out, the whole thing was just that weird.

But instead, I tilted my head to the side, shrugged my shoulders and grinned. I don't know why I did that. Possibly because I picked up on some nonverbal expectation from him (it was in the way he leaned against the wall watching me, his eyebrows slightly raised). Almost like he was daring me to do something. Anything.

 My grin proudly matched his dare and, like raising the other player in a poker game, it changed the stakes. Because that little quirk of his lips I'd seen earlier reappeared as he straightened and headed my way. Hoh boy.

"Come on girl! Let's get you home to bed so I don't have to hear you whine tomorrow about your stupid beauty sleep!"

I jumped nearly ten feet, my heart now firmly ensconced in my throat. Before I could grab Mags and shake her silly for scaring the brains out of me, she grabbed hold of my hand and dragged me completely out the front doors.

And that's when I decided that, despite the fact that I look almost exactly like my father, I really was adopted. I had to be. That way I could kill my sister, repent and not feel guilty about it in the least. Too bad I never quite believed that lie no matter how many times I tried to convince myself.

I shook off the urge to head back inside and find out what Mr. Barrel Chest, BC for short (a nickname I liked much more than the clichéd Supermodel), had to say and allowed my twerp of a sister to drag me to the car.

Even though I needed my beauty sleep; And even though I knew that I still had a mystery to solve about this stupid contest (not to mention church in the morning), emerald eyes swam before me. But I didn't need that kind of distraction right now. Mooning over the unattainable was never fun.

Niggling in the back of my tired mind was a thought I couldn't quite let go. That Mr. BC wasn't really *that* unattainable…

An eerie sensation settled over me, though I knew for a fact that no one was watching me like before. I felt as if my life, previously so organized and controlled down to the last minute, was about to take a flying leap right off of Hawk Point into the Missouri River… and there was absolutely nothing I was going to be able to do to stop it.

Dang it. Maybe rabbit holes weren't so bad after all. Compared to that cold and dirty river, they were downright cozy.

Chapter Five

"**Amanda** is missing."

Mr. and Mrs. Same, Mandy and Anabella's parents sat close together on the couch in my office, their hands gripping each other's, knuckles white, legs crossed.

To look at them, one would liken them to those Precious Moments figurines. Beautiful skin and pale blonde hair, they almost looked related. Dressed almost identically in grey London Fog trench coats over beige sweaters and ivory slacks, the only noticeable difference between them was their eyes. Mr. Same's eyes were a muddy brown-grey, startling in his slightly tanned face and pale blond facial hair. While Mrs. Same's eyes were a clear, almost transparent blue, the freakiest eye color I'd ever seen. Coupled with her peaches and cream complexion and the halo-like wisps of white blonde hair, one would expect to see wings unfolding at her back at any moment.

But it was the pain in Mrs. Same's eyes and the helpless frustration that Mandy's father projected that had my chest burning. Mandy was gone. And according to the Same's, no one had seen her since she'd left my office Thursday evening to bike home. I was the last person to have seen Mandy alive.

That was the day that Mandy wasn't herself. It was also the day that Mandy had given me the journal. And now she was gone.

My own eyes teared as I glanced down at my clenched fists, desperately willing myself to blink the tears back.

Because these kids had gone through enough within the last year. Because their parents had experienced enough hurt at what they'd probably felt was their fault for failing to protect their children.

"Do you know of any reason that Amanda would have been upset, Ms. Baltimore?"

I exhaled at a count of three. It's like these people never listened to their kids. And that question? Not one I'd ask if I'd thought my daughter was missing unwillingly.

"That's a strange question to ask Mr. Same, unless of course you think that Mandy isn't missing, but has run away. Is that what you're thinking?"

The room went cold. The icy disdain pouring from Mr. Same's eyes gave me pause. What had brought *that* on?

"It's Amanda, and I feel that it is a strong possibility. Amanda has been rather... difficult... to deal with these last few weeks." He hesitated. His wife's knuckles paled even more, like her grip upon him had increased before he continued. "Her associations have changed. She has fallen in with a crowd that we really don't approve of and she isn't happy about our disapproval."

Oh, Really now?

Since I didn't care for the icy attitude, I no longer felt the need to empathize and comfort. I felt my back stiffen as I leaned forward. My hands, having a mind of their own, were no longer folded in my lap but were clenched on top of my desk. I'd already felt my brow furrow and attempted to relax back into "my professional" expression. But I was failing miserably.

"May I ask what crowd?"

Mr. Same hesitated again. The side glance he gave to his wife was the first sign that utter stupidity was about to grace us with its presence – gah I hated being right sometimes (not really).

"She has been attending a Church near our home, despite our strict admonition against it."

I couldn't stop my head from snapping back. My eyes were probably bucking right out of my face but I was too shocked to school my features back into my mask of professional indifference.

"Is it a cult Mr. Same."

"All churches are cults Ms. Baltimore."

"Okay then." My head tilted to the left as my eyes narrowed. My stiff shoulders made it impossible to relax back into my "professional" posture. My poor little editor was in a frenzy trying to keep me from speaking my mind.

I took a steadying breath and tried again. Focusing on putting Amanda's welfare over telling her parents to kick rocks had me holding on by a very thin thread.

"Can you specify this particular "cults" affiliation?"

Was my irritation that obvious? It must have been because I could almost feel the icy blanket of contempt smother every atom in the room before Mr. Same responded.

"It is a Christian church. I don't know which sect. I don't care which sect. We are Atheists Ms. Baltimore. And we have raised our children accordingly. Religion is nothing but a form of control that prevents the gifted from achieving simultaneously serving as an excuse for the useless to continue being exactly that."

My back was starting to hurt, it had gotten so stiff.

"And you think Mandy is what, rebelling? By attending church?"

"It's Amanda Ms. Baltimore, I don't call you Ms. Balty do I? We have raised our children to respect their birth names. And yes, that is exactly what I believe."

I could feel my jaw tighten and my teeth were very close to grinding themselves into dust.

You're a professional Celine. This is your office, remember? Now focus and do your job!

Performance statements were a wonderful thing. When it was crunch time and the game was on the line, I'd always had a special something I'd say to myself to get me back on track.

It was a well-known sports psychology technique. Who knew it would work so well in other areas of my life?

Focus restored, I purposefully relaxed my jaw and switched my attention to Mrs. Same. I was looking for clarity; some mother's instinct to weigh in here. Her head was bowed and she continued to hold tight to her husband's hand. If she'd felt my stare burning a hole into her apparently empty head, she showed no indication of it. It seemed as though "control" was a loosely understood concept by Mr. Same.

To keep from snapping my leash and setting Mr. Same's nose hair on fire (which would be unprofessional AND un-Christian) I needed to change the beat of this conversation. This particular song and dance was getting old, really fast. It was time to remind him whose office he was sitting in.

"I understand that Mandy, and before you correct me again Mr. Same, I refer to my patients by the name that they are comfortable with being called, your preference is not relevant here. And to prevent confusion or the possibility of causing my patient any distress, I refer to them by that name at all times. If you would like to keep correcting me because it makes you feel better, please do so. However, you will have to continue to do so until Mandy is no longer the subject that we are discussing.

Now where was I? Oh, I understand that Mandy has voiced her concerns to both of you regarding the new behavioral modification program that you have enrolled Anabella in. Mandy was quite disturbed about the program and the amount of control... it gives you over behaviors as benign as, say, sleeping. "

"Your point?"

"I believe I have made it Mr. Same. Your concern is the "crowd" that Mandy has involved herself with. Could the source of your concern possibly also stem from Mandy's discontent lately regarding your handling of Anabella's treatment?"

"You bi…"

"That is enough William."

Mrs. Same finally spoke and the snap in her voice proved me wrong. This woman was not a woman living in fear of anyone. Or being controlled – at least not just now. Internally I glanced at the little editor and projected my thoughts – the plot thickens I say. Don't be trite he responds. Hmmm. Everyone's a critic.

"Ms. Baltimore," Mrs. Same, apparently taking on the voice of reason in this conversation, continued as if her husband hadn't been about to call me a female dog, "Your progress with treating our daughters since that unfortunate incident last year has been exemplary. Our seeking other treatment for Anabella's developmental disorder is no reflection on your capabilities. We just felt it was outside of your area of expertise. When provided with cutting edge technological solutions that could possibly help Anabella have a normal life, we jumped at the opportunity. And to answer your question, it does disturb Amanda that we have done so. But I do not think that this would be cause for her to abandon all that she knows and run away from home."

"So you don't think she ran away then."

"No I do not."

I didn't believe her. At. *All*.

"Have you contacted the police yet to file a missing person's report?"

No response. I really didn't want one either. I didn't want to know why two people that obviously loved their children (even if their ideology was slightly skewed) wouldn't contact law enforcement because their child was missing – even if there is a chance that the child has possibly run away from home. It took a moment for me to loosen my clenched fists again. Because they were hiding something. Something vital. And had the nerve to come into my office thinking I was stupid enough NOT to pick up on that.

I'd given up on hiding my nonverbals at that point. If they couldn't tell how much I wanted to put them in headlocks, something was seriously wrong with their survival instincts. Which I could tell wasn't the case since Mrs. Same stood rather quickly with her husband following suit.

I'm not sure what they saw when they looked at me. I could only guess that they were registering all of my cues and decided that angry didn't *begin* to describe what I was feeling.

"We felt that to involve the authorities at this juncture would be unwise. We have made a few calls and have begun tracing Amanda's steps. Once we have enough information we can determine the next best course of action."

I reminded myself that these were the people that wrote the checks to pay for their daughters' treatment. It would be tantamount to shooting myself in the foot to alienate them by saying what I would like to say. But before I could say anything, Mr. Same added (as if it were a speech prepared beforehand, his words stilted and monotone) "We would appreciate it if, should you recall anything that stands out from your last session with Amanda, you will contact us immediately."

The journal stood out in my mind's eye. Never being one for much detail, my recollection of the dimensions, the cover, even the small nick in the top right corner surprised me. I opened my mouth to respond but caught sight of the little editor, shaking his head vigorously from side to side. I had the feeling that he wanted me to "shut it". I snapped my mouth closed and decided to follow his emphatic advice.

"Were you about to say something Ms. Baltimore?"

Good gravy but I hated lying. Not just because of moral reasons but also because I'm terrible at it.

"I was. I was about to say that I wish you all of the luck in the world in locating Mandy. She is one of my favorite people Mr. Same. I hate the thought of her being somewhere alone or afraid, even possibly hurt."

Mr. Same and his wife shared a look that I couldn't decipher. I didn't speak snooty so I didn't even try to translate what passed between them. Instead I returned their nod of goodbye, mentally hurrying their departure.

So let's recap.

As of now, I had a journal to read, a patient to find and a contest to disavow.

And the clock was ticking.

That said, I have to say that there were two parts to my character. There was the confronter and then there was the coward. The coward hated change. It hated to do what needed to be done if that doing would lead to my having to readjust the current way of doing things. It whispered discouragement at the slightest change of course. It hated deviating from what it knew best so much that it would replay my failure reel (times that I've deviated before and experienced some sort of pain as a result) the second it sensed me considering another way.

Just like last week with BC, Mr. Barrel Chest. In the blink of an eye, I was seeing my past mistakes and past hurts. I shot him down and never considered giving him a chance. I convinced myself that he didn't want one, that I was better off walking away.

I knew the coward, his objective and his tactics, well. I knew and didn't fight it because most of the time I was in total agreement. I hated pain. Emotional pain, in particular. So I was with the coward one hundred percent when it came to avoiding any situation that could cause it.

Except for now. Because I was already feeling the ache in my chest grow. Mandy was missing and I was the only person with a clue as to why. The coward argued that it wasn't my responsibility; to give the journal to her parents and wash my hands of it.

Which is why his participation in this decision just ended.

Because the confronter, though rarely adhered to, had the power today. He'd replayed the conversation with Mandy's parents. Like why they hadn't contacted the police. Why they would think that Mandy ran away after joining a church. What was with all the hush-hush and secrets?

And then there was the journal... what exactly WAS going on with Anabella's treatment? And why did Mrs. Same stay quiet most of the meeting, as if she was afraid, only to exude more authority than her husband had the moment his behavior strayed from the prim and proper?

There were too many unanswered questions here. Too many inconsistencies. And I cared too much about these kids to give in to the coward this time. Besides, there was no avoiding the pain because it was already spreading like wildfire.

And there was no going back either. I knew that the moment I opened the journal and laid eyes on what was drawn on the first page, the description written in blood red pen below it. And as I read on with growing apprehension, I realized that this wasn't a rabbit hole at all. It was a bottomless pit... a life sucking black hole. One that would keep sucking and destroying if someone didn't stop it, and soon. Oy – Frikken – Vey!

Chapter Six

"**Dad**, I'm gonna freaking kill him!"

And that's why I still don't understand why I bothered to come home to these two. Spy games, cold wars, toppling empires had nothing on the wars fought right here in my own house.

"Kill him Cass and you go to prison. For life. Murder one. Conviction is certain because I will testify against you."

"But Dad!"

"No buts kid. Work it out, figure it out, but most importantly whatever it is, unless it involves death or dismemberment of the non-murder kind, leave *me* out."

The stomping and slamming of her door was my cue.

Cell phone, wallet and keys in my pockets and I was out the door. The one true beauty of teenagers was that they had their own transportation so I could spend my mornings like I liked them, in silence.

"Sam, we gotta talk."

Crap! I opened my front door trying to get out of the vicinity before another minor skirmish breaks out and ran into another issue right outside my front door.

"I don't have time for this Johnny."

Jonathan Davies was my oldest friend. We've been tight for as long as I can remember. Until he'd gone into the Marines right after we graduated from high school, we'd done everything together.

When he got out 8 years later things weren't the same. He suffered from PTSD; the conflict in Iraq leaving him with bouts of panic attacks, nightmares and a drinking habit that he didn't even try to kick. But me, I suffered from something else. Something worse. Black Ops service has a way killing things in a man that he didn't know he needed to remain human until it was gone.

When Johnny grabbed my arm, yanking me to the side of the house where the bushes were overgrown, I felt my eyes narrow. It was that cold rain inside my head again that should have freaked me out. Instead it pissed me off. I hadn't felt that way since my last op. A lot of people had died that day. I hated the icy sensation with everything in me, but that didn't stop the spread.

And as my training kicked in, my assessment of Johnny changed. He didn't look like the Johnny I knew. His brown hair, once thick was thinning, his hair line receding. Gray eyes, once sharp even when slightly glassy from too much drink had grown dull and unfocused. And his face was lined with exhaustion. But it was the twitch that told the story. Left eye, left shoulder.

A civvy – civilian might not have caught it. But I was trained to catch that and a lot more. The slight tremor in his body had nothing to do with the chill in the air and, though I was aware of all he'd suffered since his return, I knew with a creepy sixth sense I've always had that this wasn't one of his episodes.

His eyes might be dull, but his expression was intense and locked on me, like a sniper with a target.

"Three are dead man. Three so far."

It was strange how the training from years ago kicked in with an adrenaline rush that made you hyper-aware. Because immediately I understood three things; that Johnny was lucid, that this wasn't a PTSD episode and that he was talking about recent events. His body language, tone and word usage were telling me more than his actual words.

"What's up John?" I didn't need to go into detail about how his message just came across loud and clear and that I had his back. We'd known each other too long for that.

"I need eyes Sam. That firm Reigner, Lee and Statford over on George Street has got something to do with this. And that ain't all..."

"You're giving me grid squares John, I need intel."

Grid squares were objectives that soldiers were assigned to locate. Only they don't exist. And right now Johnny was giving me location but no target. From what he said, I knew that three people were dead, but that was all. It was going to take some serious patience to extract what I needed to know from John without kicking him into another episode. I also knew that I was about to be late for work again and that this was shaping up to be one Charlie Foxtrot of a day (which was code for cluster f...)

"Man, I'm debriefing now, you just ain't paying attention! I've been watching these folks for over a year. Got me a client that's more than persuasive when it comes to providing incentive. And this is out of my league man. I'm a small time P.I., this crap right here, this is a snake eater all the way. You might be inactive, but you still have connections and you still got the skills. GOFO man, I need you in on this."

My cell phone went off and without looking; I knew it was my Father. Sometimes letting my 15 year old daughter play with my phone had its ups rather than downs; one of those ups was her setting ring tones for each of my contacts. Willie Nelson's *Midnight Rider* was the best song she could have picked for my dad. Not only did he look like Willie, he loved Willie's music. If he hadn't been a successful contractor and hadn't owned his own construction company since before I was born, he probably would have been a Willie Nelson impersonator. Could have really made a career of that if he weren't so tall – height and breadth being something my father and I had in common (probably the only thing).

I ignored the call knowing I was going to pay for that later. First of all, I was running late. Second of all, I was running late. My dad had very little to do now-a-days with me home and running things for him. So he stuck to what he did second best, micromanaging me and nagging me to death. Good times.

Despite Johnny's GOFO – "grasp of the freaking obvious", I was still missing the intel I needed to even weigh in on why I was needed. Plus we hadn't talked money yet. If I had to blow off dad for a few days it was going to cost somebody else besides me.

"Run down the target for me." Since John knew what I meant by that, I headed for my truck, not shocked at all that John was still working his private investigator angle.

I think what struck most of his clients as odd was that most P.I.'s kept files on their targets. John didn't need files. He had a photographic memory and the most amazing recall I'd ever seen. Even as kids, though he used it as more of a party trick back then, it always made me feel like the boy had super powers. We toyed with the idea of creating a comic together once about his skill. Sadly we couldn't come up with a usable title – Memory Man just didn't seem cutting edge.

"Reigner, Lee and Stratford IS the target, Man! They work with some huge conglomerate out on the east coast. You heard of that new Brainwaiver contest right? The new tech that's supposedly just been invented with implants that you control through your smartphone? Well, it ain't new Brother. This tech has been around for a while and has found another home. I can't go into a lot of detail here. We need to meet in a secure location for me to run down the rest, but I will say this – I've got a list of the winners and the current test subjects that have been implanted with the tech. Three on that list have died. Teenagers, Man... just kids. Gone."

Something else was up, I could feel it. That freaky sixth sense was bugging me like crazy and I really didn't want to know what was setting it off. I didn't want to know but here's the thing. Back in the day, my father beat a vital truth into me. It's ingrained into every thought and every action that I take. It's why I applied to work in law enforcement, was invited to apply for service in the FBI and finally drafted into service in the CIA, running black ops to serve my country. That movie "Red" with Bruce Willis as the star made spy games look fun and entertaining. But they weren't. Far from it – and it was that truth that had become ingrained that kept me from walking away from it all.

A boy thinks of and is responsible for himself; a Man knows the truth, that he is responsible for himself and everyone around him. It's MEN that keep our country strong and our families together. Men produce men he said. I was a man when I came out of the womb. I was a man when I served my country and my family. And I am the same man that can't stand by and not do something when something needed doing.

"You have the list secured?"

Johnny stabbed himself in the right temple three times with his index finger. Mentally I winced.

"Right here man. Can't trust that kind of Intel to any other kind of storage."

How did I know he would say that?

"Alright, we do this in a secure location – where and when?"

"You at a new site yet?"

Sampson Construction and Concrete, my father's construction company usually sets up a trailer with a full office including communication and networking on site at the location where work is being done.

We'd been on this last job for about 4 months now, due to finish up in less than 3 weeks.

"Not yet."

"Call you at the site; give you the run-down of the next meet. Client's going to want to look you over."

"Not auditioning Johnny. You need me, I'm in. I'll help you out as long as its short term. Don't need some pencil-neck telling me what's what."

John hunched his shoulders and put his trembling hands in his pockets. There goes that feeling again. The cold rain became freezing in my head as visions from days long past hovered in the dark corners of my mind.

This would not end well. I could tell when he refused to look at me that there was more, more that I should know before I agreed to meet up with whoever Johnny's client was... hell, before I even agreed to take his back on this one.

"Spill it Jacked."

Jacked is what I used to call Johnny when we were kids. His initials, JCD – Jonathan Charles Davies had us drawing that parallel... and since I was usually pissed and done playing around when I called him that, it also stood for "I will jack you up" – thus Jacked.

"Man..."

He still didn't look up. My control was slipping because the cold sleet that was kicking around my sixth sense was going nuts. I could feel every muscle in my body tense and my nostrils flare. I knew my eyes were narrowed into slights by now. He was my friend, my boy, my brother from long ago. But this feeling? It was pushing me to my limits and friendship was about to become a fluid concept. Hurting him wouldn't be fun, I would feel like crap afterward. Didn't mean I wouldn't do it though.

"The list..."

"What about it?"

"That's the thing, this ain't professional no more man."

I forced my balled fists to stay at my sides. I wouldn't get information as quickly if I broke his teeth.

"Okay." I said this through clenched teeth but I couldn't help that. All of my control was invested in keeping me from kicking the crap out of him.

"Okay, see – I started on this thing as a job but it ain't a job no more. We're family right? We look after each other and protect each other. That's why you were willing to just take my back on this case without knowing all the intel. You and Dinah and the kids. You were my family, man. I never got married and had kids. I couldn't, not with my head all messed up you know. So I had that through you. And then you lost Dinah. We lost her, man. That was hell, watching you go through that, the cancer just eating her away to nothing. I couldn't take it if something else happened, you know? You guys, you're all I got."

John and I hadn't talked about Dinah since the day of the funeral. I'd been wrapped up in my own grief at the time, mine and the kids'. I never paid attention to how hard he'd taken it. Never really thought about how he came to our place for the holidays back then or sometimes just hung out at the kitchen table after work while Dinah prepared dinner for us.

We hadn't been as close as we were as kids, but we'd still had something. It's that something that calmed me now, even though inside I felt frozen solid. Because I was well versed in Johnny-ism so I knew, deep in my bones, that I needed to brace.

"It's the list man. The names... I... Sorry Man. Danny's name is on it."

Wait, what? Danny as in Daniel, my 17 year old son; he's the only Danny I knew enough to care about his name being on this "list".

I shook my head jerkily, trying to dislodge the sheet of thick ice that was spreading past my thoughts and coloring my vision, turning everything gray.

"Must be a mistake Johnny. I heard the list of winners announced on that show last week. Cassie loves that crap. Only reason I paid attention is because they said Alton when they announced the winners. Danny's name wasn't mentioned. It must be a different Danny."

"I know my own godson's name Sam. Daniel William Sampson, born November 11, 1997 also listed at your address. And I know he didn't win that contest."

"Then how…"

"He's not a winner of anything Sam. He's been *implanted*. He's got that tech already in him. And three of the other 20 like him, have died from it."

Chapter Seven

"**Mommy**, are you awake?"

I was. To be accurate, I'd been awake awhile as I hadn't slept much the night before. To be more accurate, I hadn't slept much in the past two weeks. Not since the day I started reading Anabella's journal

"I am now baby-girl"

The bounce on my bed was my warning. I hardly grunted at all when my 11 year old ball of energy landed smack on top of me.

Green-blue eyes blinked at me through strawberry-blonde lashes so like my own. I was exhausted before, couldn't even roll over. Now, not so much.

I did a good job making this kid. Eh, well, I guess I didn't do it alone. Her dad helped a little.

"Guess what?"

"What baby?"

"I made you a special present to wear when you go to your contest party!"

I didn't bother repeating for the five-hundredth time that I really didn't win anything. Like many eleven year olds the world over, Sammie was well versed in selective hearing. If I said clean your room, she didn't hear me. If I said turn off the lights upstairs, she didn't hear me. If I said, I've got a humongous bag of tootsie rolls, her favorite candy, Oh what a surprise – she heard me.

"Thank you munchkin. You got it with you?"

"Nah, it's in my room. I just wanted you to know about it."

"Will you be able to FIND it in your room?"

"Not funny Mommy."

"Wasn't trying to be sweetheart. I need that room clean today okay?"

"Uh huh. Is Britney coming over after school or is Aunt Maggie coming to get me today?"

I tried not to fixate on that "uh huh" which translates, I heard you but I didn't hear you when you ask me later why I didn't do it.

Instead I focused on her question. It was really a good question. I hadn't heard from Britney since the week before when her cousin picked her up. I'd left messages for her repeatedly with no call backs.

Maggie had been picking up Sammie for me since she owns her own boutique close by in Florissant, taking her back to the shop until I was done for the day.

"Don't know kiddo. Let's plan for you going to Mag's again. I'll call the school and leave a message with the office if anything changes okay?"

"Kay. Get up, get up, get up! You said if we got out of the house early today we could stop by Dukes for donuts. Remember? You promised!"

Ah, the selective memory skill makes an ugly appearance. It's the evil twin to Sammie's selective hearing. Because I did promise we'd stop for donuts today. FIVE DAYS ago, I promised. I told her to clean your room every single day. Did she remember that? Nope, not at all.

I should be stern but she was batting those lashes at me and pinching my cheeks like my mom pinches hers every time we go for a visit. I really shouldn't allow the cuteness to get to me. It was such bad parenting to reward her not cleaning her room with the awesomeness that is Dukes Donuts. But who could withstand the cuteness that was my kid? Not I, grins the push-over that is me.

And so I did what any "helpless against the cuteness" parent does in these types of situations. I shaped my recently manicured fingers into claws, growled my warning and attacked the belly and sides of my offspring.

Raucous giggles escaped us as I transformed into the tickle monster of justice. Colonel William Prescott at the Battle of Bunker Hill once shouted, "Don't shoot until you see the whites of their eyes!" In that vein, when my family introduced someone to tickle torture, the saying became "Don't stop until you see tears in their eyes!"

Sammie's giggles turned frantic and, despite her many twists and turns, she couldn't escape my fingers of ticklish torture!

Too young yet to learn the strategic move that is the reverse tickle attack, I have mercy on the poor kid and ended the torture when she started shouting, "Uncle Mommy, Uncle!"

We collapsed side by side, exhausted. Residual giggles escaped us both while we caught our breath. So naturally I'm a little too distracted to notice what Sammie is up to.

"What's this?"

Anabella's journal plops down in the center of my chest.

Oy Vey. That five minutes of peace had been really nice. I'd like to have that again someday soon. Sadly, relief was probably not featured in the future forecast that is my life. I'd give almost anything to go back to not knowing – back to my every day, comfortable cycle of work, home, kid, and repeat.

"It's a journal kiddo."

"Can I read it?"

"No honey, it's not for Sammie eyes. It's only for Mom's eyes."

What a cute little pout. Pink cheeks, flushed from our recent tickle-fest, pooched out as her tiny pink lips purse up. Instead of the silent complaint this look is meant to convey, I took it as an invitation to smother my little girl with kisses. This produced tons of giggles as well as the distraction I was shooting for.

And I treasured every single second of it. My Sammie wasn't missing. She wasn't having horrific visions, nightmares or hallucinations. She was enjoying her life as a little girl just as she should, with slumber parties, peanut butter and popcorn nights and fun times with family.

The moment was bitter sweet though. Because while Sammie was enjoying life as it should be, there were at least two girls out there that weren't. And even though they aren't mine by birth, my heart still bled.

Sammie suddenly pulled away and hopped out of my huge four poster bed, already on the move with the promise of Dukes Donuts putting extra pep in her step.

While I laid there, hugging the journal to my chest. The deep sigh I'd subconsciously breathed caused my arms to tighten protectively around the book. And I really wished, not for the first time in the last two weeks, that I were holding Mandy and Anabella – keeping them safe instead.

"Mommy! Dukes! You promised."

Another sigh later, I placed the book back onto the night stand where it had been, making sure my marked page hadn't been unmarked in the transfer.

We had to hurry if we were going to make it to Dukes this morning. And that singular thought had nothing to do with the melt in your mouth donut holes that were there, at this very moment, calling my name did it? No, not at all…. It was because I'd PROMISED… and good mommies kept their promises.

"Here are your donut holes Ms. Baltimore. And for Ms. Sammie, I have a special cream-filled, chocolate glazed donut with sprinkles, as ordered."

"Thanks Eileen," I grinned as I made the "gimmie gimmie" signal with my hands. I'm pretty sure that the leer on my face is obvious and a bit spooky. But the girls were used to it by now so I didn't bother to try and hide it.

Dukes Donut Shop was probably my second favorite place in all of Alton. Situated in the cutest storefront right on Henry Street, it was right around the corner from our place on East 9th.

Walking into that front door is like stepping back in time. The scents of fresh baked pastries and pies spilled over me every single time. The display cases hypnotized me with their fabulously fattening offerings of authentic whoopee pies, cookies, danish, and of course, our favorites, donuts and donut holes. The pretty pink and white walls brought back the 50's like nothing else could. It felt like that old sitcom "Happy Days" I used to watch on the Nick at Night when I was a kid.

The coolest thing about the bakery was, it's not just a fan of those that walk on two legs. Smack in the center, for pet lovers, was a little display with (what I have heard) are the best doggie biscuits ever made. Sammie thinks that we should test that theory by getting a dog. I told her good luck convincing me of that every time she suggested it. It might happen. Yep. In about 30 years when she finally cleaned her room.

"Need a pie today? We have fresh baked chocolate cream, yum." And here we go. I couldn't even get out of the door without more temptation being thrown my way. *Pastry Jezebels, all of them!*

"Em, do you not see my hips? I have to spend two weeks on the treadmill just because of these donut holes. No thanks."

Emily grinned from ear to ear at our usual discourse. She alone consistently played the chocolate cream pie trump card against me every time we came in.

Eileen's chuckles reinforced my suspicion that they must have a running bet going to see how long it took to get me to buy one. I might buy the pie one day...or not. I was serious about the treadmill. I shuddered and mentally slapped myself back to my happy place of donut holes sans guilt.

Sammie and I grabbed our bags and scooted toward the entrance, the morning crowd already making it hard to maneuver.

"Mom can I eat in the car?"

Opening the doors and buckling up is quite a job with our respective treats clutched tightly to us. But we didn't drop them... they were Dukes donuts, a rare treasure. We never dropped them.

Normally the rule is no eating in the car. But the wafting scent of donut and chocolate are calling our names. You only live once right?

"You can if you promise to clean your room today, okay?"

"Uh huh."

Here we go again. Too late to discuss it though since the kid is literally stuffing the chocolate sprinkled treat into every crevice of her mouth.

I needed a different tactic. Throwing my purse and the journal into the back-seat, I popped a donut hole into my mouth and started the car, then pulled away from the curb.

Pressing the speed dial number for Mrs. Same's number, I clutched my cell phone while making the U-turn that would take me back to Henry and toward Sammie's school.

I hadn't seen Anabella since she'd gone into the alternative treatment that's been spawning the activity recorded in that horrifying journal. And I hadn't heard from either Mr. or Mrs. Same regarding Mandy's status.

I left another voice mail message and disconnected as I gave my car, affectionately known as my little putt-putt, a little gas. And then my cell phone rang.

Thinking it was Mrs. Same returning my call, I answered without checking the caller id.

"This is Celine."

"Ms. Baltimore? My name is Andrew Townsend. I am an attorney with Reigner Lee and Stratford. We represent Cipher-Louis Technologies, Inc., the sponsors for the contest you've won. Is this a bad time?"

I watched my eyes narrow in my rear view mirror, my grimace of distaste even more apparent with bits of glaze crusting over my mouth and cheek. Classy.

"I'm driving if you consider that a bad time."

"Right. Can you tell me when you're available to come in for a meeting regarding your winnings?"

Never. Never is good.

"I would have to check my schedule and get back with you Mr. Townsend."

"Of course. But, Ms. Baltimore, if I may be frank – please know that the contest entry serves as a legal document electronically signed by you. I only mention this because it is in your best interest to meet with me as soon as you are able to avoid possible litigation."

Are these people serious? I have never heard of anyone actually being SUED for not accepting a prize they've won.

"I will get back to you when I have a moment Mr. Townsend."

"Thank you, Ms. Baltimore, I look forward to hearing from you."

"The pleasure is not mine." I disconnected immediately before he realized what I actually said.

This supposed pleasure of winning something I didn't even enter to win was starting to become a pain in my generous, donut hole endowed behind. Which reminded me, mental note: chocolate pie or not, I needed to spend an extra forty-five minutes on the treadmill tonight.

The little editor is silently laughed at my notation. I wonder if he was laughing at the extra 45 minutes or the fact that my inner self just answered, "uh huh" – and we both already knew what that meant... and where Sammie inherited that skill from.

Chapter Eight

"**It** is the Piasa again that talks to me this time. I'm scared because he usually comes at night. It's day time now. "I have a riddle for you, young Ana," he says. I do not like his riddles. They hurt people. They hurt me. I try to run away like I do at night but I can't move. My feet are sinking. I cover my ears even though I don't want to. His voice is really pretty, just like always. I won't know the answer to the riddle. I'm not smart like Mandy. But he won't tell Mandy so that she can help people. He only tells me. He is mean. He wants people to die. My hands are burning so bad, I have to let go or it will burn my face. I have to hear his pretty voice. I have to hear him sing. 'Same, Same, one cup one half in. Mane is where the battle begins. State explodes, Sell the line, Love joy no more; my time to fly, to even the score.'

I hate him. It is so hot now I cannot breathe. I scream for Mandy, Piasa laughs. He whispers that nobody can help me. But Mandy says don't believe him, he lies. I listen to her because I'm not smart like Mandy. I try to remember what she told me to do the next time Piasa comes. She gave me something to say. She said if I say it really loud, Piasa would leave me alone. What was it? Oh, I remember, Mashiah! Save me! I scream it right in Paisa's face. He screams so loud it hurts my ears. And now he's gone. Its day time again and my Resource Teacher is looking at me funny. I guess it's because I am still writing in my book Mandy gave me. No that isn't it. Something wet on my face is scaring her. I must be crying. But my ears are wet too, and my nose. I touch it. I feel dizzy. My hand *looks funny, like there are two but I know it's only one. Now I know why she is screaming louder and she sounds really scared. My ears and nose and eyes are leaking blood. I have to stop now. I will write some more later when I'm not so sleepy."*

My cell phone ring tone blared, a din of noise in my tiny office.

I picked it up to check the caller id, glad that I was alone. The ring tone was Vincent Price from the Thriller video... and creepy, coming right when I'd finished reading that last paragraph. I'd jumped so hard I almost swallowed my tongue.

Unidentified Number.

I sent it to voice mail. Lately I haven't been answering those. Despite the hang up calls I've been getting recently, I used to pick up just in case it was a potential client. That effort hadn't been worth the aggravation of getting yet another click in my ear.

I rubbed my temples and looked at the clock. I know I should be heading out of the door for this stupid meeting at that law firm but I still didn't move.

From my first to my third appointment the shooting pains signaling the oncoming headache had arrived with increasing frequency until, by the end of my last appointment, a full on migraine had taken shape.

Migraines are stress induced for me. While it could have been the lives of my visiting clients that set this one off, I knew it wasn't.

I still had no phone call from the Same family about the girls.

Rifling through my desk drawer for the Aleve I had stashed, I tried not to think about that last paragraph.

But I couldn't help it.

I popped the pills dry, leaning back to swallow. My eyes stayed closed as I tried to relax.

But I couldn't. Fear, from the moment I began reading this thing hovered in my office like a dark cloud. The ramblings, the visions, the predictions and riddles. All of those horrors began the day after Anabella received that implant.

It wouldn't be hard to believe that this was just the active imagination of a slightly autistic teen. Everyone who lives in Alton knows about the Piasa and the legend surrounding it. Heck, half of the businesses and a main street are named after the thing.

The local Illinois Indian tribe folklore read that the Piasa beast, a monster with the face of a man, antlers, fangs, scales, wings, claws and the tail of a fish inhabited the bluffs along the Missouri river long ago. The first written record or picture was from a French Priest, Father Jacques Marquette. The tale of its reign of terror on the Illinewek Indians is logged historically and there is even a state park site with the painting of the monster depicted above the caverns out on the great river road.

It wouldn't be a stretch of the imagination to believe that this thing fueled the nightmares of a child that lived in the area.

What I didn't understand was the details I'd read about me specifically in more recent entries. Details no one should know but me.

The alarm chimed on my cell phone. My first instinct was to grab hold of my throbbing temples but my hands were already there. I didn't even realize that I'd been rubbing my temples again.

I fought the urge to blow off this meeting and stumbled to my feet to gather my things. Jacket, phone and purse in hand, I shut off the overhead light, locked up and gingerly move down the stairs.

I beeped the key fob unlock button to my putt-putt, trying hard to stay alert to my surroundings despite my headache. The Aleve was kicking in but it's still hard not to get distracted by the pain.

So I almost miss the black pick-up parked right across the way on Broadway. It stood out because it looked brand new, despite the dirt in the big tires and dust streaks over the glossy black paint. And because I don't remember ever seeing it before.

Since I'd rather err on the side of caution, I made a mental note to ask the ladies in the downstairs Banquet Center about it tomorrow. That's the one good thing about knowing gossips; they usually knew everything about everybody.

And these ladies loved to work their gossip with pride and skill... like it was an Olympic sport.

The inside of Reigner Lee and Stratford was as gosh-awful ugly as the outside. I'm no art scholar and never claimed to be despite my "artsy-fartsy ways" –a proclamation of the gospel according to Mom.

But architecture is the reason that I fell in love with Alton, Illinois.

From the cobblestone streets on State Street to the historically statuesque houses all over town, Alton brought sexy back to architecture in a big way for me.

Huge southern wrap around porches, look outs built into attic rooms that allowed an astounding view over the bluffs, not to mention beautiful historical brownstones moved me to spout poetry, I loved it so much.

Some houses were built close together San Francisco style while others were spaced 3, 4 or more lots apart with plenty of space for gardens, children's play areas or gorgeous views.

I was struck dumb for a moment by the building that housed my office. My passion for the artistry of the area had grown astronomically from there. An old masonic temple building, The Temple Banquet Center had been preserved beautifully from the authentically laid stone work to its huge Doric columns and balcony significant to architecture from the 1800's.

Hence my disgust with the building I stood in now, the law firm of Reigner Lee and Stratford. Located in upper east Alton on George Street, its modernistic design of triangular glass patterns sat like a humungous zit on the face of beauty that is Alton.

A monstrosity of geometric design complete with satellite dishes everywhere, if the building were a person, I'd karate chop it in right in the throat. Don't even get me started on the inside.

Pure white or clear slick surfaced furniture surrounded me from the moment I stepped through the door. I felt like Beetlejuice in his here to fore un-produced sequel where he goes to heaven. Only it's not heaven, it's a fake - it's really hell. It's at that point that he realizes he'd rather be anywhere else than there, like in the attic dancing to Harry Belafonte or in Purgatory's waiting room with the witch doctor.

The pristine nature of the place was just plain creepy. It was a law firm not a hospital for cripes sakes!

"Ahem, May I help you?"

And no surprise, it came fully equipped with snooty, "desperately in need of a sandwich" receptionists, also draped in white from head to toe... how charming.

"My name is Celine Baltimore. I'm here to meet with an Andrew Townsend?"

The receptionist crinkled her delicate nose before leaning slightly to her left, touching her ear.

Actually, the earpiece was a nice touch. Perfect for fake-heaven's waiting room, it was translucent, almost invisible.

At this point I wondered who cleaned this joint. More importantly, how in the world can they afford to pay them to keep it this pristine? The finger prints alone would drive me nuts.

"Mr. Townsend requests that you be seated Ms. Baltimore. He will be down to retrieve you momentarily."

I nodded in what I hoped was a regal fashion and turned to the wall behind me across from the receptionist area.

See-through plastic futuristic type chairs jutted out of the walls before me. They reminded me, just in case I'd forgotten, that I was still a plus sized girl.

Not super-plus where I could literally to break the thing, but a size 14 which is perfect for my height (that's what I tell myself anyway). I'm just curvy enough to be uncomfortably snug should I deign to sit in one.

The ensuing debate with my little editor is seriously intense. I don't want to take a chance that anyone is watching me squeeze into that chair, but I haven't a clue how long Mr. Townsend will take to "retrieve me" as it were.

My little guy stamped his foot and pointed to the seat insistently, what a great communicator he is.

I mentally shrugged. It was a good idea to sit because my headache wasn't completely gone. Not to mention, as cute as my stylish heels were, at three and a half inches my feet were feeling the pressure so I could really use the break.

But still. She just told me to sit like I'm a third grader waiting for the restroom or something. I'm a grown, successful woman. I'm capable of making up my own mind about whether I wanted to sit or not, and as far as I was concerned I...

"Ms. Baltimore?"

Dang it.

Well this was embarrassing. Apparently I CAN'T make up my mind about whether I want to sit or not.

 Refusing to blush about the fact that I was just staring at a chair as if it would bite me on the rear end, I executed a nearly perfect runway turn. Mags and I had practiced them every time we went shopping at Nordstrom's. Who knew that the skill would pay off?

Having turned, I almost choked on my own saliva. Wow. I meet two exceptionally handsome men in as many weeks. What lottery did I win and how can I enter it again? Or is winning without entering becoming "my thing" – like Ross from the old show Friends, only his thing was "divorce".

"I'm Andrew Townsend. I'm very pleased to meet you Ms. Baltimore."

Was it my imagination or did he really just put emphasis on that "very"?

The hand held out to me was masculine and strong. Equipped with long tanned fingers, one of which (the pointer finger) sported a single black onyx ring in the shape of a triangle, that hand could probably tell stories.

Stories that, despite the alarm bells my little editor was sounding in my brain, I really wanted to hear.

Chapter Nine

She'd gotten out of the car like she was on her way to an execution.

Celine Marie Baltimore. 34 years of age, divorced, one daughter.

She was the second winner listed in the Intel John had provided. Since I couldn't just walk away from this thing I had to look past the red and white haze trying to cloud my mind and vision. Instead I needed to adopt a calm, methodical approach.

After spending all day searching every inch of Danny's room and hacking into his emails along with the files on his computer, I'd found no leads. That only left his cell phone for me to search somehow later since he carried it with him at all times.

When my service training kicked in, my body performed every task on autopilot. As always, I'm highly functional but I struggled mentally to keep myself coherent... to not "check out". Just the thought of my son being used as a lab rat for tech that's killing people has me itching to go Elvis and start taking the people at that law firm out, one by one.

My being on auto-pilot was why, when I saw her exit the Temple Banquet building, familiarity tugged at me but I still couldn't place her.

It wasn't until I got a full frontal the moment she turned toward my truck parked across the way from her car that I recognized her. At about six feet tall with the sunset caught in her almost too thick to manage hair, she should have been impossible for me to forget.

It was the lady from Fast Eddie's. Recall played havoc with my senses as the scent of vanilla and something else hit me. Yeah. It was definitely her. She'd run smack into my chest so hard I had to take a step back to keep us from falling. Grabbing hold of her had felt like I'd caught a cloud of soft fluff that was all woman. That's when the smell of her perfume had slammed into me like a Mack truck.

Want and need had brought every cell of my body to attention so quick my head spun. I hadn't wanted a woman like that for years, not since I lost Dinah. And that was before I'd gotten a good look at her.

I thought I'd seen the last of her that night. Fast Eddies is a pretty hot spot. People from St. Louis as well as folks travelling from all over swung through all of the time to hang out there. I figured her for one of those types since I'd never seen her there before.

Turned out she was local. I knew it was irrational and I couldn't explain it, but the fact that she was Alton made her mine... that and I felt like I knew her; needed to know her more than just in passing. She was mine to protect. According to her file (a file I'd made on everyone that made an appearance on "the list") she was divorced. That meant that there was no man around to keep her safe but me. And there had better not be a boyfriend in the picture either. If there was, he wouldn't be for long. She was mine. Period.

I followed her at a discreet distance while the freezing rain in my head intensified. The direction she was heading in was taking me right back to my target so I wasn't surprised when she pulled into their parking lot. I'd been staking out RLS for a couple of days now. And just like with Danny's room, I had no leads just yet. Until I followed her here. Did she have the tech implanted already?

Why else would she be going there unless she did? The thought that she could already have that crap in her made me sick to my stomach. My jaw clenched as my grip on the steering wheel tightened so hard my knuckles turn white.

The cold rain had turned to black ice mixed with a red haze again... but this time I didn't even try to stop it. I just sat there and I waited. Trying to get control would be a wasted effort at this point.

My cell phone rang and I was tempted to ignore it. Checking the caller ID, I inhaled a steadying breath before pressing the green call button.

"Enoch Bartholemew Sampson!"

She knew I hated that name. It was the worst name I'd ever heard in my life. But it was also the name that could make the dark ice recede so I felt human again. But no less exasperating. I didn't have time for this.

"Yeah Ma, what's up?"

"Your father just told me you took two weeks' vacation with no notice! You know that he's not supposed to be out there working with his heart condition!"

"Ma, Dad is out there every single day telling me what to do and sometimes redoing everything I *did* do. You tell HIM he's not supposed to be out there with that heart condition."

"I'm telling you! You'll just have to cancel whatever shenanigans you and Johnny have going on and come to work tomorrow. Your father needs you."

My head fell forward into the wheel and just stayed there. Shenanigans? Crap but my mother was nuts.

"I can't Ma. I promised Johnny I'd take his back on this. If it wasn't important I wouldn't have asked for the vacation."

Silence on the other end. It went on for a while. So long I started to wonder if we got disconnected somehow. I raised the display to eye level to check when I heard in a tone that I hadn't heard in years...

"This doesn't have anything to do with your previous work does it baby?"

And just like that, I'm back. Back in that dark tunnel where Mara is shouting, pinned down by what we thought were Syrian thugs. I'm back there smelling the gun oil, the burning stink of so many discharged weapons. And blood. Mara is down, gut shot. Her dark clothes and dark hair matted with sweat, in the night she's hard to see but I see her laying there, waving me away instead of calling me closer when the shooting stops. Rounding that bend of filthy boxes and crates I see why. A boy, no more than 10 with a semi-automatic weapon in his hands crouched there watching me, trying so hard to be brave. No more ammo left in his gun, he's shaking and sniffling, ready to die for something he hasn't got a clue about. Three of his friends lay there beside him, two wounded, one staring sightlessly in death into the darkness. I'd died a little with those kids that day. And then the sleet in my head took the place of whatever it was that died. I thought the sleet had faded for good after I came home to my family. It had all but disappeared. Until the day I lost Dinah.

"Baby?"

Her voice was just above a whisper which meant I had to talk and talk and fast. I protected those that belong to me, even from what I had become. No need for her to know all that. No need for both of us to suffer.

"A little bit Ma. But mostly it's about helping families and keeping people safe. I got a responsibility to fulfill in that Ma. I messed up with Dinah. Out there playing war games and protecting people I didn't know, I wasn't here to catch the cancer and protect my own family. I can't let that happen again, you know?"

It's better that she thinks that this is just about Dinah; I didn't lie to my family. But taking liberty with how I worded the facts isn't something I considered lying either.

There was a pause but I knew from past experience it wouldn't last for long.

"Dinah was not your fault Enoch. And I don't ever want to hear you say that again. The good Lord knows what He's about and people are always His business. Your daddy taught you responsibility but the other side of that coin is just as true which you've managed to forget. You do everything that you know how to do son. You work every gift and every strategy you know how to win whatever you need to win. But when it's all said and done, those things that you can't control, you give 'em to God. And you let it go. You understand me?"

"Yes ma'am."

Best words ever invented to stop a Mama on a rant… Yes Ma'am.

 "Good baby. Now you go ahead and take that time you need to fix whatever you need to fix. I'll just have to pitch in at the site and call on a few of your cousins to help your Daddy out. I love you son, and I'm praying for you."

"Thanks Ma."

I disconnected the call thinking I should probably pray too… for my cousins. Shaking my head not even trying to think about the pissed off phone messages that were going to be waiting for me from my kin next week, I refocused.

Two people that belonged to me were caught up in this mess I had to fix. That meant that at least two of my people could die if I failed… And the only lead I had was that Reigner Lee and Stratford is running the show somehow.

My mind and body locked, sensing something just over the horizon. Someone else might die before this thing was over. And if I had my way, the casualties would only belong to RLS Law Firm. When I finish with them there would be nothing left for them to even think about rebuilding. I promised this very thing to myself while I kept watch for Celine Baltimore's exit. That was another thing my Father had bred into me, something I never failed to do. I always kept my promises.

Chapter Ten

I tried not to be obvious in my appreciation for Andrew Townsend's attractiveness. It's not impossible to do but it dang sure felt like it.

I shook his hand firmly even though my own hand was shaking slightly.

His firm grip didn't surprise me since the handshake went perfectly with the man.

Tall and broad shouldered at about 6 feet 2 inches, he stood just short of my 6 foot 3 inches in heels. His clear gunmetal blue eyes were perfect for his strong clean shaven face. His lips had a bit of a bow shape; he would almost appear effeminate were it not for the strong chin and sharp nose that had a bit of a bend to it.

Perfectly cut and styled dark blonde hair framed his almost too pretty face. It wasn't hard to believe that this guy was probably used to getting a lot of female attention; he definitely had mine.

But I couldn't let him know that. It would make our upcoming chat a lot more difficult. Which is probably why they chose him to meet with me this time around.

"Follow me please."

Mr. Townsend turned smoothly and led me to the stairwell obscured behind the receptionist atrium.

The entrance to the stairwell was seamless. It is apparent from this side of it that the glass leading up the stairs on my right is really a one way mirror that looks down into the lobby. Therefore, it was also a place where one could easily check out someone such as myself who, in my propensity for foolishness, stared vacantly at harmless office furniture.

I shook my head in disgust. He was probably smirking at me in contempt right now thinking of how I went from forlorn to uppity in two seconds flat. I sighed quietly at my own hopelessness. This was definitely not one of my more stellar moments.

We reached the top of the stairwell. The scenery changing so drastically that I wondered if time and space have bent in on itself, placing me in a different building or perhaps a different time line.

Time travel not being possible (as far as I know) I assumed that there was a decorator out there with much better taste than the one that designed the lobby. The upstairs décor that involved rich wood paneling, wall plants and the beautiful earth tones of the plush carpet were much easier on the eye.

Approaching a fairly large conference room on our right I realized that this conference would include more than just the two of us as Mr. Townsend directed me inside, shutting the door behind me.

Grateful for the small favor of escaping fake heaven-hell, I had no concerns with taking a seat in the large very comfortable looking black leather chairs that circled the beautiful oak table. I didn't wait for the invitation either. My own little private rebellion was in full swing. *Take that you neo-modern Nazi's!*

"Thank you for agreeing to meet with me regarding the contest you've recently won Ms. Baltimore. I'd like to introduce you to Ms. Delilah Robinson and Mr. Lance Finney."

Wow. I nodded my hello at the Obsessed Hollywood anchors seated across from me and marveled. There wasn't just one but two television personalities right here in little ole Alton, IL. What was sad was that I didn't like either of them well enough to ask for an autograph. What a waste.

Greetings exchanged, I got straight to the point. I was never one to waste time and idle chit chat with people I didn't know and didn't want to know was exactly that so...

"Again, Mr. Townsend, I didn't enter the contest."

At that Mr. Townsend seated himself directly across from me and right beside Ms. Robinson. They made a striking couple, reminding me of Mr. and Mrs. Same. It was almost eerie how both couples looked so perfect together. Almost like they were hand crafted in pairs which would be totally insane.

Mr. Townsend took a deep breath while Lance and Delilah glanced askew at each other. He folded his hands together in dove tail fashion and in slow motion, raised his head to look at me across the table. And I didn't back down from that stare either. I was from the Midwest, he would have to come at me with something more than a staring contest to intimidate me. If this was all they had I was gonna eat this meeting for lunch, get them off my case and get home with enough time to take my kid to a dollar movie. All of these thoughts were quickly flashing through my mind as we sat there, gazes locked, glaring at each other, eye to eye.

I could almost detect a nearly imperceptible smirk. I couldn't tell exactly what he was thinking, but suddenly I had a bad feeling about how this was going to go. And the Darlings of KMCU sitting in on this meeting did not bode well for me.

And just that quickly, the man's demeanor shifted. Charm appeared to ooze out of Townsend's pores. If his attractiveness weren't enough to get me to nod my head stupidly and obey whatever it was he was about to say, the way that he was now looking at me probably would have been enough to convince me.

Except I'd already exceeded my quota for falling for hot guys this month, and I meant that literally as well as figuratively. One hot guy camped out in my brain was enough to fuel my fantasy reel.

Two was one too many, I'd end up blowing a gasket trying to take on this smooth talker. And besides, he had soft hands. Manicured ones. Metrosexuals were so not my thing. I preferred to fall into mad, unrequited love with manly men, like that guy from Fast Eddies.

Mr. Townsend was just about to speak when Lance interrupted, probably losing patience.

"Ms. Baltimore, I don't believe that you understood the conditions of the contest that you've won. I won't argue whether or not you actually entered the contest, however I would like to point out that, were someone to fraudulently have entered you, they would have to have known some very intimate details about you, not to mention sensitive verifying data like your social security number and address. While someone could have quite possibly stolen your identity, it is very difficult to believe that someone would do so with the purpose of entering you into a contest where you would win a cash prize, a party on a casino boat and the most expensive technology one could buy to date. You do understand why we are finding it very difficult to believe that this would be the case?"

The first lawyer I spoke with sang this same song to me the day I called, only not as politely.

I knew how crazy it sounded. Heck, there is a part of me that would have probably jumped at the opportunity to do this under normal circumstances. Only these circumstances weren't normal.

My patient has this thing implanted in her head. And the last bit of news that I have about her comes from her journal where she is bleeding out of her eyes, ears and nose. I don't know where she is, how she is or if she is even alive.

What I do know is that I would let them take every cent I have, including my practice, before I allowed them to put one iota of that death tech in me.

But saying no outright wasn't an option either. I'm no private investigator so I don't know much about what I can do to get the information that I need. What I did know is that this contest may be my only way to find out what's going on with Anabella.

I just didn't want to get killed in the process. That meant I just might have to find another way. Staying on these people's radar was just too much of a risk. So I countered their logic with a little bit of my own.

"I understand all of that and would even agree with you were I sitting on that side of the table. But the fact remains that I am on this side of the table Mr. Finney. And just like its not plausible that someone would steal a person's identity to do all you have stated just now, isn't it equally as strange that someone who would have actually entered the contest and won the prizes you've named would suddenly decide they don't want it, even under the threat of litigation?"

"Touché Ms. Baltimore," Mr. Townsend stated with a smirk that was no longer imperceptible but flagrantly flaunting its sheer loveliness for all female creation to admire.

I nodded and waited. I know from past experience with lawyers that the comment wasn't a concession, it was a preface. I was not wrong.

Apparently they'd decided on a tag team confrontation to convince me of my obligation.

Ms. Robinson was up next, leaning forward slightly, her hands below the table and her eyebrows raised.

"How about a compromise? What if Andy here has his IT team research the whole shebang, what computer was used, ISP addresses and IP providers, stuff like that. And while he does that, you and I can just hang out. All you have to do is go with the flow. "

Hang out? What are we, twelve? And I'm not the most technically savvy person in the world but even I know that its "IP addresses" and "ISP's as in internet service providers". I hated it when people used technical lingo and didn't have the faintest clue about what they were talking about.

Mr. Finney continued where Delilah left off, "Accept the cash prize for now and just stash it in an account somewhere so that you can easily return it to CLI in the event of proven fraud. "

I considered all of what they were saying until I couldn't think anymore. Placing both hands behind my neck I bent backward a bit to stretch and clear my head. I instigated this moment of seeming consideration to further observe Lance and Delilah while they waited for my answer.

Lance and Delilah didn't look like matching bookends together, not like Delilah and Mr. Townsend did. They were a contrast of opposites in fact. And anyone that actually watched their show could probably tell that they disliked each other on a whole other level.

Even the word hate would be a fair descriptor of their obvious disdain for one another. Delilah sat there in her pretty pink blouse with the lacy collar, blond hair swept up in a pony tail and frivolous gold-bangle bracelets. She was the epitome of the blond bombshell.

Lance however, was dark and brooding. He was a study of rich browns from his chestnut hair and caramel eyes to his fashionably cut suit.

The slight curve upward of his eyes that hinted at Asian heritage wasn't as noticeable as his almost too full lips that would look better on a woman. Were his face to age about ten years, I could see a weak chin developing. And his eyes, while the color was impressive, were spaced too far apart. Having studied figure drawing, this was something I'd always notice about people. It didn't help that my dad would always say, the farther apart the eyes, the more cruel the man. All of that together had me shifting uncomfortably since I had his undivided attention.

It would be shallow to say that I didn't like this guy just because his eyes weren't close enough together. But it would be true. Cause I didn't like him, not at all.

"Go to the party," Lance continued as if there hadn't been a break in the conversation.

"I'm sure that Andy will find something to corroborate your story long before they actually get to the implant phase. "

Mr. Townsend flinched slightly. I noticed it the first time when Delilah called him Andy. He flinched again when Lance just said it. His jaw tightened slightly then relaxed like nothing had happened.

Mr. Townsend concluded with, "Ms. Baltimore, you would have our deepest gratitude in that, with your cooperation, we have avoided an incident with our client who has been promised very concise results, while you get all of the benefits of the contest win. This compromise would work for all parties involved."

For a moment, while Townsend was speaking my vision started to gray around the edges and it was difficult for me to concentrate. I blinked rapidly and turned my attention to the other two people in the room. They looked just as attentive as they have from the moment I entered, appearing to feel just fine. So whatever was going on, it was just going on with me.

It was hard to describe the hazy feeling coming over me and even more difficult for me to understand it, let alone mention it. I shook my head once, then again, trying to clear my vision and shake whatever this was off.

Because I knew what they were saying to me. And everything made sense, but... For some reason I just felt wrong. Out of sorts. Apathetic. I am considered many things such as OCD per my loving sibling, hyper to the point of irritating per my adoring parents; but I have never EVER been described as apathetic.

I tried to shake off the feeling one more time, breathing a sigh of relief as my vision started to clear. Only to have that relief cut short when it struck me as odd that Mr. Townsend was, at this moment standing beside me. He'd been sitting right across from me and suddenly in the blink of an eye… he wasn't.

"Are you alright Ms. Baltimore?"

My mouth was dry and I felt like I'd just swallowed an entire bag of cotton. Opening my mouth to respond was a chore. And the more I struggled to do this the angrier I got. I was angry because I knew somehow, beyond a shadow of a doubt, that these butt-heads just pulled some weird mojo hocus pocus crap on me, probably in an attempt to force my compliance.

My little editor is passed out in the corner of my mind. That was my first clue. I just had to do my best to be diplomatic without him.

"I will need time to consider the offer Mr. Townsend. I need to think this through. I have a child to consider so you understand why I can't make these types of decisions on the fly."

He was still looming over me and it was starting to freak me out.

It seemed as if he were looking for something, searching my eyes like the fountain of youth and the mysteries of life were bottle-capped inside.

"I do realize you have a daughter Ms. Baltimore. Her name is Samantha right? I understand that she is eleven years old?"

I can barely see him now, but not because I can't focus. It's because I'm squinting so hard. So while I can barely see his face, amazingly, everything else became clearer than my near priceless crystal song bird sculptures. I could hear the squeak of each chair; the hum of the heating system and slight tapping of Lance's foot. Every single sound was suddenly magnified. I went from squinting to flat out glaring at Townsend, my jaw stiffening as my hands balled up into tight fists. Because it took everything in me not to jump up and slug him at the not-so-subtle threat he just made to my kid.

And he had the nerve to smirk at me... again. Hmph; funny how it's not so cute anymore. And then he started yapping again like I would hear anything he had to say at this point. This guy seriously didn't know when to quit!

"Eleven is such a fun age. And really, we don't mind your bringing her along with you to some of the festivities if you like, all except for the dinner party, which is for the over twenty one crowd. We even have a pilot program for the implant that we are pushing through congress in hopes of test running it with select elementary schools and students in order to improve our youths' learning capacity and performance. We'd be happy to put in a good word for Samantha, perhaps get her into the program. Would you like that?"

He did it AGAIN! It wasn't worded as a threat. Anyone else probably would have been flattered. But I saw THREAT in big ugly red letters and had to quench my growing desire to crush this guy like a cock-a-roach.

I said nothing else, which to me – said everything – right before I rose stiffly from my chair and gathered up my purse and jacket before heading toward the door. I let him have the last word. That was totally fine with me.

Because the truth remained that, when you threaten a bear's cub, she didn't go on a rant or put on a performance for the world to appreciate. She just proceeded to rip your arms from your body before snatching your heart straight... outta... your... chest. I could have warned him and told him that he'd provoked the mama bear in me, but I didn't. He didn't deserve a warning. But something told me that he WOULD deserve every single second of pain and misery that was coming his way. And God would still love me. Because I could repent and ask forgiveness afterwards. See? I was totally diplomatic. Better, I would come up with my very own strategy to drop these dirt bags to their knees by causing a litigation and media nightmare that they wouldn't want to ever repeat. Great plan right? It was so perfect, I could almost believe myself when I announced in my head, I don't need the little editor for everything now do I?

Chapter Eleven

Watching her walk out of RLS made something in me stand up and notice. Not in the same way it did at Fast Eddies either.

It was a battle to resist the urge that insisted I get out, walk over there and shake her till her bones rattled while screaming at her to stay the hell away from this place. But something was off about her so I decided to do what I did best, watch and wait.

I'm guessing that it was the way she moved that had every alarm going off in my head. At the bar she didn't walk slow or calm, she moved in a hurried, frenzied way, but still confident. If I could put it into words, it was like her body wasn't doing everything she wanted it to do fast enough. She put all that together in a way that was sexy as all get out. And what was strangest is she probably had no clue on the effect that the combination of conflicting traits had on men. How it attracted them. How it attracted me.

But looking at her now, from the moment she walked out that door, her steps were slow and evenly spaced, almost like she was deep in thought. And that might have been okay if she wasn't shaking like a leaf, something I shouldn't be able to discern from this far away. But I could, partly because she had one of those little efficient hatchback cars, the Honda version, standard obviously, with no tinted windows or anything.

With no impairment whatsoever, I watched her grip her steering wheel and stare blankly into space but the air around her seemed to almost sizzle like the air off of a baking side walk on a hot summer day.

And just like that I knew. She wasn't distracted, confused or what I feared for a moment, drugged. She was furious. Mind numbing, teeth gritting, shoulders shaking, furious. And now I really want to get out and check on her but for a different reason.

Before I could move to get out of the truck she started her car, gunned the engine and took off out of the parking lot, turning on what should have been dang near two wheels onto George Street heading east toward E. 4th street.

She made a hard right onto 4th, her tires squealing.

Leaving me speechless.

It didn't take long for me to decide to follow her, just to make sure she got home safely. I wanted to know that she was okay and, while I really wanted to know what it was that had her so fired up, I figured that could wait.

I tried not to think about the fact that I also just wanted to know her, who she is, what she does, just - *her*. I could still smell traces of that vanilla plus something else scent that made me desire things I hadn't desired in a long time.

I still saw that quirky little smile and the shrug of her shoulders when she stood at the front door of Fast Eddies, so cute – a total contradiction of her "I am woman, hear me roar" character.

I wanted to fix this. I needed a solution soon because I needed to make sure my son lived through this and I wanted more time with her. And I would have exactly that. That's promise number two that I made to myself.

It didn't have time to think it through. She wasn't getting away from me a second time. So I took the corner at 4th myself like I was in a race for my life to tail her. I just might have been; for my life, for hers and for Danny's.

***

"Hey Danny man, wait up!"

I could walk faster to pretend that I didn't hear him. My head hurt like a friggin' beast, but if I ignored the captain of my basketball team it was like committing team suicide or something. I would never get passed the ball on the court. Especially since Rob was also the point guard.

I slowed my pace to match his as he ran up to me. Man I didn't have time for this. I wished my head would stop pounding already and explode if that's what it wanted to do. Put me outta my misery.

"Dude you were an absolute monster in practice today! What's got into you? You dating that Kelly chick you've been crushing on or something?"

Robs face swam in front of me. I knew I was answering him but it felt like my tongue was taking up my entire mouth. I heard my own words but they sounded slurred and my voice sounded really deep like somebody slowed down my vocals with the mixmaster music software on my computer.

"Nah man. Just upping my game. Practicing. You know how it is."

"Uh no, I don't actually. I haven't been on fire like that for a while. But straight up, whatever it is you're doing man – drills, imaginaries – whatever it is, I seriously need to get in on that."

I knew I was blinking a lot too but I still saw all gray, no matter how much I blinked. Like the world around me was fading into a black and white version of itself. This is what was weirding me out but I couldn't let Rob pick up on my panic. I had to focus. My man J warned me that I couldn't let people know when everything went all funky. I couldn't let them in on my edge because then they would be next in line to get one too. And I had to face the truth, my game was average before they put this thing in me. Now I was close to unstoppable.

"Sorry man, no time, I have to get home and check on my little sister. That girl is working my nerves like it's a full time job with benefits and bonuses."

Taller than me by about 4 inches, Rob was staring down at me a little funny, his brown face screwed up with what I imagine could be concern. After a minute of that I could barely make out his expression because his face started doubling up on me. What was really wigging me out was that his eyes were changing colors; everything was smoke grey… except his eyes. They went from their normal brown to a glowing green then a burning yellow and that was when the shape of them started changing… it was so messed up. I wondered if somebody slipped me some ex or something. I don't mess with drugs, especially ecstasy. I was at a party with my cousin Brittany once and saw these kids messed up on that stuff. Nobody could get near me when they were on that crap after that. I learned that day that you don't do drugs - drugs do you. You aren't in control and the worst thing you can be is out of control around a group of people that can record you with their phones and put your drama all over you-tube. No thanks.

Shaking my head to clear it I felt my damp hair slapping my ears, still wet from the shower after practice. That helped me focus a little but Rob was still frowning down on me even more now. And his eyes – man they are definitely yellow… and growing. It took a second but I saw the shape his eyes were beginning to take and wanted to crack the heck up. Cause somebody definitely slipped me something. Living in Alton, it's not hard for me to recognize that thing since its everywhere and when I say that I mean it is literally all over the place. I hate the legend of it and it was freaky that the stupid Piasa was suddenly grinning at me with the most evil grin I have ever seen, straight out of my boy's eyeballs.

"You alright man?"

I shook my head again hoping the Piasa would go away because it ain't real and I was feeling the urge to run away, screaming like a little girl, even though I know that I know that I know, this thing was NOT real.

"Yeah. I'm good. Why?"

"Dude, uh... did you fall in practice?"

"Rob, I have to get home man, so what's your deal?"

"Well uh; I haven't ever seen blood – that much blood anyway- coming out of somebody before. "

"What?"

I looked down at my shirt, which was pretty hard to do because my head was swimming like it was trying to win the Olympics. Huh, true story. There was blood on it. With my left hand still holding tight to my gym bag, I reached up with my right, which was still clutching my car keys, and touched my face.

What the heck? Scales? I didn't have scales!

"Uh Danny, I think we better call an ambulance man."

Rob's face by now had expanded and even though I heard his voice, it was coming out of the face of the Piasa. The beast had like, taken over his whole body or something.

"Ambulance?"

My voice was moving so slow I kept my words to a minimum. Rob knew what I was asking though.

Fangs opened wide to speak in a pale man's face that had huge antler-like horns on his head. Man, if this got any freakier I might pee my pants like I did in preschool.

"Man you're bleeding. I'm calling 911."

"It's just a nose bleed dude."

I had to calm him down. I couldn't go to the hospital. I'd signed an agreement. Any medical treatment I needed was to be provided by them only. I had their card on me somewhere, but either way, it was just a nosebleed. I just needed to staunch the flow, get home and lie down. Nose bleeds weren't fatal... Oh, there was also that big-as-crap scary, legendary creature that didn't really exist staring me right in the face. They'd told me things would be almost normal; that there were only a few side effects like headaches and a little insomnia. Otherwise everything would be totally normal. Yeah right, this was normal, just like dousing myself with lighter fluid and setting myself on fire was... totally normal.

"Your nose isn't the only thing bleeding. Blood is coming from everywhere, man. You hear me? EVERYWHERE."

Hmm. The Piasa had some big freaky wings. Who knew? I mean, the picture showed wings but nothing like this. These things were massive. Wait, what did he mean, I'm bleeding everywhere?

I looked down at my shirt again and it was saturated with blood. So much so, the color of the shirt was getting darker, just a dark gray in my black and white world, but still. It was hard to see my jeans since I was sitting down on the ground beside my car. Wait, when did I sit down?

"Wait Piasa. Here. My bag. Card. Front pocket."

"Man did you just call me the freaking Piasa? What in the name of the big bang theory are you on dude?"

"Pia- Rob man. Get. Card. Or Cell. Speed dial. 2."

Piasa-Rob was frowning at me now but I knew he understood.

I felt a hand rummaging through my front jeans pocket. So weird. I hoped the cheerleaders had all gone home from practice. I felt exhausted. I should be too tired to care. But Kelly is fine. I don't want her to think... whoa dude!

"Other. Pocket. You. Freak."

Piasa-Rob shook his head and mumbled, switching pockets like I asked. Sorry dude. I'm just not that into you, I thought. Then I chuckled. It was a wet, soggy sound as he put my cell to his ear and touched the display.

"Hello? This is Robert Allen, I'm a student here at St. James Academy."

Piasa Rob was saying something to me; only his fanged face didn't match his words so I wasn't getting it. What did he think? I read lips? Clueless fictional beast, what good are you?

"Yeah, no. I don't know what you just said, but my friend here Daniel Sampson is on the ground in our parking lot BLEEDING OUT OF EVERY ORIFACE!"

Wow. Piasa-Rob sounded pissed. What was he mouthing now? Dude, file those fangs down already and I could probably understand you!

"We're in the parking lot on the east side of the building. You need to bring an ambulance. He's still loosing blood and I don't think my YMCA life guard training covers stuff like this!"

Piasa –Rob wasn't talking anymore. I'm not near the river at all, but I heard water rushing around me. I looked up at the beast, no longer freaked out since it's obvious by the way the edges of my vision are growing darker that I'm about to pass out soon. He looked right back at me, so intently that finally the words he'd been mouthing at me slapped my mind so hard I almost passed out right then.

"STAY AWAY FROM ANABELLA!"

What? Anabella who? The only Anabella I knew was the little sister of that Jesus Freak Mandy. We don't even run in the same crowd. I'm a jock and; well, she's a Jesus Freak. She takes the fact that we go to a Catholic high school a little too far.

The beast punched my brain again with those words and if I'd had the strength I would have given him the finger, despite the fact that I'd nearly lost it long ago when my dad saw me do it to that Ingersol kid that lived down the block. He was a bully. And I didn't even know what it meant. I still didn't know what it meant. All knew was that my dad's grabbing my finger and twisting it till I agreed to never do that again meant it was the epitome of disrespect. And that ugly thing would get NO respect from me. Nobody told me who I can and can't hang with, not even my dad. I didn't bother flipping him off though; I was too busy feeling the cold concrete of the parking lot under my face. Apparently I didn't do things half way. If I was going to pass out and everything, face planting on concrete made passing out somehow more official.

"Danny man! Wake up!"

Nope. All I had the strength to do now was breath. And as the gray around me slid into darkness that was inching toward me from every corner of my vision, I honestly felt like, even breathing was overrated.

Chapter Twelve

"**Mom**, can we grab some ice cream before we go home? Pretty please?"

"Sammie, no means no."

"But MOM."

"Means no…"

"Mommy."

"Means NO you demon child!"

Mumbling and grumbling, the usual procedure also known as verbal pouting from an almost spoiled rotten only child, commenced as I crossed the bridge into St. Louis to pick Sammie up from Mag's place.

There was only one way to deal with my mini-me. Which was a welcome distraction from plotting my revenge against some high and mighty attorneys. And the subsequent begging of forgiveness from my All knowing God – who, of course, would know that I'm not really sorry until, you know… *after*.

It had been a whole week and I still had no clue of what I was going to do about it. Yep, a distraction would be good right about now.

"You should have told me that Dr. Dufenshmirtz stole your vocal chords and that you needed ice cream to treat your tragically torn larynx!"

Ah, there they are. Giggles and snorts. My kid. Her laugh was so goofy it could make *laughter* keel over and pee its pants cracking up.

"Moooommmmm."

Heh. Only eleven year olds could stretch the word mom into infinity with the patience of a true Jedi Warrior in order to get their way.

"Hey, would Phineas or Ferb complain about no ice cream? NO I tell you! By golly they would march up to one another until Phineas confidently announced-'Ferb I know what we're gonna do today,' and then they'd build their own ice cream fountain out of sheet metal and milk! So stop whining kid and get creative!"

More snorts and giggles. Who knew that the cartoon plot of Phineas and Ferb would be my Red Cross tonight, saving me from taking that reverent journey to our favorite ice cream shop in St. Louis, Maggie Moo's. Which, of course my sister absolutely LOVED because of the name.

"Momma, I've got something to tell you?"

Pulling off of the highway and making a right onto Lindbergh where my sister's shop was located by the old Jamestown mall property, I tried really hard not to deep sigh in Sammie's ear. Because when she says those words in that tone, what I really heard was James Earl Jones' Darth Vader voice saying, "Mom. Its about to go down!"

"Spill it Baby."

"Dad's coming over this weekend."

Only what it sounded like is, "dudscmngohvrdishwknd."

Yeah. I needed this like I needed time to speed up and bless me with wonderful gifts of aging such as arthritis or osteoporosis.

"Why."

It was supposed to be a question, it really was. But after years of dealing with my ex-husband and his various less attractive, younger and skankier versions of my more illustrious, big-boned self, my tone adapted for survival.

Better flat with no inflection than with the attitude I longed to slap onto the word. Which I would NOT do because, despite the fact that my ex-husband desperately needs a physician (put simply, he is NOT well), I must not indicate this fact to our very impressionable parrot-like young miss. There's nothing like your ex screaming into your ear through the phone that your offspring asked what a skanky wench is because she overheard her Auntie Maggie say it to her Mom in reference to his newest lady friend, Doreen. And who names there kid in this day and age Doreen? The woman was twenty-six, not fifty-seven for crap's sake!

"He wants to talk to you."

Turning into the parking lot of my sister's shop, I gritted my teeth and stifled the urge to say, NO DUH into the phone. I tried very hard to protect my kid from the sarcasm that flies out of my mouth unchecked just incase the little editor isn't on his J-O-B. Sadly, after all of these years, I'm still not very good at that.

"Okay baby. I'll get the details when I get inside."

The quiet "kay" I heard before disconnecting ripped my heart out. She always said it like that when she knew that Derek and I were about to go toe to toe.

Guarding her from that was useless. I wished our drama wouldn't ever touch her, but no matter how hard I tried to stifle it for her sake, the more impossible the man became.

Because of course, my life isn't difficult enough as a single mother that works part time, runs her own business and is currently being harassed by the largest law firm in all of the Midwest.

And just like that, I have to ask myself, Celine, what are you doing?

Who am I to take on the largest law firm in the Midwest, let alone one of the top ten technology companies in the world?

I was just a social worker. A glorified one with an LCSW tacked behind my name, but a social worker nonetheless.

Eyes clenched shut I gripped the wheel with all of my strength. A part of me wanted to rip the thing right out of the chasse.

Why did I have to do this? Why did I have to find out what's going on with Anabella and Mandy? Why does it have to be ME that suffers because of the Same family's, heck, other people's poor choices?

I allowed myself that moment. But just that moment: that 30 seconds of pent up anxiety at this feeling of helplessness and self pity before I let it go. There are times when I would go into prayer about these things but right now I didn't bother. Because I knew for certain, I could try to invite God to this little pity party all I wanted, but He hasn't ever shown up before so I'm pretty sure He isn't going to make this one time an exception to the rule. He knew that I knew what he was about... He was God. He was power and He was love. He wasn't about complaining or whining, he was about solutions. And what He had to say about my issues, He knew I wouldn't want to hear... not at that time anyway.

Trust me.

So simple. And irritating when all you wanted was for someone to sing along with the "poor me" lyrics to your "it's all so unfair" song.

Closing my car door harder than I should have, I winced and took in my sister's shop. Brushing away the emotional dregs of self-pity, I focused on the great job Mags had done with her place.

Honestly, it was the cutest little boutique I'd ever seen. Catering to the growing population of ethnic cultures that are beginning to infiltrate the North County St. Louis area, the store reminded me of Claire's, a cutesy little mall store for little girls.

While I'm not ashamed of my Irish-American heritage, my sister and I have always had a fascination for all things ethnic. From soul food and authentic Mexican food to the baby "china town" on University

City's Olive Street where it is lined with different types of Asian novelty shops, grocery stores and restaurants.

Our love for all things ethnic stems from what we were taught as kids – every culture and race possessed undeniable beauty- a beauty that is God-given and fueled the pride of each nationality. Truly intelligent people lovingly appreciated the differences just as one appreciates diverse and varied works of art. One is never better than the other, just different. No less beautiful and no less perfect.

Mags instilled these ideals into her shop for pre-teen and teenaged girls. From the marquee sign proclaiming "DiverCity," to the window displays of exquisite Mexican, Asian and African jewelry and clothing displayed, the shop glowed with arrays of pink, electric blues and beautiful browns.

With the little coffee bar in the back and what Sammie and I called, "the baby book store," the small shop had become a hit to teenaged crowds lately.

Hearing the bell jingle as I walked through the door, I smiled when the scents of cinnamon and vanilla hit me hard. You'd think the variety of smells would clash, but somehow, sis made it work. Once past the scents that greeted you at the door, the more subtle smells of jasmine and patchouli seductively lures the customer to the right where the coat racks stood beside the knick-knack shelves that sported lit candles and, my favorite, crystal figurines.

I freaking adore this store.

"Daughter mine!"

And, that's my dad. Who, as usual, was, "yelling like a heathen," as my mom would say. Because apparently he wanted me to know that he was here. I had to know that because it was imperative that I greeted him first and foremost as was his due.

Which is why we jokingly called him King Henry the 8th when we were kids. But once we were in high school and had taken a class or two in English literature, we discovered what Henry the 8th was really like. So we stopped calling him that. Immediately.

Fast forwarding to the present, since he'd been retired now for about 5 years, Dad spent a lot of his free time at the store making repairs. Or fishing.

Daddy rounded the corner from the back "employees only" section of the store, stomping through the coffee bar area and into the store proper before I could finish hanging up my coat. About two inches taller than I, there was something about Dad's presence that turned him into a living, breathing tower of Dad-ness; intimidating in my youth (especially when I was being sneaky) but on days like today, a huge comfort.

Not even waiting for me to make a full turn from the coat rack, I was squished into a hug so perfect, I was catapulted back in time to when I was ten years old and had burned my hand trying to make s'mores at the kitchen stove.

He'd grabbed my hand and some butter and slathered it over the burns while he instructed Mags to grab the tiny medical kit we kept under the sink. I'd cried and screamed for ice or cold water but he'd calmly held my hand and spoke so soothingly that I'd had to calm down to hear him.

"It won't help daughter mine, it's a temporary fix; one that never lasts. It's the easy way my darling girl, and a trick. Don't ever fall for the easy way. The price you have to pay is always greater than you expect."

He'd begun to rub the burn ointment onto the burns and I'd calmed further, feeling some relief.

"Life is pain daughter mine. You've got to grow strong so you can handle that pain and get to the joy on the other side. That's why you don't take the easy road girl. Easy hurts you more in the long run. Understand?"

I didn't understand then. I'd just nodded and fell into the most awesome and safest hug in the world. I didn't fully understand that truth until I married a man because it was easy... in the beginning. We didn't argue or fight much. We had very little drama and he seemed totally supportive and loving... in the beginning.

Hugging my dad just a little bit tighter I squeezed my eyes extra tight to keep the tears at bay. Because I don't know how we ever thought to call him Henry the 8th. King Henry was an idiot. But my dad was wiser than Yoda.

"You alright?"

Squeezing him again just because I could, having conquered the tears, I leaned back a little and smiled his smile right into his face.

Which is what he always accused me of when I was up to no good. "And don't you dare smile my smile at me girl, I know what it means because I invented it!"

I couldn't help but grin at that thought which only succeeded in causing him to narrow his eyes at me. And before he could accuse me of anything that I was or was NOT guilty of, I beat him to the punch.

"Daddy! Are you losing weight again? You know how Mom feels about you getting so caught up in your projects that you forget to eat."

Heh. What better way to make that expression of accusation disappear and replace it with one bearing a guilty sheepish smile? As if that weren't enough, he shrugged his shoulders at me and grinned MY GRIN right back into my face. Men. Biggest kids ever.

Shaking my head and laughing I let go and turned just in time to catch my rail thin dynamo, moving so fast all you can see is mostly legs and blond ponytails.

Catching hold and hugging her tight I whispered a prayer of gratitude. Because I would rather deal with baby-daddy drama than have my girl become ill or come up missing.

Suddenly I didn't care about the whys or the answers to my why me's as I'd wrestled with God in my car. I was holding in my arms a pretty convincing argument for why. I would want someone out there to care, to do SOMETHING if it were Sammie in trouble. It was just that simple.

I liked that answer better than the one I heard whispered deep in my heart, the one I chose to ignore.

It's again, short and sweet but powerful nonetheless. And, again it irked me. It was just three little words that had me so conflicted. I wanted to be grateful for my beautiful girl and throw something at the wall in a fit of frustration at the same time.

Because while God doesn't attend pity parties, He apparently doesn't mind express mailing His response to your "pity party" questions – and the, "why not you?" He answered me with is really so NOT what I want to hear... and much worse than the usual, *TRUST ME.*

Chapter Thirteen

"**It's** my son Ms. Baltimore. He's missing and I don't have any other leads but you."

What the haymaker?

When I woke up this morning I had no clue that my day would be going in this direction. I knew that I would have to deal with the lawyers and the ex husband soon but I was determined to ignore them until I had no choice.

I was still clueless about how I was going to address the party situation. Lance, that TV guy with the wide-spaced eyes, had left me no less than six messages. Which really wasn't helping. I don't do so well under pressure when making tough decisions. Instead I evoked an age old "Baltimore" family trait. I task avoided.

So I'd pressed the "ignore call button" for Derek and the lawyers at least fifty times while trying to focus on the mystery that is Anabella's visions. They could be just hallucinations but that Piasa one sounded a lot like it was providing clues. Only when I got to the office and opened my desk drawer, the journal was gone. Like the wind. Teed off, I slammed the drawer shut so hard that one side of the ornate little handle broke off. Just freaking fantastic.

And the parade of stupid that is my life kept on marching from there. My quick run for coffee turned into a slow run due to long lines (new staff training in the coffee house) and my spilling hot coffee all over the place because people were bumping me around like I was the bonus round in a video game really didn't help matters any.

But that's life right? You have good days and bad days. Except this parade just kept on marching with more eager participants joining in.

Two of my remaining six regular clients no call – no showed on me. That and the missing income from Amanda and Anabella's visits meant making the office rent was going to be tight this month.

My hospice supervisor at my part time job called and asked me to be on call this weekend because their last available social worker had a death in the family. Which meant that Fast Eddie Friday was out. Sadly, it also meant that I was actually available to meet with Derek about whatever it was he wanted to talk to me about. Dang it.

I could save us both the time and effort and just say "NO" to whatever it was he wanted. But I knew from past experience that he wouldn't settle for that. Everything had to be a big production with him. He should have seriously considered going into Drama – maybe get his own reality show; The REAL EX-HUSBANDS of the MIDWEST; complete with tractor pulls, bib overalls and some type of muscle car. Nah. Child support enforcement serving absentee fathers would probably kill that thing dead in the water.

Life continued on and showed me that Murphy (my nickname for Murphy's Law. Apparently we have a love/hate relationship that I absolutely love to hate) can be cruel as well as spiteful and vindictive. I knew that he could be, but I felt, just for a moment, that somehow Hope felt like intervening and wanted to make up for this mornings challenges.

I'd been sitting there at my desk despondent about my wasted morning and my soon-to-be wasted weekend. My head had just fallen to the desk with a loud thunk when I heard several more thunks; only these were coming from the direction of my office door.

I don't even remember getting up to open it or anything but of course I did. All I remembered was my first thought as my mouth dropped open.

I must be dead.

That's the only thing that popped into my head as I blinked at the man standing there in my hallway. Because stuff like this does not happen to me. My patients come up missing, my ex-husband is a pain in my rear and my life gets taken over by a contest I didn't even enter. That's the kind of stuff that happened to me.

What does not happen to me is stuff like this where the best looking man I have ever run into – literally- is standing at my door and saying my name. Did I mention that he knew my name?

Dadnabbit that little editor! He should have been front and center. I should probably consider replacing him with a woman; she'd be more efficient and less prone to letting my mouth hang open like I worked for a drool farm.

"Are you not listening to me again Ms. Baltimore?"

I'd zoned out on him before hadn't I? That first impression wasn't a very good one and since I didn't want to make this kind of thing a habit I had to kick the old guy in my head into gear. Quick – say something man! I needed him to actually string two words together for me, without holding my nose this time around!

"Yeah. That's me. Have we met?"

You are so lame little editor. You finally make an appearance and THAT is what you came up with?

"We did a while back at Fast Eddie's. I never got a chance to get your name though. I'm Enoch Sampson but you can call me Sam. May I come in?"

"Well that's going to get pretty confusing."

"What my name? Sam's simple enough."

I didn't get why he was frowning at me like I just set his drawers on fire.

"Ri-ight. Sam is a pretty simple name but that's not what I'm referring to."

"Okay. So what's confusing about my coming into your office exactly?"

"Nothing."

I don't know if it was my slightly exasperated tone of voice or my shrug that had him frowning down at me AND putting his hands on his hips in that, "Lord give me patience," stance.

I didn't really care either. I guess I was too busy enjoying the view.

Man. Those green eyes hadn't lost their luster had they? And that dusting of facial hair had me thinking that all he needed was an ax to pose for a lumberjack calendar. I'd so buy that.

I tried to keep my eyes from crossing with lust but it was so hard to do... especially when he bit his lip like that and his head kind of tilted just a little to the side. I had to remind myself that nice Christian girls don't drool all over men they hardly know. But that still didn't help.

A mental slap from my little editor brought me back to reality because I really didn't know what I'd said to bring us to this communication standoff. Let's see, there's his showing up then saying his name, Sam. With his name being what it was and the fact that we call Samantha Sammie or Sam on occasion, this could get really confusing if he were to... Oh!

I smacked myself in the forehead and chuckled as I opened the door wider for him to step through.

"I'm sorry, sometimes I subconsciously assume that other people have mind melding capabilities that allow them to join in on my mental conversations. My daughter's name is Samantha and we call her Sammie or Sam as well."

"Ah." He stretched the word out a little as his hands traveled away from his hips and burrowed into his pockets.

Please, please, please oh eyes of mine, stay above the waist. I've got enough to repent for later.

A little irritated at my libido and its propensity for getting me into trouble I couldn't help the slant of my thoughts.

Because seriously? He went from Alpha- male powerful to appearing self conscious and cute in just two seconds flat – just from putting his hands in his pockets! Who DOES that?

And who knew that it would be so. Dang. Hot!

"I probably shouldn't expect that though."

At first I couldn't find two words to rub together to start a fire, now I couldn't stop them from taking over. Oh wayward tongue with your silly fickle ways, thank you so much for all you do (not).

"If others could actually hear what went on in my head they'd either throw me off the bluffs or jump themselves. You know that old commercial with the frying egg – this is your brain on drugs? That's my brain on good old oxygen. If I'm breathing I'm probably thinking something insane."

"Uh huh."

At that point his shoulders were almost to his ears with his head tilted to the side. And I'm too embarrassed by my verbal diarrhea to get that the little half smile I remembered so well is pulling at his lips. I was like a train wreck about to happen. I know that I should absolutely positively NOT be looking at those lips. I blamed the twitching. It looked as if he was trying his best to keep that grin at bay but It wouldn't be denied.

He wasn't much of a talker was he?

It started getting hot and my small office was growing tinier by the minute. My rubbing my hands on my jeans so fast that they felt like they were about to catch fire may have had something to do with that.

I should have at least bothered to check my hair or clothes in the mirror before I'd answered the door. If I had spinach or something in my teeth I would never be able to live down the embarrassment.

And then I reminded myself with a sigh of relief that I hadn't had spinach since yesterday. Yay me! I have a reason to thank my regular and somewhat obsessive dental hygiene.

I should have invited him to sit but then I would have had less of him to look at.

Good gravy, the man's physique was so broad and perfect it was almost mind-boggling. The only thing that could come close to this magnitude of hotness is if someone genetically spliced the DNA of a bear with the hottest human male in the world; and the creature got all of the good parts from both species and none of the bad.

And worse, he'd been standing there looking absolutely perfect in black from head to toe – from his tight black tee and black jeans all of the way down to the black timberland boots on his feet. The man oozed charisma and hot maleness all over my tiny office. I deep breathed and realized I had actually been holding my breath. I should have had a seat instead.

"Is it okay if I sit down so that we can talk? I really need your help."

And that's when my brain actually started working again. It was a lot like someone jump starting a car battery. My thought process went a little like this:

Huh? Oh! Ooohhhh. This was not a social call? But he's so beautiful. And I so need something good to happen to me right now! That was my denial phase. And then:

Dadnabbit! Time to put on my professional face and do what I do to make the baby-bucks around here. I so hated having an alter ego.

Like Clark Kent and Superman. Only I wasn't really that super now was I?

I slipped into my pro persona easily on a daily basis. But doing it in front of this guy, yeah, not so easy.

I cleared my throat a couple of times as I walked around to the other side of my desk.

"Please do, by all means Mr. Sampson." I'd said, which wasn't all that bad since what I really wanted to do involved me falling into his lap and petting that muscular chest until my fingers fell off.

And so here we were, sitting in my office and staring at each other after He'd just dropped that bomb on me. Had I heard him right? His son was missing? Because apparently two missing teens and a missing baby sitter wasn't enough on my plate.

How did I get here again? And why am I all of a sudden the patron saint of lost teens?

"I'm sorry, Mr. Sampson. Why exactly am I your only lead?"

He was leaning forward over his knees with his hands clasped between his legs. The look on his face was earnest and I could see from the faint lines appearing on his forehead that he was obviously strained and concerned for his son. And knowing all of that my heart broke a little for him. But that didn't change the fact that I didn't know his son, or at least, I didn't think I did, so the link to me and how I was his only lead remained unclear.

"Brainwaiver."

He said it through clenched teeth and I could have pretended ignorance and questioned what he said, possibly ask him to repeat it. But he didn't have to repeat it. I'd come to despise that word with a passion so I could probably hear it spoken in several different dialects and still feel that shiver of abject hatred run down my spine.

"How can I help?"

I probably wasn't meant to see him exhale but his shoulder's sudden relaxation was a telltale sign.

"Meet me Friday at your place? Its most likely more secure there than here."

I also saw the tension easing in his forehead, which made me feel better for some reason.

And it wasn't a struggle to agree to meet him since Friday was my on-call day anyway.

What struck me as odd though was that he didn't ask me for my home address. He pulled a piece of paper out of his pocket with my address on it and a question mark. I nodded my head yes, confirming that it was my address and that was it. There'd been no need to really say anything else.

So as he got up to leave I'd silently contained my freak out about this whole scenario and watched as he approached the door. He'd turned then, looking at me for a moment, almost like he forgot something, but, having changed his mind I guess, he nodded his goodbye and left.

I watched him walk out the door, his back straight, confident and strong. And suddenly I felt exhausted again. What in the world was going on in little old Alton, IL?

I was tired of feeling tired.

I was sorry for him about his son. I was sorry about Mandy and Anabella. More importantly, I was sorry that the only news I would have for him Friday is bad news. Because the only clue I'd possessed about this whole psychotic situation, Anabella's journal, had just come up missing.

Thunk. That was my head hitting the desk again, except this time, there was no knock on the door to keep me from staying down there for a good long while.

Chapter Fourteen

Walking to my truck was the hardest thing I'd ever done.

And now I had to wait until Friday to see her.

Scenting her again was like walking into a room of pure, unadulterated longing. My heartbeat tripled the minute she opened that door and I had to fight my own body as the instinct to grab onto her and hold her to me played havoc with my control.

And I definitely had no time to dwell on that fact. I'd already determined that she was mine so there really wasn't any point in mooning over the woman.

I had plans to make and people to contact. It was growing more obvious every day that Johnny and I wouldn't be enough to crack this nut; I had to call in some back up — starting with the list of ex-marines and former operatives that Johnny and I compiled. These were his and my guys and gals from the corp. With a bond forged in battle and blood, they would always take his back. Just like I did.

And if they weren't available then it was going to get really ugly really fast. Cause then I'd have to go to my "other" list. But my son's safety was worth raising all hell which is what calling on some of my old team would accomplish.

I catalogued those feelings I'd been experiencing for Ms. Baltimore to be experienced at a later time. I had to because they meant something to me. They were the first things I'd felt in a week. I'd been nothing but numb since the day Danny didn't make it home.

Turning on my blue tooth, I hit speed dial to update Johnny on where I was at. He answered in a gruff sleepy voice as expected since he was a night owl and it was still early yet.

Giving him a quick rundown of what I'd learned it didn't take long to get his agreement on calling in our old teams. The hard part was getting them to show up as soon as possible. These folks weren't in the corps anymore. They had lives and families, jobs and responsibilities. Johnny assured me that it wouldn't be a problem and disconnected. He didn't have to explain that either. The bottom line was, when you've bled together and stitched up each other's wounds – you'd know for a fact that your corps brother or sister wouldn't call on you unless it was urgent. And this whole situation passed urgent weeks ago – the moment those three kids came up dead.

Having started the ignition I paused just for a moment to get my head together.

I'd only been in that office for about 30 minutes but it was long enough to catalogue everything that I saw.

From the placement of the furniture I could tell that it hadn't been moved recently. The carpet didn't show any changing indents or drag markings. But it did show slight footprints – methodical and patterned from one area of the office to another. They led to places in the office where the occupant wouldn't go every day such as the window sill, book shelf and the small table by the couch. It was also clear that items on her desk had been adjusted recently. The lady kept a pretty clean office so the small, almost miniscule areas around certain items on her desk that were more dust free than others were a definite red flag. Either someone had been in there searching for something or someone had planted a bug.

The beep in my headset indicating an oncoming call interrupted my thoughts as I pulled off.

"What's up Cass?"

I hated this. I promised my kids that I wouldn't ever lie to them. I couldn't bring myself to tell her that her brother was missing yet. I let her think that he was staying over at a friend's. Since they didn't run in the same circles at school and never really saw each other, it wasn't a stretch for her to assume exactly that.

What was bad however was breaking the news to my parents. Dad had gone extra quiet. He knew what that meant, that I was on the warpath for my son. His silence was his consent. Thankfully my mother insisted I send Cass over the minute school let out yesterday on the pretext of helping her out since the Christmas holidays were right around the corner.

"Hey Daddy!"

Loved my girl.

"How's your day kid?"

"Grandma reminded me to call you about something weird that happened at school yesterday."

My grip on the wheel tightened as I turned off of Broadway onto Harris. I was going to do one of two things when I saw my mother; give her a high five or hug her until she couldn't move. Smarter than any government operative I'd ever met; she had a hidden gift of listening and ferreting out information. To the people she's talking to it would seem like regular every day stuff. But my mother would dig without you realizing that she was digging. This is why my sister, two brothers and I never got away with anything.

"Oh yeah?"

I tried to breathe easy so Cass couldn't hear my excitement over the phone. I needed another lead like I needed air.

"You know the captain of the basketball team? Robert Allen?"

I did. I also knew that the basketball coach had seen Robert run to meet up with Danny after he'd left the locker room last week. No one had seen Danny since.

"Yeah honey."

I tried not to allow my impatience to slip into my tone but I needed her to hurry up and I needed her to do that yesterday!

"His mom was at the school yesterday morning, totally Teed off! I mean she lost it Dad, right there in front of everybody. She was screaming at the basketball coach and threatening to sue the school and junk. I was going to ignore it cause Dad, that was way embarrassing for Rob. So I stepped out of the gym hallway and ran right into Kelly, that girl that Danny likes? First, she asked me had I seen Danny. I was all, NO, he's my brother not my boyfriend. Then she was all, well something is going on and you need to find out if he's okay. I never liked her Dad, really, the boys only like her because of one reason."

"Uh huh."

Get there baby, come on. Give me something. Anything.

"Any way, I was like, why wouldn't he be? Then Kelly said that Robert's mom was mad because Robert was missing. She accused the coach of helping him run away from home or something. I guess he'd been mad at her the night before and they had a big fight. He left for school the next day and hadn't been home since. Some guys on the team were over there whispering that the last time they'd seen him was when they'd seen Danny at practice a week ago."

Another kid had gone missing? I pulled over and before I realized it, my head was resting in my left hand, my right gripping the phone to my ear. This crap was spiraling completely out of control. But first things first;

"Cassie. Baby I've got to tell you something."

Nothing. My daughter was a chattering magpie. She was almost never NOT talking. And since she's smart as all get out, I knew that she'd figured this out – it's why her grandma told her to call me.

"Baby?"

"No Dad."

I should have been more concerned about the flatness of her tone than her words. But I was caught up in pain that was all mine so the words were all I'd grabbed hold to.

"You have to listen to me now Cassiopeia."

I could hear that her breathing had increased into the receiver. Before I could continue she interrupted, talking so fast that I had to mentally play it back slower to understand what she was saying.

"Brit still hasn't called me back. It's been two weeks and even Aunt Helen's said she hasn't heard from her. She says Brit never ignores her calls. Do you think this is related somehow? Is everybody coming up missing Dad? What's going on?"

She almost screamed that last part. I could hear mom trying to calm her in the background but I had no answers for her right now. And I didn't believe in coincidence. It simply didn't exist.

Before I could give my girl assurances that I didn't even have at the moment, my blue tooth beeped. There was a call waiting. The caller id showed unidentified number on the display.

"Not sure baby. I gotta go okay? Tell your grandma to clue you in. And I need you to stay at your grandparents for a while. Is that cool with you?"

"Yeah its fine. The cousins are all here except Brit. Jeff's even home from school for Christmas break. He said to tell you hey."

"Alright kid. Gotta go. Call you tomorrow kay?"

"Love you Daddy. Stay safe?"

I mentally promised my girl that I would do exactly that as I switched callers.

"Sampson," I answered.

"Got a call from a friend who gave me this number; says you're in need of some tech support?"

At least three of my family members, one of them my son, were MIA. This war had just gotten so personal it was ridiculous. Short answer to that question? I needed all the support I could get. And that meant calling in my crew too.

I was no longer gearing up to accept the fact that someone might die before this was over. I'm done with that. Someone was definitely going to die. And I planned to bury RLS right along with them. That's promise number three.

***

"She still hasn't called you back yet?"

Lance didn't answer as he leaned back to prop his feet on the desk. He rested his head in his linked hands behind it to stare at the ceiling.

Why did the vixens constantly need to be reminded of their place? Especially Delilah. Heaven forbid that someone would actually ignore her. He knew without looking that she was shaking with rage. When would she get it that her anger meant nothing to him?

She was a pawn just like he was. The only difference? He got paid more. Plus he could force her to do whatever he said, whenever he said it.

Reminded of that fact, he reached for his smart phone resting on the desk. And again, without looking he knew that Delilah's rage had just flown up another notch. Because she knew what he was about to do.

She knew exactly how he would use it to put her in her place.

After years of being the one overlooked he was finally the guy holding the big guns. His family, one of the elite bloodlines to settle in this country way back when, had overlooked him. His peers at his Ivy League school, the headmasters, teachers and coaches had all overlooked him. And the first woman he'd given his heart to, would have done anything for, had overlooked him. But to her in particular, he was thankful. Catching her in bed with his older brother, both stoned out of their minds, showed him the truth.

That power wasn't about earning people's respect. It was about taking it. So he didn't ask for permission when he contacted several of his father's "elite" buddies and exposed his father's mind games and corporate plots to them. He didn't blink when his father "mysteriously disappeared". He'd simply taken over the handling of the family accounts and became the "grovel to" guy. He didn't wait to inherit power. He took it.

And his big shot brother the actor who'd slept with the one woman he'd wanted? When he could have had his pick of anyone?

Lance let him keep his place as the face of the family in Hollywood, content to keep his finger on the pulse in the background with the "little people". Because he pulled the strings.

As he selected the Brainwaiver app on his touchscreen, Lance wasn't swayed or bothered by the keening sound he heard coming from the other side of the desk.

Delilah would learn just like they all did. Eventually. She'd better if she wanted to live much longer.

The scream of misery and gagging followed by the sound of her body hitting the floor, thrashing around didn't even faze him.

The truth was he enjoyed it much more than some said he should. He knew he shouldn't be aroused by it, but he'd convinced himself that it was the power of it all that got him going. Not the suffering. But deep down he knew the truth. Because the more they suffered, the better it was. And right now it was truly beyond better, it was marvelous.

Chapter Fifteen

Saved by the dang bell!

While yesterday had been a day for the record books, today had been surprisingly calm.

Until Derek had shown at my front door an hour ago.

Then today sprouted fangs, turned into a rabid vampire and tried to tear my throat out with a viciousness I couldn't even describe.

My goodness but the man's drama should fuel the writing of screenplays! And where is the little editor during all of this? He'd probably found that rabbit hole that Mandy had mentioned, stored a portal in his little loft that is the left hemisphere of my cortex, and jumped through it at will. Usually when I need him the most; for example, like now, when I'm a snip-snip away from being incarcerated for castrating my ex-husband.

Who was actually flirting with me right.... this.... minute.

He must have lost his ever-loving mind!

I should have known something was off when I'd answered the door. He'd dressed in all black (which he knew from past experience was something I found attractive; heck, all black could make the guys from duck dynasty attractive). And it had gone down hill from there.

"Hey babe."

Really? I hadn't been Babe since I became the ball and chain, affectionately termed BNC by his pot-head friends. And that was over 12 years ago.

"Uh. Okay"

I stretched out my response to turn on the porch light. I had to check his eyes to make sure he wasn't high. Or drunk. Or high AND drunk.

"You gonna let me in babe? It's freaking cold out here."

Again, seriously?

"That would be because it's winter. But spring is around the corner. Which is how long you're gonna be out there if you came to see my daughter high."

"I didn't come to see Sammie. I came to talk to you. And I'm not high. Exactly."

"Then what are you? Exactly?"

"Available, sexy and free for the rest of the night."

And that's when I threw up in my mouth a little. It's not that Derek was no longer attractive. But the perfect turquoise eyes he'd possessed as a teen had grown muddy from years of hard living and alcohol abuse. And while I'd always been happy that he wasn't a small man (because I was definitely not a fine china type of gal) his 6'2" frame now came with a paunchy belly that seemed out of place on him.

But what I hated most about the changes that had taken place for him was his hair. Blond, it used to sport natural highlights and held a beauty all on its own. Now it hung dully to his shoulders with no life in it at all. And while I'd always liked a little facial hair, his scruffy attempt at a goatee made him look homeless, *SO* not the suave gigolo look that I think he was going for.

Despite his appearance, it hadn't been the attractive popular art student guy that I gave my heart to. Because he hadn't been popular at all. In fact, his crowd had been the chess club and art club, which was seriously unpopular in comparison to my own athletic one.

No, it had been his quiet, watchful nature. And the fact that he was a closet Alpha-male, which was and still is totally my thing.

However there was too much muddy Mississippi water under this bridge; too many bad memories and too much heartache.

Disgusted by the funky taste in my mouth now that I realized his intent for this visit I'd just walked away from the door, leaving it open for him to follow.

That had been an hour ago. I'd spent the last hour calmly reiterating the fact that I am not available; don't want to go there like ever again IN MY LIFE and that I really don't want Sammie hearing this conversation. I don't want my kid disillusioned by the discussion. There was no chance in Valhalla that Derek and I were getting back together. And since Valhalla is a fictional place, I figure that meant never EVER ever. Period.

And just when he'd grown frustrated with my standoffishness and moved from the couch onto the arm of the chair I was sitting in, the doorbell rang.

I jumped up out of my seat like the chair was on fire and ran toward the front door, almost falling as my foot caught on the edge of my beautiful (but evil at the moment) Aubusson rug.

Not to be deterred, I answered the door as if there was life saving, oxygen breathing chocolate cake on the other side. My mouth hung open again as I stared across the threshold thinking, what a perfect description for the person that stood there.

Enoch Sampson. He was the human version of a triple layer, double fudge, chocolate cake, with chocolate frosting. In contrast to his all black mode of dress yesterday, today he was a study of dark browns from his open collar, molded perfectly to him - shirt, to his perfect fitting brown slacks and dark brown hiking boots.

"Hey."

Per-fect. His voice, so deep and smooth, added a dose of Suisse mocha to my analogy for him. And I should probably answer before I started drooling because, yep, my mouth was still hanging wide open.

"Hey. Please come in."

My heart stuttered a little at the side smile he gave me before nodding and stepping in.

I turned to lead him through the foyer while running a quick mental assessment of my appearance because dang it, I forgot to check the mirror again.

Trying not to nervously rub my hands down the front of my skirt I recalled that my hair was styled in a fashionable bun, my make up was subtle (to go perfectly with the soft lighting in my living room) and I was wearing my new brown high heeled boots which I thought made me look less big and more statuesque. It's not that I was dressing to impress him (I *totally* was!)

"Who's that?"

Double Dang it! Being in Mr. Sampson's presence for just the two minutes it had been since I opened the door made everything else fade to black.

Including Derek.

The rudeness of his question had me stepping forward with a verbal smack-down at the ready. But before I could let him have it, Enoch stepped in front of me (as in between Derek and I), his body slightly turned so I could see that his arms had crossed.

"Enoch Sampson. And you are?"

Uh oh. That was an Alpha stance big time. It was definitely time to go into damage control before the verbal smack down turned into a physical one in my beautifully redecorated living room.

"I'm Celine's husband, that's who I am. And my wife doesn't see clients in her home so I need you to state your business and schedule an appointment with her during her office hours."

Derek's jaw popped and his gritted teeth over those words actually distracted me from what he'd said. He had crossed his own arms by now and had stepped forward as if he meant to physically remove Enoch from the room.

I saw Enoch's body tense as his arms dropped. Oy! I knew a fight stance when I saw one. His slightly bent knees and deceptively relaxed frame meant one thing, that the MMA was about to make an up front, personal visit to my home.

Wait… did Derek just call me his wife?

Hands out I stepped around Enoch and between the two frowning men, one hand on each chest. I am so about to let Derek have it when Enoch grabbed my hand and again, placed me slightly behind him. And before I could argue that I am NOT Derek's wife or the fact that I was just snatched out of the way without my permission, Enoch spoke calmly, like they weren't about to pound each other right into the ground despite his stance.

"Celine isn't married. And I'm not her client. I'm her date."

My eyes roll up to my ceiling as I briefly whispered a prayer for help.

Because now both men were standing chest to chest and Derek's face just turned really red. Like, magenta red almost. Sadly, I knew what was coming next. When Derek got really angry, he would spit when he talked. That meant that Enoch and I, judging by how red Derek had gotten, were about to be hit by a monsoon.

***

Sam

"Hi. My name is Sammie. Its short for Samantha but I like Sammie better. Are you a friend of my mom's?"

How exactly did you answer one of the cutest little girls in the world without sounding like a goof? I've always had the answer to that question. On the day Cass was born, those squinty dots we called eyes taught me how. They stared at me out of a tiny face, scrunched and red from screaming her little lungs out. I knew it then and I knew it now, because that answer had never changed.

You answered them with the truth.

But I had to clear my throat to remind myself I didn't have to whisper like she just did.

"I am. Name's Enoch Sampson but everyone calls me Sam."

I tried very hard to keep my smile from turning into chuckles but I was failing miserably. I wanted to laugh because first off, she'd been watching me for a few minutes before her approach, peaking around the wall that probably led upstairs. Second, she was dressed for bed in hello kitty pajamas and fuzzy socks so my guess is she should be in bed instead of down here satisfying her curiosity. Third, the moment I spoke back to her in my normal voice instead of a whisper, a delicate frown appeared causing a small wrinkle in her nose. Her mouth pursed in what seemed to me a chastening expression. Put all of that on top of the fact that she kept trying to scratch her elbow without dropping her stuffed dog while checking behind her every few seconds, obviously trying not to get caught – that's a recipe for hilarity.

I cleared my throat again but I think she was on to me since my shoulders were also shaking a little. I've always been terrible at acting.

"That's gonna get confusing."

This she said in a mutter instead of a whisper after another quick glance behind her, her two blond ponytails swishing each time she did so.

This kid was too adorable.

"Yeah. Your mom mentioned that it could."

"Yeah." She parroted trying to scratch her elbow again.

Both of us seem to be quietly assessing one another and I know from just a few minutes with this kid that, as cute as she is, she was dangerous. Because not only was she cute, but she knew that she was. And she had no problem using her powers of cuteness for personal gain.

 But, just like her mom it seems, she was also full of surprises. I'd kept my peace, curious to see what she would do next since her mom would probably be back any second now, having left the room on a personal call. Turns out I wouldn't be disappointed.

"I like Enoch better."

"Do you?"

"Yeah. Enoch rocks."

"Okay"

"Don't you wanna know why?"

Of course I wanted to know why. She definitely had me curious. But I'm not sure I really should know why. It's going to be adorable, I know it. And after these last few minutes with her I was finding it hard to reconcile her existence with the dork that had finally left a half hour ago. If this kid gets any cuter I'm going to have to accept the fact that either she was adopted or her mom wasn't the woman I thought she was and must have had an affair. But instead of all that I answered.

"Sure."

"My mom told me the he was so cool with God, that they were like best buds and everything, that God just said, you know what? You don't even have to die, you can just come up here and hang out with me. And that's what he did. So I think Enoch rocked. Because he had to for God, who is *really* awesome, to just take him with him you know?"

Wow. I had no other words for that. Except that my mother was going to freaking love this kid.

"Is that right? I don't remember reading that about Enoch. Where would I find that?

"Duh. In the Bible silly."

Down goes the stuffed dog again. I might have to mention to Ms. Baltimore that she needed to check her laundry detergent. Watching little Sammie scratch had phantom itches running up and down my own arms.

"Okay, where in the Bible exactly."

"It's in Jentsis somewhere. You should read the Bible every day. Mom says it's an awesome way to find out what God thinks. She says I think I'm right all the time just like she does so God is the tie breaker."

"How is that exactly?"

She giggled and glanced quickly behind her again before answering.

"Because He's always right."

Ah. I still don't get it but again, you can't really argue much with cuteness of this magnitude so I just kept smiling hoping her mom would show up before I did something stupid, like give the kid my credit card and tell her to go buy whatever she wants.

"So can I call you Mr. Enoch instead of Mr. Sam?"

Aww man. Did I leave my wallet in the car? I'll just give her the whole thing at this point. Dangerous isn't the word for this kid.

"That works for me. Can I call you Sammie since you like that better?"

I received a really big grin with that one. If I stayed here a minute longer this kid would have me wrapped around her finger for life.

"Yep. That works for me too. And it's okay if you don't like my Daddy. He tries hard but he's just not really good at being a Daddy."

That last part was said with a little frown and pursed lips while she gripped her stuffed dog tightly to her. As soon as she'd said it her gaze dropped to the floor, almost like she knew she'd said something she probably shouldn't have.

Or it could have been the look on my face. Because I wanted to go back in time and, instead of allowing Ms. Baltimore to escort him out of the house, grab him and drag him outside myself to beat him into the asphalt. No kid should ever feel that way about her dad.

"But he tries hard because he knows that Sammie rocks too right? Just like Enoch."

And just like that, the sun came out. That beautiful, clear, innocent gaze jumped from the floor and into my own with a smile that killed. Seriously killed.

"Yeah. I do huh?"

"Yep, even I know that. And I've only known you for a whole 5 minutes."

This time when she squeezed her dog, it was to spin and laugh a little. And I can't explain the weight that seemed to lift off of my chest. I felt lighter.

Better yet, I felt like this was going to work out somehow. That I was going to get my boy back safe.

And so I grinned while Sammie did a little power dance with one arm flexed and the other stretched out, pointing to who knows where while nodding her head to music that only she could hear.

"Samantha Cheyenne Henry! You get your behind in that bed like yesterday!"

"Uh oh. Gotta go. Bye."

One moment I was watching the power stance dance frozen in action, right before very round eyes and pursed lips reappeared as Sammie turned my way with a little wave. That was before she somehow sprouted wings and seemingly flew back the way she'd come. I could actually hear her little feet hitting the stairs double time.

And I'm still unclear exactly how long I remained there bent over in my chair, wheezing because I was laughing so hard I couldn't catch my breath.

But when I finally sat up, Ms. Baltimore's crossed arms and tapping foot sent me into another bout.

I couldn't really tell her how I was the helpless victim in all this. I was too busy trying to breathe. And I really didn't know what she expected anyway. That kid was cut from the same exact cloth as her mom. And that's exactly what I'd tell her too as soon as I could breathe again.

Chapter Sixteen

"**Ma'am**, despite your claim that you were allegedly assaulted by the young man when he placed his hand on your rear end, chopping him in the throat and kneeing him in the groin is simply not acceptable."

It was hard to miss the TSA agent's frustration as he explained this for the fifth time to my old team member and fellow ex-agent Denise Ferry. This situation right here is exactly why we called her Balboa. Raised in what was considered "the hood" in the worst parts of Miami, Denise's mixed heritage of African American and Latino ethnicity caused her to stand out in the largest crowd. Standing at about 5'8" with a physique that made most men wrench their necks to get another look, her long mahogany hair shown healthily in perfect contrast to her champagne colored eyes.

Undeniably a beauty, she was targeted by neighborhood gangs from the age of 12 to join. Girls joined those gangs one of two ways; either they were beat in or they were "sexed" in. The girls that fought their way in gained respect from the male members and status, which could lead to leadership at a later date. The girls that were sexed in became the gang prostitutes and spent the rest of their existence on their backs for the glory of the gang. They gained no respect and were always treated with contempt.

Balboa was an avid catholic and was devoted to her mother's family traditions. So sexing her way into the gang was not an option. And since a beautiful girl like her wouldn't survive the beating that the less attractive female gang members would put her through without learning how to protect herself, she'd sought help.

Denise's older brother Juan had been a boxer before he was killed accidentally by a drive by shooting. When she was a kid, he would baby-sit her at the gym where he would go to train.

Losing him at the young age of ten and with their father long gone, she knew that someone had to protect their home and their mother. And that someone had to be her.

Balboa kept going to that gym. She described it to me once as her cliff notes for street survival. She would stand beside the ring mimicking the moves of the boxers from the various types of punches to the dancing, blocks, faints and dodges. The guys there took her in and protected her - thought of her as their little sister. And that was okay by her because she was in a safe place learning everything that she knew she would need to know one day.

So when the pressure started for her to pick a side for "protection" when she was 12 she became more demanding with her training by adding Mixed Martial Arts to her repertoire.

By the time she turned 13 and her budding beauty was undeniable she was ready. She took on 6 of the 12 female gang members with status whose ages varied from sixteen to twenty five. She never gave me the details of what happened that night. All I know is at only 13 years of age our girl came into the gang with a status that placed her directly below the female gang leader and her second in command. And no one, male or female, ever dared to even think about laying a hand on her during her time there. In any way.

A smart girl, Balboa determined to get her diploma and to go to college with full support from her gang family and her mom. She never claimed to lead an innocent life but from what I gathered she was the closest thing that the gang had to a conscious. Not surprisingly, by the time she'd graduated high school she'd worked herself into the role of second in command and consult to the male gang leader and members. She had a mind for strategy and a right hook of steel; all packaged together in the most effeminate female you'd ever met. A study of massive contradictions, she was always our go to on strategy and surveillance when in the field. That had been quite an accomplishment for a 23 year old recruit back then.

And she hadn't changed one bit, from what I could tell in the 6 years since I'd last seen her; which is why I needed her now.

Except this part. I didn't need this. Shaking my head at her as she winked at me before turning to face the red-faced TSA agent who'd hand-cuffed her; I tried hard not to laugh out loud.

Because it's not that Balboa didn't understand the rules. She just didn't care. While she had a conscious and would never seek to actively harm an "innocent," she tended to thumb her nose at authority at the worst possible times. Like now.

Leaving her to find her way out of this little episode of ridiculous on her own, I headed back toward the board to watch for the other arrivals. Double-checking my cell to check the time I tried not to broadcast my impatience. Lambert Airport was a pain and a hassle for those of us who hated standing out in a crowd.

And I hated crowds. That was the one benefit of being a CIA operative I didn't enjoy. Crowds became a tool, easy to blend into for those who were covert operatives. I however, was not a covert operative nor had I ever run lead for a team. I was support. While I obtained the training necessary to fulfill any role, mine was more like "glorified secret service" than spy guy. And that's just the way I liked it.

For the first time ever I would be taking point on a mission. Not because it was a goal or something to be proud of. It was because I loved my son.

Being point entailed my being here at Lambert to pick up the first wave of our team then heading over to my company's current construction site in Kirkwood, Missouri. A secure location, the site was where we'd determined to brief everyone on the mission, the logistics and formulate a plan.

Oh Happy Day.

Since Cheryl, Rich and Max were all due to arrive within the hour and Matt was slotted for arrival tomorrow, it was a good time to go over the intel that I'd gathered a couple of days ago from Celine Baltimore. She'd been a wealth of information though she'd assumed otherwise before we got down to business.

I pulled out my small notebook and pen that I kept in the back pocket of my jeans and started going over the list when my cell went off.

"Hey Johnny."

"Sam. You pick up the packages yet?"

"I've got one here at the loading dock now. The others haven't come in yet; figured I'd wait around just in case we get some late arrivals."

"Ah. Which one did we get in?"

"The Rocky road."

"Got it. Um. That flash freeze might not hold. You need anything to handle any meltdowns just in case?"

I chuckled as, with perfect timing, Balboa dropped down into the seat next to me with her carry all and suit case daintily placed in front of me. Talk about nerve on this woman. She could beat a room full of trained fighters so quickly my head would spin, but she couldn't carry her own bags.

"Nope. It came in some type of packaging that is supposed to handle that."

I hear the faint snort through the line and shook my head in disgust. We really shouldn't encourage her bad behavior by laughing. But how could you not when the chick was nuts? Yeah, Rocky Road was definitely fitting for her, in more than one way.

"Cool then. See you at the hang out like we planned?"

"Yep."

Disconnecting I turned to the grinning female swinging her crossed-leg back and forth with its red croc skin high heeled shoe that must have cost a fortune, and stared.

"What?"

Like she didn't know. But like any sane person I parroted, "What?"

"Yeah. What?"

"Balboa."

"Don't start."

"Really though?"

"Don't. Start."

"How old was he, and I'm not talking about the government issued rent-a-cop?"

And now she's checking her nails like this conversation was boring her or something.

"At least in his twenties."

And does she have to chew that gum like it's about to jump out of her mouth, with her teeth as hostage, to run away?

"If I chopped every guy in the throat that got on my nerves..."

"There would be a lot less people going around ticking others off and getting on other people's nerves. See? I did the public a service."

"You are getting on my nerves and I'm not chopping you in the throat."

"But if you did obviously I would try not to get on your nerves. See how that works?"

"You WANT me to chop you in the throat?"

"Nope. But if you did would I be working your nerves right now?"

"No because I'd be in jail."

"And that is why chopping people in the throat is a solution no matter how you look at it."

And that was when I remembered little Sammie telling me how cool Enoch was. So cool that God just took him so they could hang out. I never thought I would find my name or my namesake's situation so appealing. Because, at this moment I was thinking, maybe God will think I'm cool enough to snatch me up too.

I think what concerned me most was that I saw her point; chopping her in the throat was beginning to look an awful lot like a solution right now. But I didn't think I would qualify as God's hang out buddy if I did that…. Hmm. Tough decision.

***

"Okay everybody, let's recap the leads we have and our preliminary plans for Monday to obtain more intel. I want everyone on the same page so there's no confusion. Sound good?"

Nods all around the room meant we were good to go. Using the projector app on my cell phone I displayed a picture of the Narrow Way Church building on Union onto the wall, they were our biggest lead at the moment.

"According to Celine, this is the church that Amanda most likely attended because of its proximity to her office, the belief structure and the progressive youth ministry they have going."

More nods so I continued.

"We've got Johnny on the church Monday to see what he can find out about the youth ministry and any role they play in this since its teenagers that are either found dead or missing."

I slid my finger on the display to change the picture.

"This is a picture of Edward and Caroline Same. The family lives on Danforth Street in Fairmount – an affluent subdivision South of Alton proper. Matt arrives tomorrow; he already knows they're his assignment. Max, you'll be outfitting him with the tech for bugs and what-not."

"Who's Matt again?"

I shook my head a little to clear it. I was exhausted and running on fumes after about two and a half hours of sleep per night if that.

Needing a minute, I looked around for my coffee cup and forced myself to be patient. I kept forgetting that we'd all gotten so used to handles that most of us didn't know everyone's birth names.

Richard McDonald, also known as Boogey had asked that question. Standing at 5"6' he was probably the least most imposing guy you knew, until he opened his mouth. At twenty-eight, Boogey hailed from Houston, Texas, loved sushi, hated dogs and was the biggest conspiracy theorist ever. Proud to be African – American (and just plain American) Boogey knew weapons and cars like chubby kids knew candy; intimately and with great frequency. Working as a mechanic now in his brother's shop he had no problem freeing up his schedule for his old crew buddy Johnny.

And he didn't ask for much as compensation; just a lifetime supply of sushi and an opportunity to see Cheryl Larson (also known by her handle, Minute). He'd been crushing on her since their first Op on partnering units 5 years ago.

Cheryl, now a hot shot Neurologist in New York City after leaving the military, was just as oblivious today of his fascination as she was then.

I'd heard Boogey's question but because my brain was on a 5 second delay due to lack of sleep, Balboa answered first.

"Matthew Killian... K.C."

I grinned because I knew someone would ask "the question".

"What's the K.C. for if his name's Matt?"

Balboa loved this part.

"His favorite movie."

And just like always, she never elaborated.

Rich's raised eyebrow and rolling hand signal to her to keep going was my signal that we were getting off track. And before I could bring us back on topic because yeah... 5 minute delay...

"Killer Clownz."

"WHAT?"

Which was the response of every single person in the room besides Balboa and I.

Enough of that; it was time to bring this back around before we all disintegrated into giggling grade schoolers.

"Back on topic guys; quick recap about the Sames. We know that they have at least one kid on the implant and in RLS custody and one missing. We also know, due to Johnny's connections that the older child, Amanda, hasn't been reported missing to the local authorities. These folks know something we don't know guys, so besides the church Max, they are a huge priority."

Maximillian or Max, also known as Macchio remained his usual stoic self and simply nodded. The tallest of our group at almost 6"7', like Balboa he was a study of contradictions. Most tech guys were assumed to be nerdy Bill Gates types. Not Max. Obviously athletic, even though he was tall he didn't have that creepy thin guy look. He wore his height well on a muscular frame. His coloring was dark and his last name – Arpaio, didn't help pinpoint his heritage; he could be Italian or Latino.

From past experience, while I knew Max as a true introvert that loved his tech, women often flocked to him because of that "man of mystery" vibe.

Despite that, a true gentleman, Max never kissed and told. His handle "Macchio" was derived from the fact that he just doesn't age. While I assumed that he was about the same age as John and I, you really couldn't tell his age at all. He looked to be in his mid twenties though that would be an impossibility having served in John's and my unit. He was a good man and I was glad to have him on board.

"Last we've got Celine Baltimore. Celine is my assignment. She's also our key to the inside of RLS. Balboa, you're with me. Max you already know the play. Our plan for Monday is to get eyes and ears into her office. After we do that, she'll invite an RLS contact over to get more info on the Brainwaiver app and implant so we have an idea what we're dealing with. It might also be a good idea to plant a few bugs on the contact as well.

Boogey, you're on standby until we determine if we need to breach. If we do it will strictly be a retrieval mission for the kids. Minute you know your assignment and have your contact's information. Proceed with caution. Before you go we need you working with Max on the hack so that you can locate any medical documentation that can be referenced to get that crap out of those kids."

More nods and a few loud exhales were my cue to wrap things up.

"Any questions guys before we get out of here?"

"Yeah."

"What's up Boogey?"

"I hate to say it but I've got to."

Johnny started shaking his head at his crossed arms and legs. I had the feeling that this confession was going to be like a freight train, once on the track it was no use trying to stop it.

"But I told yall that these rich white folks was working up some mind control technology to program the masses. Didn't I tell you? I told you!"

And on that note, I politely grabbed my keys and headed home to my bed.

Chapter Seventeen

Celine

I walked past my desk for the fourth time, desperately trying not to revert back to my old habit of biting my nails.

In three minutes I could expect to hear a knock on my office door.

I couldn't get a grip on why the sudden urge to freak out assailed me. When Enoch and I'd gone over the plan Tuesday night, I'd felt relieved. I was a little freaked to be working with ex-military and CIA types, but still relieved.

When he'd revealed that part, I'd actually thought he was joking. And then I found out that he wasn't. That's when the parade of stupid started marching out of my mouth in quick succession.

"Really, CIA? So are you R.E.D. – retired, extremely dangerous, like the movie? Oh! Can you step out of a moving car like Bruce Willis did? Because that had been BEYOND awesome! I'm just saying!"

Enoch had laughed at that. I loved his laugh. Deep and rich with a bit of bite to it, his laugh had been enough to make me feel not so weirded out by all of this.

Because at first, I'd been weirded out big time.

Stuff like this happened in movies and in really good books, but not in real life – definitely not to me. It was stuff like this that practically threw my life goal of "playing it safe and living by the book" into the dumpster of "not gonna happen".

And the only reason I was okay with that? I wanted to find these kids. I wanted Sam's son safe. And I wanted to be done with all of this Brainwaiver crap.

It had been a good night, a great dinner and while I had been on my best behavior, Sammie hadn't been.

My kid had always been bright and shiny, her only real fault being selective hearing and memory when it came to cleaning up.

And still, around Enoch she took all of that to a whole other level. Bouncy, excited and chatty, she told him about everything, everyone and touched on every subject she could think of.

It was like she'd stored years of stories in her head until someone came along that she felt it was okay to release them on.

By the end of dinner, I'd been exhausted just listening to her.

Yet inordinately pleased.

Because Enoch had nodded the whole time, interjected here and there to show he was listening, and didn't seem to mind that she dominated the conversation one bit.

And that's when I knew I was in trouble. Attraction I could handle. Being hot could only hold my attention for so long.

But with Enoch that wasn't an option. My reaction to him every single time I saw him was feral. A reaction that wasn't getting any better with exposure like I'd hoped.

Add that to his obvious patience with my kid and what looked like a stellar relationship with his own... I was falling and I was falling *hard*.

But I really didn't know him yet. And I wasn't one of those kinds of people that trusted easily. That was also why I didn't date much. I hated wasting my time. And I couldn't just tell a guy that ten-minutes into the date I already knew it would be a fail (sometimes of epic proportions).

Because the little editor, if nothing else, was extremely polite. Therefore, I'd be stuck playing nice the entire night when all I really wanted to do was get home, fall into a good book or watch a movie with my kid.

But not with Enoch. From the little time we'd spent together, despite the circumstances, we'd just... clicked. I'd be my goofy self and earn that gorgeous side smile of his for it. We'd talked about some of everything under the sun even while giving Sammie most of our attention. So imagine my shock when things got a little awkward the moment Sammie had left us to get ready for bed. I was not a shy person. Not even a little bit. In fact, I was so far from shy that my name was listed as an antonym under "shy" in Webster's Dictionary! There was absolutely no reason for it! I'd been great – communicative, up-beat and a text book hostess that entire day.

I was cool and copasetic when Max, one of his team members, had been by earlier to sweep the house for any listening devices. I asked about that and was told it was so we could "debrief" here. Man! I really got a kick out of that spy lingo.

If I was all of a sudden going to "go shy," it should have happened during Max's visit.

But it was Awe-some! He was a tall guy but not one of those really thin ones that looked like their stomachs were ingesting their backbones. He wasn't as attractive as Enoch but definitely registering as a huge blip on the hotness scale. Embodying the saying "tall, dark and handsome" to the fullest; he was dark everywhere from his breathtaking olive skin tone to his blue-black hair and dark brown eyes. And he was a brooder. Women loved brooders. It was something about their eyes – bedroom eyes I think they call them.

And, while all of that was great, it wasn't why I said he was awesome. The man had slipped on some glasses and BAM! Instant hot genius guy. And when he got to work I was so fascinated by *watching* him work, that it was easy to forget to be nervous around all of that hotness. We joked, chatted and laughed while walking through the house with his little detection jigga-ma-thingy. By the time we were done, Max was more than just a "blip" on the hotness scale to me. He was a good guy. A sad good guy (which any woman could see, the shadows and silent suffering all in his eyes), but a good guy nonetheless. Call me crazy, but in a way, I felt honored that he seemed so comfortable around me. I had the feeling that he wasn't that way with just anybody.

After being probed, prepped and made ready, my house was vetted as a clean place for Enoch's scheduled "chat".

Knowing it was safe technologically to talk to Enoch was a different animal than knowing I was safe alone with him. I didn't fear for my life or my body.

I feared for my sanity.

Because cautious, reserved, play it safe me wanted to do nothing more than lie on his chest and let him surround me. From his heady male scent (I really had to find out what cologne that was. It had a promising future of consistent use... on my pillows) – to his rugged good looks and deep emerald eyes; I wanted to drown in him.

And that's probably where the awkwardness came in. It should have been funny, how confused he'd looked at my newly developed stutter. Or when I started nervously rubbing my hands together. Then rubbing them up and down my skirt. Over and over... and over.

It was ridiculous really. No little editor to be found... no interesting conversation or jokes. Just me, breathing all funny and acting like a goof. It had to stop or I'd have to surrender my Woman Card at the next "I am woman, hear me roar," meeting. Claude have mercy, I hadn't been this nervous since I went on my first date in high school!

At that thought I'd squared my shoulders and did what any self-respecting woman that valued her sanity would do. Excused myself to go to the ladies room.

Only I tripped over my used-to-be (and still evil) favorite rug (again) on the way. And fell. Hard. Right in front of the most gorgeous man I'd ever met.

That's me, graceful swan that I am.

A few things happened all at once. The little editor made a sudden appearance just to hang his, "out for the night due to extreme embarrassment" sign.

My face received his message, knew that it should be embarrassed and flushed a bright pink that, in the least attractive way possible, clashed with my strawberry blond hair (despite my fabulous new highlights).

And I'd bitten my tongue.

So when Enoch bent over me to check for signs of life, I didn't get to pronounce with some small amount of dignity, "I'm okay."

No. Around my swelling tongue and with teary eyes, instead I said with absolutely no dignity and no help at all from the little editor (the traitor), "Ith othay."

Nice.

And through all of that, with his handsome face bent over mine and those beautiful eyes offset by that really nice forest green tee (goodness but that was such a great color on him), he'd smiled that little side smile at me; managing to make me feel slightly less the fool.

Feeling a bit better, it took a moment for me to get moving. Because instead of getting up I'd wanted to brush his dark brown hair back (it'd fallen over one of his eyes). I'd wanted to do that and bring him a little closer to... inspect things. Like his eyes. His lips. All of him, maybe? And because he appeared upside down to me (his forehead hovered above my lips) I felt like I was stuck in some funhouse effect, falling into those hypnotic green pools he called eyes. Just like Alice, falling down that rabbit hole.

Which served as the bucket of ice water I needed to get my head back in the game. We weren't there to play footsies. That wasn't a date. Kids were missing. And from what he'd told me, some kids had already died.

With his help I'd gotten up, gone to the restroom to put myself back together and returned, no longer nervous, shy or stuttering. I did have a slight lisp because of my swollen tongue but that couldn't be helped.

And we'd discussed the plan.

And so here I was, pacing my office and trying not to run away in terror. Because I had to do my part. This thing was bigger than me. Which meant that this was my only shot at helping Anabella, Mandy and Danny. At least, that's what I'm telling myself to keep from hiding in the bathroom.

At eleven a.m. on the dot a polite knock on my door had me scurrying over to it, nervously fiddling with my blouse, skirt and hair before I pulled the door open.

All I could say was this: the hinge of my jaw was going to need a serious overhall by the time this was over. The mouth dropping that had occurred over that last month had been extreme to say the least. Just like right now. My jaw dropped so hard it snapped. Because it wasn't Andrew, who I'd spoken with and set up the meeting, standing at my door.

It was Lance. Creepy, Too-wide-eyes having Lance.

And at that moment my previous terror took a right turn into abject horror.

***

"We need eyes Macchio. Double time it."

Fingers flew over the keyboard from the back of the modified SUV.

Max didn't have to respond that he was working on it. He was an action man. He knew that you could hear his fingers flying. Common sense says that he was trying to make that happen. And that was fine by me.

Because I needed to see what was happening in there, like yesterday.

The audio we heard coming from the office was clear. And the first thing I heard was the fear in Celine's wavering voice.

And that just did not work for me. I needed to see who was in there causing that reaction. Every single alarm in my psyche rang like crazy and the ice storm behind my eyes was slowly building. I had to calm myself because my response to this unknown threat was about to turn physical in a big way.

"Got it."

"On screen Max."

Again no response but I didn't need one, I could almost see him nodding his assent as he made that happen.

Alton was small. A tiny little town compared to the major cities like St. Louis or Chicago. In small places like this it was really easy to stand out. Standing out was the kiss of death to a surveillance team.

We couldn't set up outside of Celine's office without garnering some type of attention. Instead we set up in the parking lot of the gas station on Broadway about 2 miles out, well within range for the state of the art equipment Max was running in the back seat.

I didn't know why we couldn't get a visual at first and I didn't need to know. That is what we had Max for. But I did need to know why Celine was freaked.

Focusing on the image bleeding into the screen on my laptop, my eyes narrowed in recognition.

"I need everything you can find on this guy Max."

"Name?"

"Lance Finney."

"Age?"

"Between 25 and 30."

"Got it."

I didn't bother to be amazed that this was all of the information Max needed to get me the intel. He was just that good. The best actually. Which was why he'd left the CIA. He knew a lot more than they realized about everything that he shouldn't know at all. Things well above his clearance. Things above the President of the United States clearance. Macchio was the walking dead and he knew it. Because one day, someone would come along that was better than him; and since digital footprints could never be completely deleted – only hidden really well – it was just a matter of time.

Celine's slightly calmer voice brought me back to the present as I again focused on the screen.

"I thought I would be meeting with Andrew?"

"I gathered that you would. However Andy couldn't make it and he asked me to step in for him."

Celine's pursed lips and slight frown was her only response. Easy to see Sammie was her kid right then. You'd have to be stupid to not read that reaction. And I had a feeling that this guy was far from stupid.

"So. Let's get to it shall we? I understand that you have questions about how the implant and application work yes?"

"Mmmm." Celine spoke through tight lips and gave a stiff nod. It was clear that she did not like this guy. At all.

Lance Finney was in profile to the camera but the smile on his face had me itching to run the two miles that separated us full tilt. Because there were several kinds of people in this world. There were moral folks, decent folks and selfish folks. And then there were the truly sadistic folks. The one's that classified as evil with no apparent conscious or empathy; no compassion. Society calls them sociopaths.

As children they pulled the legs off of grasshoppers and watched them gimp along and suffer with glee. They pinched babies and hurt those smaller than themselves with the clinical expression of a scientist looking at a germ under a microscope.

They studied pain and relished it. They basked in the smell of fear and convulsed with joy at controlling those they deem powerless. Truly evil in every intent of the word, these are the ones my Mom used to tell me were stoned to death as children in the Old Testament. If I remembered right, she said that God told his people to kill them and purge the evil from among them.

I never really understood that sentiment until I joined the CIA. And again today as I watched this dude with his creepy smile.

Taking this guy out would be doing the world a favor. And before I allowed him near Celine without me close by ever again, that is exactly what I would do. Promise number four.

Chapter Eighteen

That last punch tore the skin over my left eye and I hit the ground with another "umph".

I had learned the hard way that anger wouldn't help so there was no point in getting frustrated.

Picking myself back up slowly for the fifth time today I shook my head slightly to clear it before stretching my neck to the left then right.

Calm breath. Remember your goal. The person you are fighting isn't your worst enemy. You are your worst enemy.

My eyes opened as the young woman with long dark hair caught in a ponytail on top of her head, dressed in a sports bra and biker shorts barked at me, "Again."

Her handle was Balboa and according to Enoch, she would be handling my hand-to-hand combat, stick fighting and MMA training.

According to me, she was an evil– Zoe Saldana Barbie doll with fists of steel.

Her goal in life? To be born again as Sonya from Mortal-Kombat while torturing me for my uncoordinated and clumsy ways.

I put up my guard making sure not to drop my left this time and I jabbed with my right.

I'd been at this with her for over a week and I finally felt as if I was improving.

And I had to. I had to improve because the alternative was not acceptable. I never wanted to feel the way Lance had made me feel, ever again.

For the first time in my life I'd felt like a victim. And I didn't like it.

Reticent to continue the meeting with him instead of Andrew when he'd arrived, I knew it was necessary to keep him there nonetheless. And I'd never in my life regretted being more right, on both counts, than I'd been that day.

Remembering fueled my punches and blocks with a passion that probably took Balboa by surprise. And I made it a point to remember and relive every second. Because that would be the last time he'd ever see me that way again...

Lance had sat before my desk as if it were his interview and not mine.

"So. Let's get to it shall we? I understand that you have questions about how the implant and application work, yes?"

I answered in a non-descript way, nodding a little for him to continue.

"I'll summarize how the implant works in the same way it was explained to me. I'm sure you took a health education class or two in college so you are familiar with how your body responds to stress?"

What a condescending bucket-head. He said that as he glanced at my LCSW certification framed on the wall behind me. I guess social workers don't rate on his "people most likely to buy a Bentley list". And why was I not surprised? Well, never one to miss an opportunity to lower some one's expectations of me further, I responded.

"I was an athlete in college as well as high school so yes, those types of classes, as well as courses on alcohol and drug effects were mandatory."

If I didn't know any better, which I didn't I could have sworn that he sneered at me a little.

"Fabulous."

Pin-head.

"Shall I continue?"

"By all means."

"I take it that your stint in athletics provided you ample opportunity to understand how adrenaline works. Basically the body's own performance steroid, during moments of stress the hormone's biochemical role is to increase your heart rate, force muscles to contract and increase respiration."

I nodded for him to continue.

"While there have been designer steroids that stimulate this effect, prolonged exposure to that physical state would soon result in deterioration of the heart and blood vessels and could result in heart disease or a stroke."

Yes, yes. I know this. Steroids Bad. I was an athlete for cripes sakes! I nodded again to show that even former athletes can follow simple sentences.

"The implant is like a computer; it bypasses the stress feature by accessing the messages that the brain wants to send to the body with the end goal as well as current goal in mind. Then it maps the least problematic way to accomplish the body's goal and begins to stimulate the necessary functions within the body to bring the desired end goal to pass, one process – or several systematic processes at a time."

What? I didn't communicate this with words assuming that my raised eyebrow and crossed arms did it for me as he continued.

"In essence, the implant finds out what you want and begins to use your body to make what you want to happen and, depending on what that is, it could do the job by forcing one biological response or several. It will continue to do its job until the goal is accomplished."

Okay. Creepy much?

"So the body serves as a host to the implant?"

"No. Host indicates a symbiotic relationship where the implant benefits somehow by being utilized by its bearer. The implant is a computer. Some artificial intelligence exists but its main function is to achieve the desire of its bearer. It simply does what it is told, either in the way that I just explained it, or by the application it's wirelessly connected to."

"So the implant is not biomechanical in nature then."

"Now I didn't say that."

No? I felt my eyebrow go up again. Which is funny, since I've done that twice now and didn't even realize that I could.

"The Implant has to be biomechanical in order to be incorporated into living tissue and not have the body attack it as a foreign entity. However that is where its bio functions end. It could never "possess" the bearer or force the bearer to do something that they wouldn't normally do."

Lie. Huge lie. I don't know how I knew it, but my little editor was in the background pointing both fingers, arms jabbing back and forth while doing a little dance. Translated: liar, liar, pants on fire.

"Uh huh." Is what came out instead.

"You say that as if you don't believe me."

Because I don't.

"I'm just not sure how to translate that clearly scientific explanation into cause and effect. Perhaps if you gave me a few examples…"

Ugh. And there goes that creepy grin again. I tried hard not to rub my arms in response. Sort of like when you think a spider or bug is crawling on you. Even though you look and don't see one, you can't help but rub your arms anyway.

"Gladly. Let's assume that you are a teenager with a dermatological issue… like acne."

"Okay."

"By going to the Brainwaiver application on your smart phone you could select, "derma" for skin, then select the body part in question, "face", then select the issue, "acne". The app will respond to your selection with, "resolve?" The bearer would select the appropriate response then pick from the possible resolutions that the app lists."

"And then it's fixed? Just like that?"

"Just like that. The process is completely biological however, so the bearer may not see the results for hours yet or even overnight."

"Okay. So let's say I wanted to fix my weight problem?"

"You have a weight problem Ms. Baltimore?"

Funny man. If his eyes weren't so far apart I'd make like the three stooges and jab him in them with my two fingers. Sadly I don't think my fingers could have spread that far to do him much damage.

"Let's just agree to disagree then. To answer your question, if that actually were the case, " *insert creepy grin here*, "you could utilize the app suggestion under weight management and follow the prompts."

"And I would just lose weight, overnight?"

"It would depend on how much you want to lose for how long it would actually take. Also the manner you would like to lose it in. For example, if you wanted to increase the benefit of your workout –or gain the discipline to work out – you could set the app to do so. Your body would respond accordingly with appropriately stimulated dispensations of adrenaline, endorphins and HGH. This method would probably get you to your goal quicker than should you select a different option that handles how your body processes sugar, fat and waste."

Wow. That sounded really good. Too good. Because I knew that there was a catch. And that catch had people bleeding from their eyeballs or coming up missing. And that pretty much was the end of my brief fascination with app assisted weight loss. It was time to bring this meeting to a close.

"Well thank you so much for stopping by Mr. Finney. Your answers were candid and informative. I look forward to attending the party. And I guess if you don't ever find the person that falsely entered me into the contest, I won't be disappointed."

I said this as I got up to escort him to the door, sure that he followed me because the cold draft of "ick" racing down my spine told me so.

Only as I reached toward the door knob to open it, before I'd even slightly felt the cold metal on my hands, I was snatched, spun and pressed against the wall beside it, Lance's body flush against my own.

Eyes wide my breath hitched as I struggled to move my arms and push him away.

And he let me do it. For a while. I pushed, pulled at my arms, bucked and strained, and he just stood there watching me do it the whole time. Until I'd had enough of that eerie horror movie vibe.

"Let. Me. Go." I'd gritted that through clenched teeth, still fighting, praying that the tears I felt gathering wouldn't fall and humiliate me. Because I didn't want to give this guy the pleasure of seeing me cry. And to him it would be a pleasure. There was no doubt in my mind about that.

More struggling ensued to the point where I was just about to completely botch our plans by screaming for help when Lance, almost looking bored, stepped away.

"No need to panic Ms. Baltimore. I was just demonstrating to you what the implant makes possible for you. I've had it now for over 6 years. There have been some upgrades, however, even while it's an older version; mine remains cutting edge on the technological front. There are very few limits to what I can do. When the implant was first installed, I needed the software for commanding it just as you would need the app when you first begin. However over time it has become a part of me. Whatever I need, it responds accordingly as you just witnessed. You are far from weak Ms. Baltimore. But the implant allowed me to hold you with next to no effort on my part."

Seething, I pushed away from the wall and got as far away from him as the room would allow. I had no words for the jerk and I wanted him gone like vapor.

"I apologize if my demonstration upset you. That wasn't my intent."

Yes it was. It was totally his intent.

"However, I knew that the demonstration would hold more… weight… in convincing you of how the implant is really in your best interest. It really brought home my point, wouldn't you agree?"

I nodded as I hugged myself with gritted teeth. I doubted the desk between us afforded much protection from him, but I needed the illusion badly.

"Good. Then I am sure I won't have to come looking for you since you will definitely be attending the party?"

His veiled threat didn't deserve my words. A nod is all he was going to get since I was trained as a child that the middle finger was not an appropriate response from good Christian girls.

"Fine. Good. Well, it was wonderful seeing you again, please don't hesitate to call me if you should need a ride to the festivities."

And he'd walked out of that door taking with him the illusion that I was going to come through any of this unscathed. He'd shattered my safety with a move that didn't faze him and watched my horror unfold with a boredom that was more frightening than malice would have been.

So when I heard another knock on my door, thinking it was Enoch I ran to it as if my life were hanging in the balance.

It hadn't been Enoch.

And that was how I met Balboa. Standing in my office, watching me wipe angrily at the spilling tears with the heels of my hands, right beside Max.

I didn't know where Enoch was. They didn't tell me. Max just got out his cell and walked back out into the hallway to make a call. I over heard him say Sam and she's alright. But that was all I got to hear.

Zoe Saldana's Barbie image also known as Balboa had stepped up to me with a Kleenex in her hands.

She didn't invite me into a hug to comfort me or ask me if I was okay. I'd taken her tissue and she nodded like I'd just said something though I hadn't. And before I could speak she barked at me for the first time, "If tomorrow is too soon, let Sam know. Wear work out clothes. I hope you can take a punch."

Then she'd turned on her high-healed black boots that I would absolutely maim other shoppers for, and flounced out the door.

She'd been kicking my butt like it was her bread and butter ever since.

I would have preferred that Enoch had been on the other side of that door with a hug and promises to keep me safe. But God knew that what I'd needed was a hotheaded Barbie doll to show me that things aren't always what they seem. I'd walked in that first day underestimating her. That had been mistake number one.

And the next time that Lance faced off against me, it was going to be his. Because true to this last week's routine, I have weapons training next with Boogey. And I loved his motto: if you can't beat them – don't join them; blow them away.

Lance the creep's face swam in my minds eye as I ducked another punch and countered with a roundhouse kick to Balboa's open right side. Her nod of approval as she picked herself up off the mat was my signal that we were done and I'd done well.

Gloves off and running up the steps I headed toward the gun range where my new Sig 716 AR Rifle and Sig p320 pistol with 9 mm rounds awaited. *Beat him or blow him away*. I smirked as I ran faster. Because either one of those worked for me. I wasn't picky. Not at all.

Chapter Nineteen

"**Ladies**, I'd like for you to meet my daughter, Cassiopeia Sampson. Cass this is Celine Baltimore and her daughter Samantha Henry."

"You can call me Cece and..."

"I'm Sammie!"

I cleared my throat as Celine glared at Sammie. She'd asked the kid to be on her best behavior around my family but since that entailed dialing her sparkling personality back a little; it was like asking a fish not to swim.

I tried not to look at Cass because then both of us would fall out laughing. And that would really embarrass Celine. Making a good impression on my family and daughter was obviously important to her. And I was relieved that it was. Because after all this crap was over I wanted to officially begin our dating relationship. But first things first, I had to find my boy.

"Nice to meet you Cece, and Sammie."

Cass's small smile was genuine but I could tell that she hadn't been sleeping. The dark skin below her eyes, which were heavy with exhaustion practically, screamed that fact. It'd been two months now and she wasn't privy to the info I had, she didn't know that Danny was still alive which meant there was hope.

"I like your name! Its just like those stars Mom calls the.. the... tonsilashuns! Can I call you Cass too? Wow, you're tall! How old are you?"

Cass grinned, her hazel eyes laughing up at me while I chuckled. This was exactly what she needed. A little dose of Sammie could bring a mummy back to life.

"Take her in and introduce her to your grandparents Cass." I nodded toward the great room where the family was gathered while taking Celine and Sammie's coats. Turning back the way we'd come in I headed toward the big closet in the hallway.

Watching the blonds walk away, hands held and swinging while Sammie bombarded Cass with a billion questions back to back, I felt something shift inside me.

"Hey. You okay?"

Celine had come up behind me as I'd finished hanging up their coats. Turning to answer and not realizing she was so close I held my breath. If I leaned forward, just two inches, I would be kissing her. Which was not a good idea. Because I had the feeling that, once I started, I wouldn't want to stop.

But that didn't stop my eyes from practically swallowing her whole as if I hadn't seen her in years.

Hair pulled back in a bun with little tendrils hanging at her temples, her blue eyes shone so seductively at me, I was hard pressed to remain where I was. Snatching her coat back out of the closet and rushing her out the door to get her alone would be so rude that I would never hear the end of it. She would be worth it though.

"Enoch?"

Ah man. And that mouth. I wasn't a catholic but if Hail Mary's or whatever would help now I would say them if I knew the words.

I hadn't been with anyone since I lost Dinah. And lately my body had really been reminding me of that fact.

I'd been watching Celine train for weeks now. And to tell the truth, from that night I'd met her at Fast Eddie's; my body had been on a one-way trip to frustration-town.

Her once soft curvy form had transformed into leaner curves with a hint of muscle. Her face had become sleeker and her rounded chin developed a slight point, drawing a man's focus right to those pink full lips. All of this just made her bright blue eyes even more stunning and her passionate expressions that much more inviting.

Had I not wanted her before now I would have been a little disgusted with myself for being shallow.

But I'd wanted her from the moment I saw her. And I was still finding it hard to adjust to the emotional roller coaster that wanting her had me a frequent rider on.

Like the night Lance Finney had grabbed her. I'd never known that much rage in my life. Not even when my wife was dying of cancer. Hurt and anger I experienced, yes. Desperation and grief especially. But I'd never known a rage that literally turned my vision so red I couldn't process anything.

So when Max had grabbed me after I'd jumped out the truck, thrown and destroyed my laptop and started running toward State Street, I hadn't realize I'd done any of that.

All I knew was that I had to get to her and I had to kill Lance. In that order.

Next thing I knew I was on one knee on the ground, the entire right side of my body disabled. Numbed and unable to move I was finally able to process that I had been moments from jeopardizing our mission. Once my vision cleared I'd gruffly told Max that I was good and he released his grip on the nerve that he'd been disabling. And when he let go I'd climbed into the backseat to watch as Celine hugged herself protectively behind her desk and nodded at Lance.

Teeth gritted I'd turned to Balboa, the red rage threatening to burn away all common sense again, "She starts hand to hand and weapons training tomorrow. Assess her level and take her through it. Activate Boogey and have him acquire the equipment and handle the set up. I want her more than proficient before the party next month."

"Got it." Balboa nodded, pulled out her tablet and typed away, what about, I had no clue.

I'd then turned to Max.

"Check her status once he's clear. Have Boogey pick up his tail I want ears on his vehicle stat."

"Yep. You alright?"

"I need to run man. I have to... I need to... Just call my cell when you know."

I didn't wait to see what they would do. They had their assignments and I had mine. Because it was either calm down or kill Finney. My mind and body preferred the latter.

To say I'd been impressed with her progress would be a huge understatement. Celine took to training like she was born to it, a transition made easier by her daily workouts and prior athletic training. She reached and surpassed every benchmark that Balboa had set. Boogey had already cleared her for license to carry status, declaring her proficient with the AR rifle and more than proficient with the 320. Boogey had been impressed. Boogey wasn't easy to impress. Neither was Balboa.

"Enoch?"

I shook my head a little to get the last few weeks out of it and focused. But remembering helped me in a way that just looking at her wouldn't have. I'd been three seconds from taking her home to put an end to our polite "sniffing around each other" phase. I'm a man that knows what I want. I've wanted her for too long. So maybe it was time I made that clear.

"Celine. Just so I know we're on the same page. You do know that when this is all over I expect you to be with me exclusively right?"

"Uhhh..." If the deer caught in headlights look on her face hadn't been so surprising I would have actually laughed. How could she not know that this was coming? It was certainly obvious to everyone else. In fact, when she wasn't around the team couldn't stop talking about it. I had to finally threaten them all with Ben-gay in their underwear if they didn't shut up and leave it alone.

"Celine?"

"Yeah?"

Deer. Headlights. Seriously?

"Woman, you have to know that I have wanted you since the moment I saw you. And if you even think that it isn't obvious that you want me back, you need to check a mirror. You wear your heart on your face Babe. So I don't doubt that it already belongs to me."

And here she goes. I can't tell if she looked more insulted or embarrassed. But it didn't matter because either reaction would cause the same result, so I braced.

"You don't know me as well as you think you know me Mr. Sampson! I will have you know that..."

"Hey Dad?"

Whew. Fifteen years of fighting with her brother just paid off in this one little act of salvation.

"Yeah baby girl?"

"Gram wants to know if you guys are coming in to join us anytime in this Millennium."

Smart aleck kid.

"Yeah, be right in."

"Kay." Sneaky grin plus laughing hazel eyes multiplied by a little blond version of the beauty standing in front of me... what was I getting myself into anyway?

As Sammie peaked around Cass's side to grin at us something told me that the answer to my question was better left unknown.

Because it wasn't like I could go anywhere. They were mine and I already belonged to them.

So when Celine glared a, 'we will talk about this later,' glare at me. I just exhaled, rolled my eyes up to the ceiling like my dad often did – he said it was to ask the Good Lord for strength- and followed her inside to the dining area.

I might as well get into the practice of doing that now anyway. Because with those three, I was going to need all of the strength that I could get.

***

What ever happened to romance? I mean, I know ours wasn't the usual boy meets girl story but how do you go from, "you need to train to fight so suck it up," to, "you're mine ugah ugah me yours uhga buhga!"

These couldn't be the best thoughts to have while fiddling with my office door.

Unlocking it was a like a Greek tragedy having an epic adventure during the apocalypse. Especially when you had a hand full of junk that you carried up two flights of steps because you didn't want to make another trip down and up again on said steps.

Grunting at my own pitiful laziness, I finally wrestle the door open with a bang.

Slamming the door closed for its cranky constitution I threw the bags filled with credit card fodder onto the couch, then collapse right beside them, all while thinking about last night.

Last night and Enoch's giant revelation – Hi Celine, I'm actually a cave man. See my club? I own you now. I bought you with two cows, a goat and a chicken.

What a Bone-head.

But was I wrong to be a teeny tiny bit turned on by that? I mean, I am woman hear me roar and all that but still. It was nice to be wanted. Especially by someone I wanted, though he'd lost his rabid mind trying to tell me how I feel! You can't just tell a woman how she feels! She knows how she feels! You're supposed to tell her how you feel! With flowers and candy. Or a date with dinner and a good movie. At the very least with popcorn and an oldie but goodie playing on Netflix.

I hmphed and pulled my cell phone out of my pocket since it was vibrating.

Enoch again. *Ignore call* again.

How about that? How do I feel now Mister "everybody knows you're hot for me blah blah blah!"

And before he could even get started I gave the little editor the hand. I don't want to hear it. Common sense isn't that common and when I'm acting like this it's a rare jewel of legendary proportions.

I don't care that Enoch was right. I don't care that he was telling the truth and just nixing all of the preliminaries because in truth, no one really has time for that. With all the drama we had going on and with the party less than a week away, we had to focus on the objectives so that everyone got out of this thing alive. I know that he was giving me a heads up. That doesn't mean that I don't want flowers, candy, romance and walks on the beach dadnabbit!

I deep sighed and reached for my phone to call him back hissy-fit free, when something I should have noticed before caught my eye.

First, my office bathroom light was on. I always turned the lights off everywhere in my office when I left for the day. Second, whoever it was hiding in there was casting a shadow.

It didn't even cross my mind to run. Enoch's training played back in my head and I recalled him saying, "Fighting is your last option. And even when you fight, it's to disable the opponent and run. Worst case scenario, kill the opponent if that is the only form of disablement left to you."

But I didn't even think about running as I slid my heels off and quietly removed my jacket. Because this was my office. And the last time that I was in it with someone who made me feel helpless, I promised myself that I would never allow that again. I wasn't going to run. I was going to beat the stew out of whoever was in that bathroom and then drag them to my team. I didn't know what they would do with them, I didn't really think water torture or pulling out toenails was their thing. But I didn't care. Because I was taking my life back. Starting now.

Humming out loud so that my intruder would think they've gone unnoticed I got up from the couch and headed toward the bookshelves behind my desk, which was also along the same wall where the bathroom door opened from further down. I started shuffling the books and then dropped one onto my desk and pulled out the chair.

I then snuck along the wall to stand next to the opening, knowing my intruder would peak around the wall to see if I was sitting down sooner or later. And when they did, I planned on taking their eyes out.

My sneak attack was foiled as a little blond head slowly inched around the corner of the wall.

"MANDY!"

I whispered it chokingly before reached around to snatch her to me in a full body hug.

She was alive. Thank you Lord, my girl was ALIVE.

Chapter Twenty

She opened her mouth to speak but I quickly placed my hand over it as I vigorously shook my head in the universal "no" signal.

Using hand gestures I had her stoop down and stay low in the bathroom while I gathered an old hat from my desk drawer along with my sweater and spare tennis shoes.

Quickly we dressed her in my things and stuffed something under her clothes to make her look like a round old lady from a distance, the whole time not saying a word.

Keeping her in the bathroom I went back to the couch and grabbed my phone, dialing the last number to call me.

"Really Celine? Because yelling at your voice mail is on my long list of things that I must get done…"

"Sam." I said it so that he would catch on immediately. I never called him Sam. And for that reason we established during day one of my training, if I ever needed help but couldn't say anything, I would call him Sam.

"I'm there in three." Disconnect.

In less than five minutes I had Mandy down the steps, out the door and climbing into the back seat of the black Escalade SUV.

Pulling her to me again I tried not to cry. I couldn't speak because my throat felt like it was closing from the effort of holding in my tears. The only way I knew that she was still in my arms was the beat of her heart crashing against me as she exhaled harsh choking breaths.

Enoch was however, not a very patient man. He gave us exactly ten seconds for all of that before he exploded quietly in a flat tone.

"Talk to me!"

"It's Mandy." I pushed the words past the blockage in my throat in a gurgled rush as I pulled back to get a good look at my girl.

She wasn't hurt thank goodness. Her streaked brownish blond hair was a mess, lanky and in desperate need of a washing. Her cheeks were a little gaunt because she'd lost some weight and her brown eyes were sunken, missing that light of mischief that was uniquely hers.

My girl was alive but she wasn't good. My gaze met Enoch's in the rear view mirror. I knew that he saw the worry all over my face. We needed answers before I contacted her parents but first, we needed to get her to safety. Confident that Enoch was taking us to my house, I focused on my patient.

"Talk to me girlfriend." We'd always had a casual communication style. I was her therapist, not her parents. Building trust meant that she could tell me anything without fear of reprisal or judgment. And that was most likely why she was here now.

"Please don't call my parents."

"Why? What's wrong?"

She shuddered and burrowed deeper into my arms as we turned on Henry. This was bad. All of her non-verbals were screaming abuse at me. But in this day and age, state custody wasn't any better, nor was it an option when you were dealing with "old money". And the Same's were definitely "old money."

"Talk to me kiddo, I need to know how to help you. I don't know if you don't tell me."

By now we'd pulled up into my driveway, the truck's ding signifying Enoch had gotten out and closed his door to come around and escort us up.

I was about to ask again when Mandy blurted, "Are you going to the party? For the contest you won?"

Stuttering and a little freaked that Mandy would even know about our covert operations I pulled her close and whispered harshly.

"How? How do you know about that Mandy? This isn't a game kid. This is dangerous stuff. So spill it and spill it now."

Enoch opened her door and the interior light came on, illuminating her face with haunting clarity. The tears that I couldn't see before continued to race down her cheeks, her expression pleading for forgiveness. At that moment I knew. I knew I was going to hate what she said but before I could brace she answered my question with a stilted whisper.

"I know because... because... I did it Ms. Baltimore. I'm the one who entered you into that contest."

And just like that my heart shattered. I never knew it was possible to feel so hurt and so betrayed. Apparently I loved these kids like they were my own. Because only someone who belongs to you has the power, with one sentence, to shake your whole world.

Saying nothing I turned to open my truck door. I heard Enoch's soft, "Come on," to Mandy.

Getting up the steps to my front door was a concerted effort. So much so, I couldn't say anything, just fiddled with my keys to get them into the deadbolt. I needed a minute to get my head together. Because as betrayed as I felt, this kid had been destroyed by something. By someone. And I had a feeling that they would be looking for her soon to finish the job.

***

Danny

I tried to focus but the light was horrible, hurting me and burning into my eyes. I tried to open my mouth, to ask what was going on but something was in my throat, choking me.

And my hands were tied down. I bucked and strained, trying to get out. I heard an awful grunting animal growl coming from somewhere. I couldn't think but I knew I was somewhere I didn't want to be, so I fought some more.

As I struggled the sound got louder. I fought even harder to get away from that thing before I heard the other voices.

"Calm him down Rosario. He's choking himself. And for crying out loud put him out before I kill him just to shut him up!"

I paused and blinked really fast trying to clear my vision. The light started to fade and I realized that the noises had finally stopped. Had that been me? Had those horrible sounds been coming from me?

I could feel my heart rate increase and just as I was about to scream a face appeared over mine, but upside down.

The face was attached to what appeared to be a doctor or someone dressed in full surgical gear; mask, hat and gown.

The voice became clearer and I soon grasped that it was a lady talking to me, telling me to calm down.

I wanted to know where I was but I couldn't ask. And what was weird was, that same growling voice, the one I'd heard before that freaked me completely out, was speaking again. Only it was words this time. And it was asking the same words that were going through my head.

The ladies eyes got really round, like she heard it too. I stopped moving and listened harder, trying to project what I was thinking to see if this was really happening.

"My name is Danny. Danny Sampson. What are you doing to me? Who are you people?"

The needle in the lady's hand clattered to the floor as she backed away from me. I couldn't turn my head to look at her but it didn't take a genius to know that she had taken off running out the door along with the other person that had been in the room.

I closed my eyes and tried to think. Think Danny think. Dad said that you never really forget anything. You have to remember how you ended up in this place. What do I remember last? Basketball practice.

My eyes popped open as the memory flooded through me and I nearly passed out from fear at the shock of seeing someone else hovering over me.

She was upside down too. Only she was a kid. Couldn't be older than Cass, maybe a couple of years younger in fact, still in that pre-teen cute kid stage.

Her white blonde curls fell over onto my face and her laughing brown eyes matched her wide smile.

And just as I started to think them, she started answering my questions.

"Hi Danny. My name is Anabella . I'm younger than your sister Cassie and I do know what you're doing here. You don't have to be scared anymore or worried. It's all gonna be okay because your Dad and Ms. Celine are coming soon. Your dad is Sam... who's Sammie? Huh. That's going to get confusing. Anyway they're gonna help us blow this popsicle stand."

I have got to be losing my mind, was what came to mind after hearing all of that. Either I was going crazy or this was one uber-freak out of a dream. From this moment on, no more horror movies, that was a promise. And Sampson men ALWAYS kept their promises.

That's when the kid suspended over me started giggling again.

"My sister says that alot, popsicle stand. Doesn't that sound funny? And wasn't it funny that those horrible doctors ran away scared? It's what they deserve you know."

Why? Why did they deserve to be scared?

"Because they hurt us for money. But there is one nice lady. She's new." In a whisper the girl continued, "She's not supposed to be here."

Alrighty then. *Hey, can you help me get loose?* I figured, since she could hear my thoughts and everything, it was worth a shot to try projecting them again.

"Okay, but it's gonna hurt. You should wait until tomorrow. Then they will do it without hurting you."

How? How do you know all this? And how can you hear what I'm thinking?

"Mandy told me that God makes special people like me for a reason. And no matter what, it's always a good reason."

And this is the reason God made you? To hear what I'm thinking?

"Nope, it's to help people, people like you to see the truth."

What truth?

"That you have to pick a side silly. You have to choose. Choose to suffer but have light as a buffer, or choose the dark and lose your heart."

Great, not only was I tied to a bed with tubes down my throat, but I was stuck in here with a mind reading kid that thought she was this generation's answer to Dr. Seuss.

I wasn't surprised when she fell off of the bed cracking up and giggling after I thought that. She must really like Dr. Seuss.

***

Sam

Fighting the bile back down into my throat I continue to shake my head in disbelief.

I couldn't believe it. I'd fought for this country, killed for it, watched team members die for it. For this? So that people could do sick stuff like this?

I watched Celine as she said goodbye to her parents. We'd just dropped of Sammie and Mandy so that they could spend Christmas Eve and Day as far away from Alton as possible without sending up any red flags.

We didn't want this to blowback on our families, but we were done. We had to do something and do something now.

Celine got into the passenger seat and I immediately pulled off to head to our command center.

Everyone had texted they'd be there except for Johnny. I hadn't heard from him since he started focusing on the church. I wasn't too worried since, after what we learned tonight we knew the church wasn't our problem. Far from it.

Celine took the batteries and sim cards out of both of our phones as we doubled back from Alton and headed back out hwy 367 to hit hwy 270 going south.

I glanced over to see how she was handling all of this. Her tight jaw and balled fists screamed the curses that she refused to verbalize.

Reaching over I grabbed her left hand to loosen them up so that I could slide my fingers between hers.

"It's going to be okay Babe."

It was pitiful and inadequate, but it was all I had.

Her eyes were shiny but her tears didn't fall. She just gripped my hand like it was the only thing keeping her from drowning and turned to gaze out her window. I knew that she was praying right then, with all of her heart. For strength, for guidance and for those girls. And for the first time since my wife lay before me dying, I prayed too. Because this was bigger than us in every sense of the word. And if God didn't intervene, there would be no hope for anyone, anywhere. Ever.

Chapter Twenty One

"**Tell** me that this is a sick joke man. Tell me you are freaking kidding me."

Boogey paced back and forth in angry strides while Balboa looked on quiet and watchful. Max wouldn't look up at all which was telling. Because something told me that he knew about this kind of thing. That it had happened before.

K.C. leaned against the wall, arms crossed and staring down at his feet. A look of utter disgust was on his face, which surprised me. Because we were all hardened ex-military types. Nothing should have surprised us. But this did. On a scale of one to ten, this one was a past infinity.

And something told me that Boogey's rant was just starting. Conspiracy theorist that he was, this hit home like nobody's business.

"So what you're telling us, is these people, rich people with like EVERYTHING in the freaking WORLD; hand over their kids as a sacrifice to this sick stuff?"

Since we'd summarized it the first go around it was time to break out all of the facts. I couldn't let my disgust run us away from the details because we needed to plan accordingly and accurately.

"Apparently there are supposedly thirteen elite bloodlines. Each branch of the bloodline is responsible for providing a male child and a female child to their tradition of preserving their elite status.

They're goal is to remain pure as they attempt to bring about the New World or New World Order."

Boogey was about to interrupt but I knew I had to stop him so that his conspiracy theory wouldn't confuse the issue of Mandy's revelations.

"I know Boogey, but this is the girls personal account so let me tell it as she explained it okay? Anyway, the Same family is an offshoot of one of these bloodlines. Because Edward and Caroline were the only ones to have reproduced and they didn't give birth to a son, they agreed to hand over both of their daughters to the girls' Uncle Cedric, Edward's brother. It was either that or be disowned by the family. Caroline fought it but Edward insisted that they would find a way to retrieve their children. Caroline agreed to send the girl's to their Uncle's for the summer as long as Edward promised that the girls would be brought home. Her maiden name is Renquist, by the way. A powerful family in their own right, though the Renquists aren't considered "old money" they hold quite a bit of influence. So apparently the threat was, bring my daughters home or else. "

I paused as Celine got up and walked out of the room. I had the feeling that she didn't need to hear what I had to say next ever again. She'd known at the onset of treating both girls that the treatment had been court mandated due to sexual abuse. But she hadn't known the extent of it. And neither had the courts. Having heard it all now directly from Mandy, she was still trying to cope. And hearing it once tonight already put her at hearing it one time too many.

"During their summer there the Uncle made the girls participate in some type of ritual where both of their virginities were taken on an altar. The girls were then repeatedly raped over and over again by their uncle and his masked friends before they were locked away, naked, in one of the guest bedrooms. Lucky for them the cleaning staff was contracted to clean the vacation properties once a month for the family, who wasn't scheduled to be there again until mid-March. Having forgotten about that, the uncle remained in a drunken stupor from the revelries, his friends having left the night before. The cleaning staff found the girls and contacted the authorities. The uncle was prosecuted and jailed under New Hampshire child abuse and child pornography statutes. What's sad is, that isn't where the horror for the girls ended."

Balboa cracked her knuckles and looked away. Max's jaw clenched again. He had to know that this part would be painful to hear, let alone say.

"The parents immediately got their girls into treatment having learned of Ms. Baltimore's way with underage clients. Their preliminary reports showed inordinate success and Mrs. Same demanded that the children be taken to her as opposed to the clinical psychologist that the Same family recommended."

Balboa got up and started pacing. You could actually feel the rage floating off of her in waves. It would have been less disconcerting if she hadn't appeared so calm.

Taking a breath I continued.

"Amanda overheard her father talking to his mother over the phone. She'd accidentally picked up the house phone to make a call and heard her grandmother yelling that the ritual was necessary and that without the subsequent rapes, partitioning the personality into compartments would be difficult. If multiple personalities weren't created the mind wipes wouldn't function correctly and the family's sacrifice would be for nothing. Amanda overheard her father's docile response to his mother and agreement that they should turn both girls over to a clinical psychologist to begin the process of compartmentalization. But because of the argument he anticipated with his wife regarding the change, the grandmother suggested another way, stating that it might be even better. The new technology called Brainwaiver would allow for the controls to be in place without a forced schism in the personality. The application would allow them to set protocols and seize control of the subject whenever they desired. It would even help Anabella who had been diagnosed as autistic be less of an embarrassment – her words."

"This is beyond nuts," K.C. hadn't moved when he said that, just continued to shake his head in disbelief. Because we'd all read the urban legends about MK ULTRA and mind control protocols back in the day as a lark. We'd even jokingly pointed out current Hollywood stars and starlets that we deemed "mind wiped" at one time or another. But never, not for one second had any of us come across anything in our experience that denoted to the existence of such a program. Or maybe we had and just didn't realize it. It was all too horrible to contemplate.

It no longer mattered because I wanted to get this done. The time to move against RLS was just a week away and I was done being subtle.

"Amanda's mother wouldn't believe her when she tried to expose her father so she found help in the Narrow Way youth ministry. Confiding in her youth pastor some of the details and getting his guidance, she was advised to wait and watch for an opportunity that would allow her to give her mother some type of evidence. She was forced to watch Anabella fitted with the implant, forced to watch her suffer from spontaneous hemorrhages and horrible night terrors. She was punished when she refused to take the implant herself though she wouldn't say how. It had been a while before she stumbled over the proof that she'd needed, Ana's journal. She was ready to hand the journal over to her mom and demand that they leave for the safety of her mother's family when she over heard her parents talking in the den. Her father had been talking to her mother like she was hypnotized. He spoke a trigger word that somehow entranced her and every thing her mother was told to do right then, she did. Amanda was horrified and frightened out of her mind. They'd done something to her mom and her sister was suffering. Her plan was no longer valid. So she found the Brainwaiver contest form that her mother had filled out for her. She knew that it had been marked with an indication that she was of an elite bloodline. She whited out and copied the form, created a false email profile and used it to enter the only person that she trusted in the world besides her youth pastor, into the Brainwaiver contest – Celine."

Balboa shook her head ruefully and chuckled a little.

"What?"

"Kid would make a great agent. That's all I'm saying."

Max nodded and added in his quiet tone, "She's definitely a survivor."

All heads nodded as I continued where I'd left off.

"During a restroom break in one of their sessions, Amanda went into Celine's wallet to obtain all of her identifiers by taking a picture with her cell phone. She entered Celine into the contest, and then a month later gave her the journal. After that, she disappeared, secretly hidden away in the home of her youth pastor and his young wife. Yesterday investigators targeted the church and the youth minister had become a person of interest in Amanda's disappearance. Now, keep in mind, her disappearance has not been reported to the local authorities. But Amanda doesn't know that. What she does know however, is that there were people that looked like federal agents asking questions around the church, flashing their badges and issuing threats. To keep her church members and youth pastor safe, she ran again and hid out in Celine's office."

And that was that. So here we were. We had some answers now, but even more questions.

The room was quiet for a moment before Balboa walked out, probably to grab Celine so that we could move forward with the planning.

And I wondered a few things. Were the attorneys at RLS aware that Celine was entered into the contest by Mandy? It would have been a simple thing to obtain a back-ground check. Proud Irish-

American's that her family were, their bloodline would be considered far from elite.

So it stands to reason that they knew that Celine was entered by Mandy. And that would explain why they would insist that Celine honor the application as a contract. Because she had been their only lead to where Mandy may have been hiding at the time.

But now, according to Mandy, they'd targeted the church. And if they'd targeted the church while having previously focused on Celine, I had to wonder, what caused them to begin investigating the youth minister?

I put the battery and sim back into place and checked my cell phone again. John still hadn't called or texted. And I hadn't heard from him in days. The ice storm raging behind my eyes assured me that, while I would give anything to believe otherwise, Jonathan Charles Davies had gone Elvis. A marine to his name, I knew that it was something he would never do voluntarily.

"Macchio."

"Yeah."

"I need you to find Johnny."

Celine and Balboa had just walked back into the room. It couldn't have been my words so it had to be the way that I said it that caused everyone to give pause.

It was so quiet that the keys on the keyboard Max was using clacked loudly with an obvious echo.

I closed my eyes and, for the second time tonight, I found myself praying. We hadn't established check in's. Johnny was a lone wolf kind of guy. He enjoyed doing his own thing, mostly because if he ever suffered an episode, his partner wouldn't have to deal with seeing him like that. So we'd all taken our assignments and trusted that we would meet up and debrief before the party. That meeting was going on right now. It was a day early, but still, we were all supposed to stay assessable in case the meet up changed so that we could provide any relevant details as well as agree on the final plan.

John's absence was a red flag all over the place. Because the party was next week. We'd all agreed that Celine was going but she wasn't going alone. Balboa was going with her to have her back. The team and I would be infiltrating RLS based upon the schematics of the building that Max had found. Since we already had a source on the inside we knew what we would be facing and planned accordingly.

Now all we needed was Johnny.

"I pinged his phone, it's done."

"His phone is dead?"

"Nope it's done. Even when a phone hasn't been charged for days there is a residual spark that will respond to a ping. There's no spark. Means that the battery has been removed and it's been dead for months, which isn't the case. There is another power source inside every cell phone – like a watch battery. I lasts forever almost because the pull on it is small. It's what keeps your date and time correct as well as your contact information saved, even when the battery is dead or pulled. I sent a wireless signal to the motherboard to reroute its programmed pull on the power supply to the watch battery in order to get a response to the ping, even if his phone is turned off or the battery is pulled. I got nothing. Since I talked to him two weeks ago, that leaves one of two things: the phone's been torched, the watch battery fried, or it fell into some water."

"Track his GPS on his car."

More typing. Max inhaled sharply.

"Where?"

"Bluffs, near the Alton water supply by Piasa Park."

We didn't bother shutting down, just scattered to our vehicles.

Dread washed over me and the storm in my head raged. I clenched tightly to the wheel as I sped down Geyer to hit highway 270 on two wheels.

Celine's hand closed over my right hand on the wheel.

And just like that I felt my grip loosen. I glanced over, her eyes sweet with concern and loaded with something I couldn't define.

It was my turn to grab hold to her hand like it was a lifeline. Because I already knew what we would discover and I didn't want to loose myself in the ice. Not anymore. Not ever again.

So when we all stood around Johnny's body floating in the Missouri River under the bluffs, just five miles away from Piasa Park, I buried my face in Celine's hair to lose myself in her scent and stave off the rage.

Johnny was gone. The placement of the body and how easily it was found could only mean one thing; they knew about us. And this was their message to us to back off.

Pulling Celine fully into me and holding her close, one truth resonated in my soul. I would mourn my friend later. It was time to end this and send these sicko's back to hell where they'd come from.

Chapter Twenty-Two

"**Houston** we have a problem."

I tried to stop biting my nails because it was not only a nasty habit; it created one heck of a bill at my salon. But it was something I always did when I paced. I paced when I was nervous.

And since Andrew Townsend Attorney at Law and appointed representative of Reigner, Lee and Stratford lay unconscious on my office floor, I had reason to be nervous in a big way.

It was one day before the party. One day until I played the starring role as the Belle of the Ball at the RLS New Year's Gala while my team went in and did their thing.

It was also one week after we found Johnny. One week since I realized that this wasn't me playing spy games; this was real life, real time and just plain real.

Johnny's funeral had not been what I would call the social event of the season. It had been heartbreaking. Just remembering how only a few people were there to pay their respects made me get all teary again, which totally messed with the new "rough and tough" persona that I was going for.

Enoch had arranged for the funeral and chose its location with a specific goal in mind. The pastor at Narrow Way had been surprised and heart broken at the call. He'd apparently known and become fond of Johnny, but hadn't known the true reason he'd taken an interest in the ministry and joined the church.

While it was determined that the team shouldn't attend because we didn't know who would be watching the church, Enoch and I did.

And one other person. I didn't know her, and from the hard look in her eyes, I didn't want to. Her dark brown hair mixed with all kinds of dyed-in colors along with her dark, almost black eyes, practically screamed at anyone thinking about getting close to back the heck off.

And so I did. I focused my conversation on the Pastor's wife after the eulogy was delivered and waited patiently as Enoch met with the Pastor briefly in the back room.

Once our time at the funeral proper was concluded, we'd traveled to the burial site at Jefferson Barracks in Missouri. It was the saddest funeral I'd ever been to. And to me, even with the small time I'd known Johnny, I knew he'd deserved better than that.

After that, hand to hand combat; stick fighting and weapons training took on a whole other sense of urgency for me. I no longer trained because I didn't want to feel defenseless ever again. Now I trained because someone's life, my team's who I now considered my family's lives might depend on it.

Because Johnny's had. And we'd failed him. That wasn't happening again. So I prepared for the worst. I took vacation time from my job and temporarily assigned my clients to another LCSW that I trusted.

Thinking back further, before Johnny's funeral I remembered spending Christmas day with my family and kid; loving on them with all of my heart while trying my best to hide the gut-wrenching pain and guilt that Johnny's death left me with. I wasn't very successful at that. But my people rocked because they didn't nag me about what was wrong. They loved me. Which was exactly what I'd needed.

Sammie and I'd gone to Enoch's family's to visit that Christmas evening.

She'd had a great time hanging with Cass. Those two had become the best of buds despite their age difference so the good news for me? I found a new babysitter that I absolutely adored.

Seeing Sammie excited and happy this Christmas, despite her dad's usual penchant for drama was one of the best Christmas gifts a Mom could ask for.

But the best gift I'd gotten from Enoch came as a surprise. I'd gone to grab our coats so we could say goodnight and get Sammie back to my folks.

I'd reached for the big hall closet door when a hand had closed over mine. And because I knew the feel of that hand without even looking at it, I turned to see what he needed. Only to find Enoch standing right there. Not just there, but *there*. Like, in my face, nose to nose, so close my eyes crossed *there.*

He'd whispered something so soft I'd almost missed it.

"What?" I croaked.

"Mistletoe." He whispered again, his gaze fixed on my mouth.

But I knew two things because my freaky attention to detail was just that vivid. One; there was no mistletoe over here by the closet, it was on the other side of the living room – hanging over the entrance to the dining area. And two; I'd licked my lips nervously because he was looking right at them. While his confusion over where the mistletoe was didn't quite register (my mind totally on the fact that he was so close we could share each other's skin) his narrowing gaze on my mouth did.

I wanted to step back and think this through because this was so not the time. His best friend was just murdered. His family was just a name call away in another room. And I really *really* just needed time to think this through.

But I also wanted to know what I'd been missing. So many times I'd been too cautious. So many times I'd had to think things through and, finding the cons list longer than the pros, had walked away.

I'd always believed that the phrase, "Let go and let God," was for the lazy. People are accountable for their choice to act, or not act at all. To choose to let something happen and then blame God for the outcome just never made sense to me.

This time, just this one time, I wanted to let go. And not just for me, but for Enoch. The pain that battered him over Johnny's loss was epic. It surrounded him like an icy cloak, a dark wind that you couldn't see until you looked into his eyes. And I knew that, if I didn't do something; because it had to be me and no one else, he'd be gone. He'd be physically here, but gone. And I couldn't – wouldn't – let that happen.

So I didn't move or back away. And I didn't wait for him to take it. I gave it freely. Going that last inch had been the hardest thing I'd done since I'd filed for that divorce.

Because a part of me died at that moment. There was no safety net for this leap into the unknown.

But when I felt his mouth on mine; first slow and exploratory then exploding into a passionate exchange of heat and emotion, I knew that the sacrifice was worth it. Because I'd do just about anything to keep him away from the cold. That, and it was singularly the best kiss I'd ever had.

I didn't know how much time had passed, but our kisses had gone from soft and testing, to exploratory and passionate, then back to soft. His hands had come up some time during the exchange to frame my face, holding me gently as he bit and nibbled, and I breathed.

My hands were holding onto his wrists by the time we'd stopped because, even then, I didn't have the strength to back away. We stood there in the hall forehead-to-forehead and holding onto each other just like that for what seemed like forever. My eyes still closed I focused on taking that next breath, and then the next.

Because this was too big. It was too much. I had no problem with playing Harriet the Spy so that lives would be saved. I had no problem with weapons training with a Sig Saur hand gun, an AR (assault rifle) as well as an archery bow. It didn't faze me to engage in hand-to-hand combat, Mixed Martial Arts and Martial Arts training on a daily basis. I took all of that in stride.

But to have this man. This beautiful, strong Alpha male man, hold onto me like my very presence was life itself; to kiss me like I was the other half of his soul? That was too big. And if I allowed myself to think about that, it would overwhelm me. Then I would freak and run for the hills.

There was too much riding on us. On me, for me to massively freak out and get ghost. And I just didn't have it in me to let him go through one more second feeling lost, which was exactly what he'd been. Lost in the freezing storm of brokenness that tried to consume him in his own mind.

And so I'd taken one breath. Then another. And another.

And finally, when I did get around to opening my eyes, his gazing back at me – no longer cold but full of fire – showed me two very real truths.

The first was, this man would never ever allow anything to harm me or anyone I love. And the second was almost just like it, he would never ever let me go. I was his. And he was so very much mine. So I did what I had to do. I'd let go and let God.

Best. Christmas gift. Ever.

Then I'd trained even harder because in the end I refused to be a reason for Enoch's suffering. That meant that if we had to fight, we had to win.

Which reminded me that I had a man lying unconscious in the middle of my floor. Because being in battle mode is difficult to shake no matter how trained you are. So when Balboa and I'd finished training and decided to stop by my office and grab the shoes for the gala (I'd accidentally left behind the brand new high heeled sandals that matched my gala dress the same day I'd found Mandy hiding in my office), I didn't expect for someone to lay their hand on my shoulder to get my attention.

Balboa had decided to wait in the car so I'd known it wasn't her. In fact, I knew where every member of my team was, it being so close to the big day. And because I knew not one of them would be skulking in the hall of my office; not to mention that the last time I'd felt helpless, it had been in this very spot, only on the other side of the door, I'd reacted purely on instinct.

Grabbing the hand on my shoulder with my right to hold it there, I'd kicked back with my right foot to disable the knee, sent my left elbow behind me into my assailant's throat, then letting go of the hand I turned with a full body right hook that powered into his left temple, sending him crashing to the ground. Total knock out.

Tempted to do my Rocky dance since I could hear the music playing in my head, I rolled him over just as Balboa was coming up the steps to see what was keeping me. I was not the average chick that would promise I'd take a minute and be down in fifteen. I'd told her I'd be quick because the shoes would be right on the couch where I'd left them. And while I was quick taking Andrew down, I wasn't very quick in reacting to my mental screams of "Good gravy! It's Andrew! What do we do now?"

So Houston, we have a problem. Because I just blew our cover. Those weren't just self-defense moves I'd used. That was boxing and MMA training that even a novice would be able to pinpoint with little trouble.

Which means that I've been training. And when Andrew came to, he'd probably want to know why I'd been training. Huge red flag.

As Balboa broke down the issue to Max on her phone, I decided to speed dial Enoch. As team leader he needed to know that we just went off script so he could chart us a new path. Because I'd blown a hole in our current one the size of Texas.

***

Sam

I don't believe in karma or bad luck. I don't believe that Murphy's Law attacks people on a regular basis to make their lives miserable just because he could (despite Celine's insistence to the contrary).

But I did believe that our plan had to be born under a bad sign. Because we were one day away from operations and set up was already in place. And we had to change it in a big way.

"Don't worry about it Baby. Quit beating yourself up. The plan was dead anyway." I said this as my mind scrambled for a solution because I was not exaggerating.

Celine kept pacing and biting her nails. My woman. Cute and deadly. I tried not to grin as I imagined her taking this guy out in the hallway. But I couldn't really stop it completely because what can I say. I was proud. She did good. She did better than good. And I needed to see that to know that she was ready. Because losing her was not an option. Period.

"I know, I know..."

I stepped into her path and grabbed her hands in one of mine and with the other tilted her face up so she could look me in the eye. Beauty. And all mine, as soon as this was over.

"You saw what Max got off of him right? The party's been moved. To RLS. Where we just had security and cameras to deal with before, now we have hundreds of witnesses to add to those concerns. The plan was dead before you touched him. Okay?"

Slow blinking at me, her eyes indicated that she understood. And I probably should have moved away right then. But I liked touching her. I liked feeling how real she was. Plus that scent of hers always brought me calm when I needed to think. And I needed to think harder. New plan, new strategy and new placements. All with one day to make that happen.

Involuntarily my hand moved from tilting her chin into a caress down her cheek. Soft and sweet. Quick and powerful. Contradiction and challenge. It's like she was made perfect; just for me. Dinah had been what I'd needed as a young man. Completely soft to compliment my rough edges and need for adventure. She was all nurture, for me as well as the kids.

I didn't realize how much I'd changed. How much I needed someone who was more of a match. Who could give just as good as she got in any arena, but still be soft and sweet when I needed her to be. Versatile. Stealth. I'd found all of that in Celine. I'd found her right when I'd needed her most. Whispering a silent prayer of thanks, I kissed my woman on her forehead to ease the worry I knew she was feeling.

More focused now, I moved away and did a little pacing of my own.

This Andrew guy had been given a message to deliver to Celine. A message that stated the location of the party had been changed at the last minute.

The question was why? It was a written invitation that he'd had in his hand when he'd grabbed her shoulder. So why didn't they mail it? Unless the change was recent.

The change in addition to Johnny's death and Mandy's arrival were all indicators that they knew something. And they were suspicious of Celine.

Suspicious enough to deliver the change of venue in person; in such a way that would frighten her? I really didn't like that thought...

"Max."

"Yeah."

"You get anything off of his phone?"

"Random emails and a few anonymous texts. Nothing incriminating though."

"Do you see the Brainwaiver app on there?"

"Uh," I heard him fiddling with the phone and then he continued, "nah. No Brainwaiver. But according to Celine, if you've had the implant long enough, you don't need the app."

True. But if he did have the implant, chances are, he would have responded faster to Celine's right hook. She was getting good, but she wasn't prizefighter material just yet.

"How long will the stuff KC gave you to keep him out last?"

"Why?"

"I'm trying to decide if we want to play with his mind a little and send him back..."

"Or if you want to hold him indefinitely to see what he knows."

"Exactly."

Celine, now leaning against the wall by her couch raised her hand like she had a question.

"Yeah Babe?"

"First, I'd like to go on record and say that I am not on board with playing with people's minds. That's what we're trying to stop them from doing. And second, would seeing what he knows involve, uh... um..."

I shook my head and paced again as I interrupted; because, she had a good point on one count and I needed to ease her mind on the other.

"We don't torture people Celine, if that's what you're asking."

"Okay." She mumbled looking hard at her nails before raising her hand back toward her mouth.

"Stop biting your nails."

She paused, her eyes rounded like I'd just told her that someone had defiled her favorite sweater with barbeque sauce and mustard.

"Eep," was all that came out of her mouth. Good. I'd distracted her like I'd intended.

Oh she huffed a bit, casting around mentally for a good set down to put me in my place. But really? What else could she say? It wasn't the best habit to have. And it probably sent her Salon bill through the roof.

Trying to hide my grin I turn back to Max.

"K.C. wants to know if we need a pick up." Max always knows what to say to bring me back to the task.

"Yep. Put him in the bunker on site."

"How long we gonna hold him?"

Walking over and taking Celine's hand I pulled her forward and walked her to the door. The new plan already taking shape, I had to pick up a new suit, get a haircut and a rental, and call in another favor; and it was already past 6:30 and getting dark.

"As long as we have to."

I felt Celine's grip tighten on my hand but I didn't think I should elaborate. Because to keep the rest of my team safe and make sure that today didn't blow back on her, I'd do what I needed to do. Compared to that, I didn't need her to know that playing with his mind would have been a far better alternative.

Chapter Twenty-Three

Nina Irwin stood on my porch seemingly waiting patiently for me as I locked my truck doors and started up the steps.

Seemingly because I knew that everything about this young woman spoke one language: impatience.

Just like her short affirmative to meet me had when I'd called her two hours ago. Just like her response had been at her uncle's funeral over the cause of death.

"Hey." I said it as I reached the porch and stood toe to toe with her. No longer a kid at 22 she stood tall and thin, about 5'9. Her multi color hair always managed to surprise me, possibly because I'd practically raised her. Her hair once a rich brown had matched eyes so brown that they appeared black. Nina had once been as happy and bubbly as Sammie; that is, until she'd lost her parents in a car accident and her Uncle had come back from Iraq a completely different person.

"Hey," she responded almost as if the word were ripped from her throat against her will.

Her tight lips and the arms crossed over her chest told me how much she didn't want to be here. And they would have to because she was no longer a person that expended unnecessary energy on words. She was kind of like Macchio in that respect. But she didn't used to be this way. She used to practically glow with energy.

Frowning and shaking away the memory, I unlocked the door so that we could get this out of the way.

We had two things to discuss and I had to grab a couple of hours of sleep before morning arrived, bringing with it the final set up for infiltrating RLS. I was getting my son back tomorrow. I needed rest to bring my A game.

Throwing my keys onto the hallway table I headed straight back to the kitchen knowing she'd follow. She knew this house better than I did, having practically been raised here when I was on assignment overseas.

I hadn't seen her since Dinah's funeral so I was still trying to grasp the changes in her before I got down to business. I don't really know all of the details but I did know that right after she returned to base once we'd buried Dinah, she'd been court marshaled for decking her superior officer.

She never had to tell me that he'd done something to deserve that. Because I know he did. Nina wasn't one to act on impulse once she'd entered into the Air Force. She had a quick mouth but wasn't quick to lash out. In fact she usually responded physically only when a physical threat was prevalent. Otherwise her cutting tongue was all the weaponry she needed to put folks in their place.

But she wasn't here to answer questions about why she'd been ousted from the Air Force or even what she'd been up to. I'd known that losing Dinah was like losing a second mom for her. And because we weren't as close as she and Dinah had been, I'd known that she would have to work that out on her own.

And now her uncle had been murdered. It didn't take an I.Q. of 200 to realize that she was going to want to be in on bringing in the killer in a big way. This kid was Johnny all over again, only in female form. Obtaining justice for him would be a priority. I saw it in her eyes as soon as she'd stepped into that church for the funeral.

Thinking about all of this I walked over to the coffee maker, pulled out the filter cup to rinse it and grabbed the coffee out of the cabinet.

"What'd the Pastor give you?" She asked it so quietly I almost didn't catch it.

Hand suspended above the filter cup and I forced myself to dump in the scooped coffee. I needed time to answer that. But first I needed to know what she knew.

"What makes you think he gave me anything?"

Arms uncrossing she closed the small distance my kitchen permitted to stand right behind me. Training kicks in subconsciously as I slightly adjusted my stand and continued to scoop the coffee out of the can to drop it into the filter covered filter cup.

"Because it was obvious that he had something for you. And the left side of your suit had a slightly thicker bulge than it had before you went into the back with him. It looked like it was the shape of an envelope."

Pouring the water into the tank of the coffee maker, I placed the carafe in its designated spot and pressed the button to start the brew before turning to fully face Nina.

What happened to this kid besides the loss of her people? She had been sweet and so happy once. Now her hardened expression gave away absolutely nothing. Her face was familiar, but the kid I helped to raise was a totally different person.

And just knowing that made me second-guess my decision to bring her on. Because I had to correct my original assessment. This person standing in front of me didn't look like she was about getting justice; she looked like she was about getting revenge.

And because Johnny and I had trained her ourselves to make sure she was protected before she'd signed up to join the Air Force and save the world, I know that she had the skills to get exactly what she wanted.

She'd lost so much so young. That fact alone had me answering her question before I realized what I'd obviously decided to do.

"It was a letter from Johnny."

Her mouth got tighter as her spine stiffened. Otherwise she didn't move, just stood there impatiently waiting for me to continue.

"And a key to a post office box."

Taking a step back, Nina executed an almost perfect military turn before heading over to the kitchen table where she grabbed a chair, turned it with the back facing me and straddled it. Arms crossing over the top, she nodded her head toward the counter by me where she'd just been standing.

Looking to my left I realized she'd been nodding to the cup sitting there; apparently waiting for its portion of the brewing coffee. A cup that wasn't sitting there before. Did I say that this girl had skills? Because she definitely had skills.

Pouring us both a cup I delivered hers to the tabletop and had a seat at the table to doctor mine with Splenda and creamer before we continued. As soon as I'd dumped in the last packet she started talking as if we'd had no interruptions whatsoever.

"What'd the letter say?"

I took a sip of coffee and closed my eyes to savor the taste. Man that was good.

Stretching out my legs I lowered my cup and then focused on those dark eyes filled now with inquiry but no less hard.

"Gave me the name and contact info of Johnny's contact. Along with a Black Card – American Express with an undetermined limit to access funds for equipment. You know how John was about contingency plans."

She nodded after taking her own sip and placing her cup on the table before she responded, "so you know who your benefactor has been since you'd started working the case."

"Yep."

Both of us continued to enjoy our coffee for a bit more before she said what I knew she'd wanted to say since I saw her standing there in my kitchen looking hard and ready to do damage.

"I'll do whatever you need to fill the empty slot on your team in exchange for a favor."

"Not gonna happen Nina."

"I want him."

"We don't even know who did it Neen, let alone who was responsible for the kill."

"Then collect the intel I need and find him. I want him. That's the deal."

"Nina. That is not the focus of this mission. We are there to get these kids. To get Danny. Who you practically grew up with; he's like a brother to you, remember? That is our focus, not revenge. If we can collect enough evidence to turn over to law enforcement and bring some justice to these sickos, well that's even better. That's the job and that's the only offer on the table." I said this knowing I had to keep her clean. It took Celine, Sammie and my family to bring me back from the freezing cold prison that killing, even for revenge led to. No way would I be responsible for introducing her to that. No. Way.

"Then you are a worse friend than I thought you were Sam."

"Don't say that," I gritted out, slamming my cup down on the table.

"Because Uncle John was like a brother to YOU. He put his life on the line for YOUR kid. And you would let them murder him with no recourse?"

"That's not fair Nina and you know it. He took this case before he knew Danny was involved. And justice instead of vengeance does NOT equal no recourse."

"But he stayed on it BECAUSE Danny is involved." She'd stood, still straddling the chair and yelled this last part; her body vibrating with barely controlled fury.

I didn't respond because I couldn't. I was in shock. First, I was shocked because the ice storm that would have normally been raging right about now, the weight of guilt that I would have felt at her statement wasn't there. It just wasn't there.

Instead there was a mental playback in slow motion of something that Celine had said to me – that we are all responsible for our choices. It was why trusting was so hard for her. She'd explained that her refusal to "let go and let God" as they say, wasn't about trusting God, it was about trusting herself not to use that as an excuse to do whatever she wanted and then blame God for the result.

Her soft hands had framed my face as we'd stood forehead to forehead with her continuing, "Because the power of choice is a responsibility; the consequences aren't ours to control – only the choice itself. Therefore, I do everything I know to do. And when I can't do anything else, I trust God to do what I couldn't. Because in the end – I chose whatever happens. I can't choose the consequence; I can only choose my action and determine that I am willing to live with the consequence, whatever that may be."

In other words, Johnny had made his choice. He loved me. He loved my boy. He chose to do what he could to help out. He didn't choose to get killed. But he made a choice that lead to that consequence.

Just as we all made choices that lead to certain consequences, his loving us and his sacrifice for us were not fodder to be used to guilt me into responding to Nina's angry manipulations for vengeance. They were something to be cherished. To be respected and remembered for what it was. Him giving everything he could to protect my family.

And he didn't do that for me to throw his protection away in the name of obtaining vengeance for his murder. That would defeat the purpose of his sacrifice to begin with.

Standing slowly, I focused on the second thing that had shocked and surprised me. That those dark eyes, moments ago so hard and empty, were now filled with tears and heartbreak.

And I realized that deep down, even though Nina knew that Johnny wouldn't want either of us to risk our lives to bring down his murderer; she felt compelled to do it anyway. Because he'd been her last bit of blood left on this earth. And he'd been snatched away.

Circling the chair I pulled her to me as she struggled and fought, but I held her anyway. She fought silently but I felt the tears soaking my shirt, the huge gulps of air and the silent screams that were erupting as she struggled. She fought with the intensity of her pain, most likely because she'd realized a terrible truth that would haunt her until she let it go. To her, she was truly alone. All of her family was gone. And there was nothing I could do to save her from that pain.

I just held on as she stopped fighting and gripped the front of my shirt, still crying and shaking her head no.

I would show her that, when she was done, when all of this was done, she wasn't alone. Nina had a family, she had us. All she had to do was choose to accept that.

***

"That you have to pick a side silly. You have to choose. Choose to suffer but have light as a buffer, or choose the dark and lose your heart."

I couldn't tell how long I'd been here but I knew it had been two weeks since they'd gotten me out of those restraints.

Two weeks since I saw that freaky little girl who could read my mind and two weeks since I'd heard her freaky rendition of Dr. Seuss. And it had been for two weeks straight that they'd been bringing me into this room and putting these node-type things on my head to run tests.

And so I was past annoyed. Because I wanted to go home. My dad had to be royally freaking right now.

"Relax." The voice through a microphone somewhere boomed into the room. I knew it had to be a mic because there was no one else in there with me. Just like always. My heart rate must have been accelerating at the thought of Dad again. Whatever. If they didn't want me thinking about my family, they shouldn't have locked me away in the first place.

"I said RELAX." Yeah, like a disembodied voice was going to calm me down.

I took a deep breath and tried to focus and not think.

I tried not to think about how I should have never listened to J. I should have never allowed these weirdoes to put this crap in my body. And I should have never let J forge my dad's name on that form.

Because I wasn't the only person effected by this. Poor Rob was too.

"He's going into A-Fib!"

I heard the voices shouting in the back ground but I couldn't be bothered with little stuff like that because standing right in front of me again was that dang Piasa.

It's uber-freaky man-face with fangs sat inches from mine and drool was dripping from it's teeth; its rotten breath blew into my face with every exhale.

I knew I should run, I wanted to run but my body didn't respond no matter how much I screamed at it to get up and move!

Shaking uncontrollably, I tried to catch a breath but my body just locked up on me, like it wanted to die.

"Choose me."

What?

"Choose me. Let me in. Let it all go. Choose me."

Uuugghh! A rough tongue slid up my face leaving a sticky wet trail while I felt people running past me, bumping me where I was laid out flat on the table.

"Pick a side," another voice, the voice of that little girl whispered while my chest felt like it was being ripped apart. *"Dark. Lose Heart. Suffer. Light. Buffer."*

"ARRRGGHHHHH!"

The pain was so intense that I'd heard that wail echoing and banging around in my head, not realizing it was me.

It felt like my chest was being ripped open... like claws were digging into it and ripping it to shreds while fangs were chewing their way through my chest cavity.

And I guess it would feel that way since the Piasa was clearly sitting on my chest, doing just that.

It's ugly man face full of fangs, now drenched in what looked like my blood came up and was only centimeters from mine as it yelled at me this time while digging in deeper with its claws.

"CHOOSE ME! I WILL MAKE IT STOP. I WILL TAKE THE PAIN AWAY IF YOU LET ME IN!"

I wanted to. Man, I wanted to do anything to stop this pain. I never imagined pain like this. It was like every part of me was set on fire, like every nerve ending was being burned with such precision that the pain came in waves, right on top of each other.

But something important nagged me, just as I was about to give up and give the creature his way. My Dad. He was coming for me. He wouldn't stop. He wouldn't give up. He wouldn't let them win. So I couldn't. I couldn't give up. I had to choose for my Dad.

"Me and you against the world Danny," that's what he'd always say when I was a little kid. He'd put me to bed when he was home and not traveling. He'd tuck me in and kiss my forehead and say it like it was a promise – you and me against the world.

I'd never known what that meant, but I knew that my dad would always take my back, even when I didn't make the best decisions. He would take the time to talk to me, teach me, but he wouldn't ever leave me hanging.

And so I gritted my teeth against the pain, the edges of my vision had grown dark and I knew that I was about to pass out. Maybe even check out. But I wasn't letting this thing think it had won, not for one second. So if that meant I had to die to tell it to go play in traffic, then that's what I had to do.

What's weird is, as soon as I'd made that decision I'd heard a strange sound, almost like that little girl's giggle. I opened my mouth, not to scream this time, but to tell that thing that I'd rather suffer than give myself to it, when light exploded into the room.

It was like a bomb had gone off. I heard screams, yelling and a long beep on a machine somewhere. I guess that meant I was flat lining.

But what was really cool is that everything was gone. There was just light. No Piasa. No machine. No people. No room. But best of all, no pain.

So I guess that I'm probably dead. And if that's what it took to get me away from that ugly thing that actually licked my face; yeah, I was okay with that.

Chapter Twenty-Four

"**Invitation** please."

Enoch reached into the inside pocket of his double-breasted silver tux to grab hold of our invitation while I tried not to appear stunned as I glanced around the entryway.

Who would have thought that an entire floor of this monstrosity called a building was equipped with a gorgeous ballroom of immense size?

The beautiful young lady that took our invitation touched her ear as she bent her head over the clear ornate clipboard with a list attached.

While this was interesting because, why would one need to bring the invitation if there was a list, I didn't ask. I took my cues from Enoch and the slight pressure on my hand (which had been looped through his to rest on the top side of his arm) indicated that I should hold my peace.

"Ah, here you are. Celine Baltimore, plus one." The young lady vacantly smiled as she handed over our invitation (again, why I didn't know because we surely didn't need it any more) and glanced behind us to the next couple in line by way of dismissal to move us forward.

Glancing questioningly at Enoch, I followed his lead as he approached the vast entrance of the ballroom where everything was decorated in glass or crystal. And I mean everything.

From the classically beautiful chandeliers to the glass tables with lace runners topped by crystal centerpieces of exceptional quality, glass and crystal dominated the room. The glass dinner ware with crystal-handled silver cutlery outlining the dining sets, putting the finishing touches on the prismic, looking-glass effect. I wasn't sure if we'd entered a glass palace, or a carnival funhouse.

I'd seen that, from the invitation, the gala was themed, "Royal." What I didn't expect was for "Royal" to look like something right out of a James Bond movie... or a horror flick. Because seriously, that is exactly what this felt like.

A young man approached us wearing the exact same type of suit that the young woman had been wearing at the entrance, only more masculine, with the same exact vacant smile on his face.

If I didn't know better, I would say that these people looked like living breathing zombies. Their carriage and walk were almost identical as they moved, like automatons adhering to strict programming.

A chill raced up my spine at that thought. With the type of technology the Brainwaiver implant used that idea wasn't as far a reach as I would have liked.

Shaken from my thoughts by Enoch's movement forward, we followed the young man who'd taken our invitation – now I see why we'd kept it – and directed us to the area where we were designated to be seated.

Enoch pulled out my chair for me, which. Was. Awesome.

And I daintily placed my silver wrap on the back of the chair near his hand as I allowed him to push the chair in and seat me comfortably.

Wow. Who knew that silver and glass chairs would be so comfortable? You could barely tell by looking at them that the seated area was actually cushioned, the fabric was just that finely decorated. I bet you couldn't find that kind of material at Hobby Lobby either.

I grinned at my silliness as the little editor mentally slapped my hands to remind me to be on my best behavior.

Feeling a hot gaze on me I turned slowly to face Enoch, not surprised to find him grinning down at me in appreciation. He'd been looking at me like that from the moment he showed at my front door to pick me up. My thought? He really really REALLY... liked this dress.

And who wouldn't?

The gorgeous, silver Patra Illusion design of the gown was form fitting and hugged every curve with an almost mermaid-like drape that started below the knee and finished just above designer shoes. The top of the gown emphasized all of the hard work I'd been putting in from training with my arms bared and shown off by the gown's halter top straps. The design was accented by small off the shoulder cuff sleeves that clung to my arms like arm bracelets.

My silver Calvin Klein Asa High Heeled sandals offset the look nicely along with the simple diamond pendant and bracelet set that Enoch had brought over with him earlier. The small Tiffany's case had been a surprise and, though I hadn't said anything, part of me was glad that he could read me like a book. He'd taken one look at my widening eyes and said, "Let me know if you don't like them. I saw them last week online and had them shipped express. I can just as easily return them tomorrow." I'd been more than relieved that the jewelry was purchased with me in mind and hadn't belonged to his dead wife. Because that would be rude. And would eek me out a little.

I tried not to preen as I basked in his appreciative looks. Because I liked it that he likes what he sees. And I liked it even more that I liked what I saw. His smoke gray tux outlined his muscular shoulders and strong frame perfectly. The emerald green shirt that I'd picked out highlighted the beauty of his eyes so well that they practically glowed. He'd looked so good in the suit that he hadn't needed a tie. It would have been too much. The man could make sackcloth and ashes look fashionable, he was that photogenic. My earlier glance around at the expressions of women we'd passed on our way to the table had confirmed what I already knew. That my man was brutally buff and dripping with Alpha-hotness. So I was going to have to start practicing "the eye" again because I could not afford to send women into paroxysms of laughter when my goal was the exact opposite – to put the fear of Celine in them for ogling what I considered mine.

"Babe, what are you thinking?"

He was still grinning at me when he asked that, but I didn't care because he looked so nice right now, he could get away with saying whatever he wanted.

"You really want to know?"

"Do I?"

"Do you?" I grinned back because this was fun. And in a little while, it was going to be work time, not play time so I needed to get it in where I could fit it in.

"How about I tell you what I'm thinking then?"

Uh oh. Nope. Not here. Nope! Panicked, I tried to stop him but as usual – my guy is a bull in a china shop, a gift shop and the super market. Don't matter where he is, he pushes to get his way.

"I'm thinking that I need my own private modeling show later. Featuring you and that dress. And whats..."

My hand slammed over his mouth to stop the words, but I had to snatch it away just as quickly since I felt those full lips smiling underneath before they planted a kiss right on my palm.

Hoh boy.

"Enoch."

"Celine."

"Don't."

"Stop?"

"Enoch!"

"What? I thought we were doing word association." And then the grin – that half smile that kept on reeling me in like a dancing worm on a hook, once again staggered me. Goodness but fish were dumb. You'd think after all the worms dancing on hooks that had caught us before, we'd know better.

I shook my head to look elsewhere before that smile did some serious damage. Until I felt his arm slide behind my chair to pull me closer. I tried not to look at him then. I really did. But it was like watching an old person fall. Helpless to do anything, you know you should look away to minimize their embarrassment but find yourself in awe of the process. So much so you can't look away. And that is where I am. In awe, swimming in pools of glowing green eyes that are so compelling I want to hop into his lap, grab him by the ears and...

"Celine! So awesome to see you again."

Whew. I turned to face Delilah who'd just approached our table and uh, wow.

Her dress made me and my Patra look like Melissa McCarthy in a housecoat. Enchanting in her off the shoulder lace and chiffon number, Delilah made us mere mortal women feel like exactly that... mere. And mortal.

"Hi Delilah. Good to see you again as well."

And I stopped there. I knew that it was rude but hey, what woman wants to introduce their unofficial guy to a woman that looked like that? No one. No one that's who. My smile was plastic as I hoped that she would take the hint and walk away. No such luck.

"Aren't you going to introduce us?" She smiled this in an almost catty fashion while I considered how best to respond. Because good Christian girls did NOT scratch out the eyes of Hollywood

Diva's. It just wasn't done. Right? Right. So that left introducing them.

Hesitantly I turned toward Enoch afraid to see that the admiration he'd held for me was no longer there; instead redirected to the goddess wanna-be hovering behind me. But, while he was looking at her, I found his expression seemed curious, but nothing more.

A weight that I didn't know was there lifted as I almost jovially turned to introduce the two, only to have Enoch beat me to it.

"Names Enoch Sampson. You're Delilah Robinson right? From that entertainment show?"

"Yep." She said this with a grin, making the "p" sound pop at the end.

"Nice to meet you." Enoch said this solicitously with a polite smile but there was no other indication of interest, which had me high-fiving the little editor in my head, then following up with a fist bump that totally exploded. Because my guy was THE BOMB.

She continued to grin and, I don't know why I expected her to just walk away – but I did. I guess it was my misguided belief in common sense being common to all people; until she opened her mouth to explain that goofy grin. And made me want to gag all over the place.

"Nice. Sampson? Meet Delilah. You want to tell me what it is that makes you so strong Mr. Sampson?" Then she leaned forward, placing her hands on the table as her uh… assets became apparent from the top of her gown. Huh. Who knew that fake could appear so real? I thought that just as she finished up with, "because I wouldn't mind at all if you decided to lay your head in my lap and confess everything."

Did she just lick her lips? With me sitting right here? Seriously? Mentally I took off my earrings to hand them to the little editor because it was about to go down, when Enoch responded,

"Thanks. But no thanks. I think I'd rather stick with the woman that gives me strength instead of confiding in one that would use my confessions to steal it." Pulling me closer, he kissed me on the cheek then winked at me before glancing back up at Delilah with a nod of dismissal, "but thanks anyway."

Heh. I snuggled a little tighter into Enoch's hold just before I glanced over my shoulder to watch the diva flounce away. And I grinned. A lot. What I did not do was call her a heifer in my head while the little editor agreed in earnest. Because good Christian girls just don't do that kind of thing.

***

Sam

That dress was going to get me into some serious trouble.

I determined to focus on the layout and set up of the ballroom instead of Celine, but that dress was making it almost impossible.

Or it could be the fact that when I'd dropped her off last night before I met up with Nina, we'd made out. Like teenagers. In my truck. This was getting insane.

I'm a grown man, an ex-CIA and ex-Military man. I'm thirty-eight years old, my son has been missing for over a month... and I was making out with my unofficial but declared girlfriend.

I shook my head at the crazy that was my life and mentally scheduled another cold shower as I checked out the Louis Cypher table.

The placement of the table, how it was slightly elevated above all of the other tables indicated its significance. The average person wouldn't even pay attention to that kind of thing. Nor would they see the triangular pattern to which the tables in the room had been laid out.

It was unusual, this type of set up, for a gala. Honestly, it was unusual for any party, ball or any other event I'd ever attended. And I'd attended several on assignment.

Flicking on the switch in my pocket, I winced at the high pitched whine indicating I've tuned into Macchio's frequency.

I leaned over to whisper into Celine's ear, "Copy."

Celine lowered her eyes demurely and took my hand as if we were flirting.

She'd already been informed about the plan and knew to back my play.

"You're good. Command center in position. Raiders one and two are in position." Macchio sounded in my ear.

Perfect.

Mentally I went over the schematics of the building but my gaze had fallen down to that dress again. Crap. Chinese water torture was better than this.

I needed a distraction and I needed one fast. Because I'd promised Celine that I would honor her commitment to herself and to God. I hadn't been trying to pressure her earlier. Or even seduce her. I was just a man who wanted what he wanted. Which meant I had to work hard at not pursuing it in the way that I would normally.

Sylvester Cypher and George Louis entered under the grand entryway arms latched with two of the most artificially beautiful women I'd ever seen. The best way that I could describe them was giving me pause, because more references to MK Ultra and other mind control "supposed" myths were popping up all over the place. And these women looked just like dolls. Walking, talking breathing dolls.

And it wasn't for a lack of animation that I said that. It was their coordinated movements; the way that they walked. Whoever set this up shouldn't have allowed these women to walk in together.

Because any man would tell you that the first thing a man noticed about a woman was her sway, the way she moved when she walked. It was a signature for most women. You could pick out in a room the women that had played sports as teens and adults by the way they walked. My son would describe it as; they had a certain swagger to them. A confidence that would have had to be developed in order to become proficient at a competitive level. A man could also tell which women had learned to be seductive and manipulative early on. Just from their walk. And then there were those who just stomped everywhere they went, speed and arrival primary on their agenda, last there were those who'd been in the military – an almost imperceptible march to a silent cadence that reverberated in their minds.

And those women? They walked like none of that. Their sway was minimal because obviously they were arm candy – but probably arranged as a subtle complement to the men that they were with. They weren't supposed to garner much attention. So their smiles were bright but not too bright. They stood slightly behind either man as each one stopped to talk to different guests, even while their arms were still linked. And they didn't chat with each other when their men were otherwise engaged. They only spoke to other guests that directed a question to them.

And that's when I remembered Mandy's description of the encounter she'd overheard of her parents in the study. I'd been focused more on what the girls had suffered than the indications of control.

Touching my right temple to activate the lapel camera with microdot recording technology, I leaned into Celine again and said in her ear, "Macchio, Cypher and Louis are both on location. Run facial recognition software on the women that they are with. Do you need specs on both?"

"Nope. Already pulled both up on the Internet so I know what I'm looking for. The women are blond? Look almost like twins?"

Huh. I hadn't noticed that but, if their hair had been styled the same and if they'd been dressed in similar styles I probably would have. One dressed in a blousy tanked crystal sequined dress belted at the waist with the hem stopping slightly past mid-thigh and crystal sequined high heeled pumps, while the other dressed in a Diana style long black off the shoulder number, it was hard to see the shoes but if the heel was shorter that would account for the height difference. Smart.

"Affirmative." I whispered right before I kissed Celine's ear then sat back.

I gritted my teeth and tried to think "cold shower" thoughts while Celine glanced at me from the corner of her eye and grinned.

Yeah. I deserved that one. I'd done it to myself so I had to pay the piper and suck it up.

Facing the room again I allow Macchio to do his thing, even though he'd probably already started from what he'd found on the internet.

And then I felt Celine straighten next to me, her hand coming under the table to clench mine.

Looking to the entrance I saw why. Team Same was in the house. Literally.

Celine's gaze dropped to the table and I saw her struggle to bring her emotions under control.

We've really got to get a handle on that because my girl wore her emotions like cheap perfume. They were obvious to anyone within five feet. And we needed to do that like now since the Same's just spotted her and were on their way over.

"Babe. Look at me."

Her blue gaze, full of fire, turned back to me, her lips so tight they were white around the edges.

"I need you to get a hold on it." I whispered it as I leaned my forehead into hers.

I was so close now that I could see the tears sparkling in their depths. But I knew my girl enough to know that these were not tears of sadness that I was looking at. These were – pissed off in the extreme – tears.

"Baby. They're almost over here. Don't give them this power. We will fix this. I promise. But right now, I need you not to give them anything. Not even your anger. They deserve nothing from you. Okay?"

Her strong inhalation of breath and slight nod against my forehead was all the answer I needed. Kissing her lightly on her glistening lips, man I really liked that lip-gloss, I turned both of us just in time to greet Edward Same and his wife as they approached our table.

"Ms. Baltimore. What a pleasant surprise." Mr. Same's rigid smile had my hackles raising something fierce. I protected what was mine and my instinctual response perceived him as a threat. Just by that smile. It would be my absolute pleasure to put a hurt on this guy. And just maybe, before this was over, I would get my wish.

Chapter Twenty-Five

"**Isn't** it though?" Celine had responded. I wondered if she extended real effort into being funny or if humor just came naturally to her. Because for some reason I'd found that entire conversation hilarious. Maybe it was the way she had held her head; cocked to the side and resting in her hand with her elbow on the table. Her eyes had widened to the point of ridiculous but her scornful smile had spoken volumes.

Edward Same, probably not having any response that wouldn't be considered rude had excused himself, moving with his wife to greet another couple that had just come in.

Caroline's lack of expression and vacant smile had clearly indicated that she wouldn't be taking part in the conversation. I'd briefly wondered if every woman in the place was going to be mind-wiped before I'd received my cue.

"Raider 1, Raider 2 has cleared sector 5. Raider 3 is standing by."

"Copy that." I'd said into Celine's ear before kissing her there again because yeah, it was just that irresistible, then I'd moved.

Gaining access to the men's room with minimum witnesses hadn't been that difficult. Nearly everyone had cleared the entry hall except for a few stragglers.

Having to wait for that last stall with the vent cover I'd needed to gain entry to the ducts had been. Because the guy that'd occupied it for what seemed like hours seriously needed to have his colon checked.

I'd texted Celine just that before climbing up into this thing. And it was never as easy as they made it look in the movies either. Especially now since it looked like the duct was narrowing too much for me to fit through.

"Command, need my location." These things were nasty too, rat crap and spider webs everywhere. They didn't show you THAT in the movies either. It was why Macchio had made sure that Doc planted a protective garment bag in the vent yesterday. It had only taken moments for me to strip down to my black wet suit, store my tux and get a move on.

"Raider 1, your current location is sector 3, rear hallway, maintenance closet according to schematics."

"Copy that. Need exit."

"Exit clear at your current location. Raider 3 activated."

"Raider 3?"

"Copy Raider 1. Got your six." I grinned at that. And I was glad that Nina remembered. Johnny and I would play flag football with the kids. In the huddle I'd be holding Danny on one side and Nina on the other. Before we'd break I'd ask, who's got my six? Johnny and the kids would yell, WE GOT YOUR SIX, HOOYAH. And he'd had my six too. Johnny had our backs, right to the end.

"You better kid, that's what I'm paying you for." I heard a snort as I quoted the spy movie she used to love and couldn't help but grin.

And then I got serious. And did what I do best.

***

Danny

"Hi."

Dang it! Rubbing my head, because slamming it into the bunk bed above mine is always fun, I turned to find that kid in my room. My locked room. The one you couldn't get out of without a keycard; a keycard only issued to authorized personnel.

Made total sense.

"Kid…"

"My name's not kid. I told you, it's Anabella."

Really? My head hurts *and* I need this weird kid bugging me right now?

"Okay, whatever. Look…"

"We have to go," she whispered as she bounced; which really freaked me out because I think this was the first time I'd ever heard the kid not yelling every word.

I was about to tell her to get lost. But when I opened my mouth to say it, nothing came out.

Because she started glowing. Like, a lot. What the WHAT?

"Uh…"

"We have to go now Danny. Daniel. *Daniel William Sampson*. You have a weird name."

Okay, I would probably be having a snot fit right now (because my name is weird and Anabella isn't?) if life hadn't already taken a left turn into Weirdsville months ago. But waking up from the worst pain you've ever had in your life changes things. Especially when you find yourself dressed in ugly gray scrubs, in a room with a roommate and no memory. No memory since the pain took you and no explanation of what happened or how you got there. These are the things that had a way of mellowing a guy out.

So when a kid who could read your mind walks into your room, a room that you couldn't get out of before she got there and says, "it's time to go," I believe that my new mellow response is, "holla back crazy place that hurts people," as I grab hold of my roomie and head toward the door.

Made total sense.

Turning, I hopped up on the edge of my bunk to look over the top one where Rob was sleeping.

"Dude. Time to go."

"What?" Rob had been completely out of it since they put that thing in him. Unlike with me, he didn't have a choice. I chose this when I let J convince me that this junk would better my game. He didn't bother to tell me how much it would cost me though. So I felt like it was my fault that Rob was stuck here. He didn't ask for this. He didn't sign anything.

These people just did what they wanted to do with him, thinking that nobody would miss him or ask questions. But they didn't know his mom. And they definitely didn't know my dad.

I shook him again because he'd fallen back to sleep just that quickly.

"Dude. Get up. We got to go."

Instead of waiting for him to respond again I pulled on him to get him out of the bunk. I checked behind me to make sure the door was still open and that the exit was clear, seeing that the kids bounce had gotten faster. Not only that, but that glow was shining pretty dang bright. Something told me that if we didn't get gone soon, we'd miss our shot.

Grabbing hold of Rob I dragged him the rest of the way down off the bunk, put his arm over my shoulder and half-hug carried him as we staggered toward the kid and the door.

I was so focused on getting out of there that it surprised me when the kid walked around Rob's other side and put his arm over her shoulders to help with the load.

Freaky or no, I was really starting to think this kid was all kinds of cool.

Once we got out into the hallway she turned us to the right. For some weird reason I felt, I actually FELT my dad. I don't know how. And I'd never felt anything like it before. But I knew two things. That my dad was there and that he was close.

I pulled harder to hurry us forward and was glad that the other two seemed to get my message. Rob's step picked up a little more and the kid seemed to be handling her side of the load like a champ.

We made another right into a corridor that was labeled "Sector 4," and ran right into a lady in a lab coat. She was little bitty, no taller than 5 foot 3 with beautiful red hair caught up in a bun and sweet brown eyes. And then she grinned at us. She had a small gap in her front two teeth, but that small thing out of place made me feel like she was human. Human and not some angel that was here because I died or something. And that grin should have really freaked me out. But I was still mellow – that grin had nothing on what had happened to me last week: I'd been rocking my own personal river of Styx with no gold coins. Cause how do you know you're in a bad situation? When you start remembering crap from school like Greek mythology and use it to describe your life. Or was it *Percy Jackson and the Lightning Thief*? Either way, it wasn't good.

And it wasn't good that we'd just got busted either. I was scrambling to come up with a good reason for why we'd be standing in the middle of the hallway; two teenaged guys and a 13 year old girl, and was about to just wing it when she said, in a New York accent no less;

"Well look at you!"

And since she wasn't looking at me, I looked to where she was looking which was at the kid who bounced even more despite the load of my bud hanging on her shoulders.

"I told you. I told you I could do it!"

My head bounced back toward the lady when she responded, "Yeah you did. You've got the goods girlfriend."

My head bounced back to the kid.

"Yep. You owe me ice cream. And Dukes donuts!"

And then the lady laughed. And at that moment, I would have given anything to be 10 years older. Anything. Cause there was only one other person that I knew who laughed like that... My grandma, who seriously rocked. Like Gram, this lady laughed with her whole self, shining through her eyes as her shoulders shook and her head tilted back. I don't know who this lady was and I didn't care. All I knew is that I would follow her anywhere. Tomorrow. Right now I had to find my dad. And since she wasn't stopping us...

"Excuse me ma'am. We need to..."

"Daniel. William. Sampson." Dang it. Did EVERYBODY know my whole freaking name?

My mouth must have hung open because Rob all of a sudden looked me right in the face and decided to join the land of the living by laughing. At me. Just because she said my name. Makes total sense.

And then she finished and, well, it kind of did.

"Boy you look like yo' Dad spit you clean out! You look like him, talk like him, even stagger like him." She said that last part while laughing again. And that's when I decided that she would have to come to grips with our age difference. She would have to for us to get married as soon as I graduated.

And when I went to break that down to her just like that, the kid interrupted.

"We gotta go Ms. Sherry."

Sherry? It was good to know the name of my future wife.

"Ms. Baltimore hurts for me and misses our talks."

Who?

"She needs me. *She needs us.*"

Okay, I know I'd taken on a new lease in life but this mellow vibe had its drawbacks. Like the fact that when the kid said that last part, she looked straight at me. In my eyes. And said it in a way that I felt it; just like I felt that my dad was close. That kind of stuff right there? That deserves a major, in your face, jumping up and down and yelling, freak out. But being the new mellow man that I am, instead I just tell the truth.

"I don't know Ms. Baltimore kid. Is she a teacher or something?"

The kid hopped forward and grabbed ahold of Ms. Sherry which was cool since Rob was now carrying his own weight so we could both let go.

Thinking that she would ignore my question, Rob and I followed along at a speed walk until the kid stopped again and turned to point at me. Pointing, she promised (in that weird voice I could feel again), "Nope. We're hers."

And just when I stopped to soak in that craziness, my heart almost stopped as my dad dropped out of the ceiling like, right in front of me.

And as he grabbed hold of me I knew that everything was going to be okay. Because my dad was here. And the weird kid that could read my thoughts had probably known he'd be here... the same as I did. The same kid that told me that I was going to be a teacher to some lady that I didn't even know. But none of that last mattered as much because I gripped my dad with everything I had and only one thought was clear in all the mess that was my jumbled up feelings. *Makes total sense.*

* * *

It was the flickering of the lights outside of the ball room which preceded the loud blaring sound of alarms that gave me my first clue that all was not well with our mission. Well... that and the armed security guards that skittered hither and yon outside of the ball room.

I raised my wine glass to my mouth to hide my words as I mumbled into the mic, "Raider one, are we clear for phase two?"

"Stand by." Macchio's code for holding my position made me nervous. Especially since I saw Lance and Victoria marching toward my table. Great... Obvious much?

Quickly I checked all possible exits to see if it were more prudent to desert my post. While it would have been easy to slip through the milling crowd as many of the people had risen from their seats at the commotion outside of the room, I knew that the last thing I could afford to look like is a suspect... especially if my team hadn't cleared the children out of the building. And that little endeavor would just be the end note to phase one. Phase two involved raiding labs and rooms for all of the tech that we could find. Getting the kids safe was our highest priority... getting this crap gone, like off of the planet never to be found again gone, was a close second. Then we would be clear to move out for phase three. My favorite phase.

Phase three could be done from a distance after a benign looking thumb drive was inserted into one of the pc's attached to the wireless server. Macchio had written a cute little virus designed to cause any Brainwaiver software or applications to politely eat themselves to death.

I tried to control my smirk at what was coming by the time Lance and Delilah had arrived at my table.

"What have you done?"

My raised eyebrow as I slowly placed my wine glass back on the table probably provided a clue at the type of response Lance was about to get to that idiotic question...

"In what sense?"

Delilah's hand to Lance's chest was, I guess to halt his forward progress, looked as pale and just as frail as the crystal surrounding us. I almost applauded her effort to adopt what had to be her "good cop" face (probably to glean more information from me because, yeah, apparently I was THAT dumb) while Lance looked on with red ears and a blotchy face. It looked like he was about to explode.

And what did she expect me to do exactly? Drop to my knees and confess to whatever imagined scenario that they could only guess at? I say that because it was obvious that they didn't have a clue about what was going on. Macchio was that good. So when he was on a job that required him to "make sure that the target had "no eyes" and "no ears", he did his thing like a champ.

As the only man I knew that could completely take down someone's security without even entering the building, then patch into earlier recordings while updating the time lines to NOW... he wasn't just like a champ, he was THE champ. Then again, I didn't know that many spy types that could do such a thing. I just knew my crew. And my crew was all kinds of awesome, so if these jokers were looking for some kind of fear or hesitation from me, they weren't going to get that. With that thought I tried to drum up as much disdain as I could sense dripping from their fingernails. There was no way I could out-creep these two because they had creepy down to a science with their cybernetic enhancements and Barbie slash ken doll perfection. But I could do arrogant with the best of the best. Being a former athlete had that effect on a person, you could walk into any crowd feeling the poorest, looking the drabbest and appearing the plainest, and still do it with an attitude that sent the message, "I dominate." Period.

Which is probably why Lance's face just got all kinds of redder...
approaching an orange color in intensity type red. I figured he was
either doing his best impression of a red dwarf about to explode or
was just getting in touch with his "inner tomato". I tried not to
laugh as Bob the Tomato from Veggie Tales popped into my head,
nearly giving the little editor a fit. But the little guy was on his job
and stifled my giggle fit... cause arrogance was good, straight up
laughing at your target to his face probably wouldn't end well.

"Where is your date? His name was Sampson, right?"

I grinned and picked up my wine flute again. That was just arrogant
right? Because I didn't want to appear to be gloating... but I so WAS
gloating, at least in my head. Poor little editor, he should really
consider early retirement.

Taking another sip I lower my wine glass and as if we were in a
poker game, raised the stakes of our conversation by leaning
forward with my elbow resting on the table, my absolutely NON-
gloating, cheek resting in my hand. I was going for a visage of poise
and refinement. But my smirk was probably ruining that effect. I
fell back on our lines rehearsed prior to arrival to keep my focus off
of enjoying their obvious freak out and onto our mission and
objective.

"In the toilet." My answer was so anti-climactic all I garnered as a
response was some rapid blinking and a few twitches, then a head
shake and a cough.

But I waited. Because, as if on cue, Lance's eyes narrowed, creepily
in sync with the clenching of his fists. Hmmm.... I wondered what
he planned on doing with those fists in this crowded ballroom? This
shouldn't be this fun, should it? Because it was. I was having more
fun right now than I'd had all night.

And while it was obvious that Delilah was trying valiantly to hide her
sneer of disgust, Lance had abruptly turned away while reaching
into his suit pocket. He was probably working hard to resist the urge
to pound me into tapioca. I couldn't say much for the man, but I

could say this, he had some really good self-control going there. Must have taken anger management classes at some point. Because instead of slapping me silly, he just placed his cell phone to his ear while moving swiftly toward the ballroom exit.

A quick glance at the Louis/Cypher table told my why Lance's complexion was fast approaching maraschino cherry redness. The two tech giants (to be remembered not-so-fondly from this night forward as "the doll makers") stared after Lance with narrowed eyes and clenched jaws. It didn't take a computer genius to see who they blamed for this debacle. I watched them as they shifted their attention from Lance to each other while rudely ignoring the guests seated at their table. I absolutely hate it when people are being rude... but hey, as long as Lance was in trouble... I could totally live with that.

"Raider one is clear. Phase two is a go." I grinned into my flute I'd just picked up for another sip before hiding my startled reaction. I tried my best to hide a minor freak out by taking another sip. I say freak out and that it was minor because Delilah had immediately turned her attention to me from where she had been watching Lance march toward the exit. It was like she'd heard Balboa's declaration of the kids being clear. Which would have been impossible. So why did it FEEL like she'd heard it?

That weird sensation of uh-oh only increased when I focused on what she was saying...

"It won't matter you know..."

I tried not to react. But my hand had tightened on the wine flute, causing the liquid to shift a bit. And she'd seen that. This lady might have been plastic as all get out, but she was not dumb. Not at all.

I forced myself to relax then calmly placed the flute back onto the table. Relaxing back into my seat like I was on the crystal throne of England, I slowly crossed my legs and waited for her to elaborate. I didn't know what her angle was yet... if she was about to expound upon my future defeat or try to fish for more information. Either way, I tried not to worry. I had more than just my team's skills and my own recently acquired abilities to trust in. GOD was on my side. And if God was for me, all of the plastic dolls, cyber-people and tech devils in the world couldn't dare stand a chance against me. So imagine my surprise when the conversation started to take a totally unexpected turn.

It was when she glanced toward the Cypher- Lewis table, then shifted to her right so that her back was completely to them that I began to wonder. I didn't wonder about whether our mission would be successful or if I wouldn't be getting out of here tonight alive. Despite a small niggling doubt, I had confidence that nothing could stop us simply because I believed that God wouldn't let it. So it wasn't my team, myself or the kids that I wondered about. I wondered if Delilah had really chosen this life. I wondered if she was in it to win it using her own free will and right to choose... or something else.

And it was all in her eyes. Everything that I thought I knew about her, I suddenly began to question.

They say that the eyes are windows to the soul. If that were the case, I knew, without a doubt that I was staring into the eyes of the most tortured soul I'd ever met.

"They have been on to you from day one you know."

I blinked. I heard her. I knew what she'd said. I just didn't know where she was going with this.

"They know who you know, where you go, where you work, who you do and what you do."

I would have expected her to deliver that line with a smirk of her own. Or maybe, at least as much arrogance as I'd put into my own body language. But all I could pick up on her was sadness... a deep sadness. A tormented type of sadness.

"... they know every single minutiae of your little happy Alton life. And they won't hesitate to smash you and everybody you love into bite sized bits for their enjoyment," she continued as I began to fully grasp what she was doing and why she was doing it.

Because this wasn't gloating or threatening at its finest as I'd expected. This was a warning. The type of warning that a prisoner that's been caught trying to escape would scream out to their cell mate who still had a chance to be free. A warning that gave me an idea of what weapons my enemy had at their disposal. She was telling me to run. To run fast and to run hard. To take everybody I have ever cared about or ever loved and get ghost. And I had a feeling that this moment, this warning.... It would cost her. She knew that it would cost her. But she did it anyway. And that was when I began to wonder if the kids were the only ones trapped... the only ones that we were supposed to save.

"Babe, what's up with the alarms? Is the building on fire? Why is everybody standing around like pigs in a pen when it sounds like we should be clearing the building?"

Feeling Enoch slide into his chair beside me didn't surprise me. I'd expected it. But seeing an expression of such longing and pain flash across the face of one of the most beautiful women I'd ever seen? Right before she shut it down... that surprised me. Watching her abrupt about face as she sashayed toward those huge double doors didn't bring the relief I'd thought I'd feel a moment ago when I couldn't wait to see the back of her. I had a feeling that our mission... our objective had changed and changed HUGE. And despite the satisfaction I wanted to feel as my team called out each phase's success until there were no more objectives and we were clear to depart, I knew. I knew it just like I knew I needed Christ, air and the man sitting beside me. We weren't done. Not at all. Not by a longshot.

Chapter Twenty-Six

I snatched awake to the sound of my own voice, screaming.

I was drenched in sweat and my nightgown was clinging to me, not a dry spot on it.

Thank goodness Sammie was still spending time with her grandparents. I really don't know how I would have explained this one.

Rubbing the sleep from my eyes, I glanced over at the clock and shook my head.

My alarm had been going off for over a half an hour and I hadn't even budged. It might have been because of the nightmare I'd been trapped in, or possibly the nightmare that I knew was brewing on the horizon.

Moving slower than my normal morning zombie-like speed, I turned on the bathroom light and grabbed for the counter to steady myself. I looked down at my hands and realized what was happening. My hands, that's to say, my entire body was shaking so much that I was surprising I was still standing.

And it wasn't because I was cold. It was because I had been experiencing the worst fright I'd ever experienced in my life. While I had been sleeping. Yeah. That was new. It would have been easy enough to chalk this up to residual fear from a dream that I couldn't even recall. But I knew what it was really about. And it had a lot to do with Delilah and the Doll Makers. Mental note: write that down, it would be the perfect name for a retro 60's all girl band with bouffant hair-do's.

Resolved to get going, I finished my business in the bathroom, washed my hands and brushed my teeth, totally on auto pilot. Because I had a lot to think about. Before last night I was so sure about everything. About me and Enoch, about how everything would work out and about how I wanted to spend the rest of my life with him. Or should I say, the next thirty so years with him verses the next week.

Glancing toward my alarm clock on my rickety bedside table, I realized two things. First, I need some new furniture. If I lived to see next month I was definitely going shopping. I might even consider tacking down my gorgeous rug since Enoch kept complaining about it, but probably not... AND... I had to get my behind in gear. I had no time to dwell on the horror that was my life (or the horror that was my bedroom furniture); I had to train. I had less than a half hour to be ready for Balboa to pick me up. She'd promised that we could grab Duke's donuts on the way if I could be ready fifteen minutes earlier than usual. Sweet, sweet motivation. Should it worry me that she knew my weakness after knowing me so short a time? Little editor? Apparently he didn't care. I really didn't either – I figured I had to get my goodies in while I had the chance.

I headed back into the bathroom and turned the shower on full blast thinking hard. Because today I had some decisions to make. Yesterday was all about kicking butt and taking names; and I didn't really care about their names all that much. But today I had to think about Enoch, our kids and how the wrong choice could break us.

Moving at hyper speed (for me – it was probably normal speed for others in the morning) I multitasked my get-girl-clean and get-girl-gone modes, trying not to think about last night. Life would have been so much easier if I things had gone the way they should. Then

I could dwell on the high of life that came from achieving our objective.

Last night had been like a dream, nah – a really good book maybe; like an awesome movie, definitely. I'm talking Pirates of the Caribbean kind of good where, despite the fact that you knew what was going to happen, you were still wowed by HOW it happened. That in the end; the guy really did get his girl and the girl really did get her guy. All was right in their world – exactly how it should have been. And if people didn't like it? It didn't matter – because *they* didn't matter.

As Enoch and I danced in the area they'd cleared away after all of the hubbub had died down, I felt a little like Cinderella. Only I was the hard as nails kind of Cinderella where, she didn't need the prince to save her from her big bad step family because she'd kicked their butts out of her dad's house, dressed herself to the nines and rode her own carriage to the ball.

We danced and laughed and danced some more. And we watched. While Lance did his imitation of a blowfish on steroids and Delilah seemed to be doing her best to disappear into a crack in the wall, everyone else, amazingly enough seemed completely unaware of what was going on.

Security had stopped milling around. The police had long since left the scene. Even the Doll Makers had settled down as if the alarms had been a mild annoyance but nothing more.

People continued to enjoy their wine, dancing and the hobnobbing with the Mid-Western elite. But nobody and when I say that I mean NOBODY seemed even a little perplexed after all of the drama. Everyone was sedate, almost calm in fact. Like this kind of thing happened every day.

To avoid any suspicion being directed our way, Enoch and I had stayed during the dinner, the dancing and the speeches. The former two would have almost been enjoyable if it weren't for the circumstances. However the speeches, Oy! I wanted to take a hot poker and lodge it in my ears, that's how horrible the speeches were.

Some of the "future" recipients of the Brainwaiver tech spoke on how excited they were about what it would help them accomplish. Some of the speakers were like those people that win the lottery but don't really need the money... you know, they have great jobs, a 401K with an awesome pension and oodles of investment properties and what-not.

And then there were the others. Those that were so despondent and lost that it broke your heart. They had been rejected and abused. They had been counted out and judged not worthy. They had become an easy target to anyone and everyone that you can imagine. And they hated themselves for it. It was for them that my heart broke while I was sitting there ensconced on my throne of crystal and glass. Because they were so happy. They were so full of joy at the thought of finally being someone special, someone worth noticing... someone that they and their families could be proud of.

I couldn't imagine how they would feel once they found out the truth. Some would get through it I imagined. There is a kind of numbness that one develops after so many disappointments in life. People like to call that a thick skin. I called it an expectation of failure. Because if you don't expect anything, then you can't be disappointed right? That is exactly where I'd lived before Enoch, before Amanda, before this whole Brainwaiver debacle. It was a safe place to be. Slightly out of reach of pain because you couldn't suffer from losing something you never allowed yourself to have.

At that moment I'd allowed myself to see him. To see Enoch sitting there beside me. Strong. Proud. So handsome that I could sit there for days enjoying all that was him, basking in the power and vitality dripping from every pore. And he was mine. My man. My gift from God.

I should have stayed in that moment.

Because in the next, after allowing myself to take in the beauty that was my guy, I felt terror and pain grip me. It was as if a vice had closed around my heart, tightening steadily until it crushed my heart, crushed ME to dust. The realization that I could be so ecstatic a moment ago – blissful at the very thought of Enoch and his reunion (not to mention my first meeting) with Danny... only to realize that it could be snatched away. That this beauty, this love... this GIFT could be stolen from me. RIPPED from me... suddenly I couldn't breathe.

And, like always, Enoch read me. I don't know if it was something that he saw out of the corner of his eye or if he just picked up on my panic. Whatever it was, he turned to me so fast that I jerked back in surprise, almost falling out of my chair.

"What baby? What is it?"

It killed hearing him say that to me right then. His voice all gruff with concern and his eyes looking at me, so warm - so 'all about me,' it felt like I was being stretched and pulled apart by two opposing forces.

My mouth had moved but no words were spoken. Because I couldn't speak. I couldn't force myself to say the words. Would rather leave them there, hovering in my throat, then voice the horror that was washing through me. I couldn't give that horror any more power than it already had. To give it a voice could empower it to traverse the realm of thought and become something more.

So I did what we women do best. I deflected. A quick shake of my head and a face plant into his chest was all it took to get what I needed at the moment, which was him. His arms had closed around me and before I could blink I was lifted from my seat and pulled into his lap. Bliss. Perfection. Hope. And strength – because the fact that I was not a light weight was not lost on me.

His arms around me were the balm that I needed to keep the crud circulating in my head at bay. Dread couldn't surround me. I was wrapped up tight in all that was my guy. And even though there was a small part of me that urged me not to trust. I did. It screamed at me to not allow myself this moment of peace because it would make the pain, when it came, so much worse. I didn't listen.

Instead I held on tighter. I deep breathed, inhaling all that was Enoch. Then I did it. I realized that I could do it.

I let go. And I let God. In that moment I was right where I was supposed to be, and I knew it. In the arms of this man, it was much easier to understand God's plan. To understand why Jesus sent the disciples out in pairs. Why in Genesis God declared that it was not good for man to be alone. Because while I had been whole as an individual, by myself. God had given me the opportunity, with Enoch, to be so much more. And instead of being a burden – a precursor to an onslaught of pain that would again undo me, our budding relationship was a gift. It was a chance to build something great with someone that wasn't perfect, but was perfect for me. My first loss was not an indication of my entire future. And while I could still be okay if I walked away today, staying meant I was giving God a chance to do something powerful, something great. And I was free to have ALL of that.

Which was why I should have let myself stay there. I should have let that moment serve as a reminder; a life jacket for me when the storm came. But I didn't. I didn't do any of that. Even now, while I rushed to don my fighting clothes and slap my hair into a pony tail, I was shaking because I'd forgotten all of that, just that quickly. Because if I loved him enough... if I loved THEM enough... after last night, I have to let them go. I almost wish they'd have killed me instead. Death would definitely be kinder then a life without them. Without Him. Out of all of that hope for the future during that moment, like Pandora's box when opened, I only had one left: the hope that, since I had no choice but to do what they'd commanded, maybe they could make the pain go away.

Running for the door because Balboa was laying on her horn (my goodness but that chick is so impatient) I prayed for the thousandth time since my encounter in the ladies room last night, that God had an ace in the hole. That He would show me another way. Because my enemy knew me well.

Hands down, if I had to choose between my safety verses the safety of those I loved, there was only one choice to be made. It would be them, no question. And not because I was all magnanimous or holy. But because I was a coward when it came to loss. I'd rather die and see them happy, then live and watch them be systematically stripped away from me.

"Let's go girl! And don't think I'm not making you work for those donuts yeah? Donuts that good need a butt-kicking to keep the universe balanced."

Clown.

A part of me, the part that was *still* me, snickered and giggled. Even while I was dying inside. Plus I'd finished my dose of self-pity for the day. Because the earth was still spinning. And God was still good. And I'd decided, right then, that I was still letting go and letting God.

I jumped into the passenger side of Balboa's rental and snatched ahold of my seatbelt not a moment too soon. All Balboa, she hit the gas and squealed into the U-turn that took us back toward Duke's.

I didn't bother freaking out because of her driving anymore. Nor did I wonder if she might just put me out of my misery by killing me in a fiery wreck. Because while life, at times for me, could be ironic, goofy or even joyous; it had never EVER been even close to that easy.

****

Sam

"Dad, you with me? Dad?"

Danny's voice sounded so far away it echoed, even though he was standing right next to me. I was cold inside. And out. Not exactly the wall of sleet like it used to be, the cold still numbed me. Whereas the sleet had just been in my head, this new cold radiated out over my body, slowly saturating every part of me.

And I knew why.

Because something was not right. It was wrong in a way that was so wrong, thinking about it nearly exhausted me. I didn't know where to look for my enemy. I didn't know the "who" or how whatever was coming would attack. Never in my military or CIA days have I dealt with a dread like this. And despite hearing my son call my name – after not being able to hear it for months – I couldn't shake the chill. Too many factors were involved. Case in point: Our release of that Andrew guy. Yeah, we'd kept him in a sensory deprivation state while speaking Russian and Czech the whole time. It was Macchio's idea to make him think that this was a terrorist kidnapping. Based on the client list we'd hijacked from Andrew's cell phone and laptop in his car, that wasn't a far stretch. I hadn't been proud of Boogey's hotwiring the man's car and dumping it; but desperate times called for desperate measures.

Bottom line, releasing him in a deserted area in East St. Louis had been our best idea, so I hadn't fought it. The end goal had been accomplished: to keep him from linking any of this activity to Celine. To cause him to doubt what he remembered, including the punch that knocked him out. The truth is, after all we'd done to ensure Celine's protection in that, Andrew was the least of our worries. Why had the police presence cleared so quickly after the alarms? Why had there been no follow up investigation of those attending? We were good... but were we really THAT good?

Focusing on the now as best I could under the circumstances, I took a minute to get my bearings. Which meant I scanned. I took in everything going on around me to give my focus something to hold on to. I needed it to ground me. It was that or risk the operative in me taking over. Which would be bad on so many levels. So I kept scanning.

Several kids I'd never seen before lounged around our meeting room at the site. They were dressed in gray tops and bottoms that looked like scrubs. The kids' ages ranged from toddler up to Danny's and Robert's age group. Some lay on tables, still knocked out from anesthesia they'd been dosed with, while others played around on the floor with handhelds, toy cars or Lego's; stuff that I'd grabbed from my folks' basement.

There were black kids, white kids, Latino kids and Asian kids. There were a few chubby kids, more thin kids, some sad kids and a few happy go lucky ones.

It was like some weird Stepford kids movie where a Utopian society spit out all of these children that wore the same clothes and were quiet most of the time, never disagreeing, never arguing... never questioning.

Except for those that had already had their implant hacked. Cheryl or Minute as we called her, had been going all night, monitoring responses to the hacking to make sure it wouldn't cause damage, while Macchio had been doing his thing. And by that, I meant hacking his heart out and disabling every driver or link he could locate that could be tapped to access the implant inside the kids. Because it would be a shame to get them home to their lives, having seen the success of our mission, only to have them be tracked by the tech and reacquired. Step one to ensuring their freedom had been frying the Brainwaiver databases housing their information with the virus from phase two. Hacking and disabling the implant had been stage two of that process.

So it had been a rough night for Minute and Macchio. But a good one. Yet I still couldn't shake the feeling that something was off.

After we had made every play that we could make and the party "last called" us on the dance floor; we'd made sure every loose end that we could anticipate was located, cut and burned off. Every member on our team had been accounted for. It had to have been possibly the smoothest mission I'd ever been a part of.

Yet even with all of that, taking Celine to her place had grated. I wanted my family together. My woman, her kid, me and mine, all in the same place meant I had eyes on everybody. Which I'd needed like I needed to breathe. And I'd wanted it enough to force the issue. But Celine argued. She raised valid points. I even understood her logic. I still fought it because I didn't like it. In the end, she'd made too much sense. Multiple target points for the opposition meant more time to counter a strike if we needed to. Balboa and Boogey had taught her well.

And even though she insisted that nothing was wrong, that she was hormonal and emotional due to the ups and downs of this drama i.e. losing John, getting the kids safe, disabling the tech for good... I knew better.

It was something that Celine didn't know about me yet. The minute I'd called her mine, I started cataloguing every nuance of her personality. From her facial expressions to her little quirks and borderline OCD behavior, I knew her. And if nothing else, I knew that she would never bore me. The woman was too much of a goof. In everything.

But especially with her rug. What was the deal with that rug? She'd trip over that thing, sometimes 10 times in a day, and would have to stop each time to straighten it back out. Then look at it. Then straighten it some more before she left it be. When I happened to kick the thing up, even if I tried to fix it (which I stopped doing because she would only come behind me and straighten it some more) her face would get all crunched up. I'd offered to tack the thing down only to get her eyes on me, rounded like I just offered to butcher her only child and feed her the entrails. It only took once for me to ask her why I got that look. Because her answer, "What if you tack it crooked? It would mess up my floor pulling it up to try and re-tack it over and over until I got it to lay perfectly," was more disturbing than watching her do it. Yeah. That kind of nonsense was a taste of my future life with my future wife.

And I was more than okay with that. She wouldn't get the reason why I took the time to know her like that; why I learned to read her like a book. She wouldn't be okay with it if she did. The fact remained that it was my job to keep her right. And to set her right if she wasn't right no matter how crazy the reason her "not being right" was. Like last night when she hadn't been right... not even close.

But I let her have that play. I let her do what she asked me to do. I figured since I was seeing her today anyway (she had boxing and weapons training to tend to) I could get another read on her to make sure everything was all good. With that reminder I shifted my focus from the other kids and back to mine.

My boy. It hadn't even been 4 months but to me he looked taller then he'd been before. His chest and arms had been athletic but just a little on the gangly side still, the boy in him fighting hard to hold on. To keep the man that he was to become at bay. But now I could see the boy in him had given up. A man's chest and arms stood before me... one that was nearly the spitting image of me when I was in my twenties. It should have set off all kinds of alarms that this thing had somehow sped up my son's development, kicking him, at least physically, into a maturity that shouldn't have been his for another four or five years. But I was too grateful to have my boy back. A younger version of myself stood before me, with my dead wife's eyes and my father's chin. Looking at me with concern like I had been the one snatched away from everything I knew and experimented on.

I couldn't stop myself from doing it if I wanted to. And I didn't want to. So my body followed the urging of my thoughts with no hesitation, my hand latching on to the back of my son's neck and pulling him close to me, his forehead resting solidly against mine.

"Yeah." It should have been a question, an inquiry based on him calling my name a few minutes ago. But I think he knew what that yeah meant. He knew that it ran deep. And that it was the answer to his question. We were going to be alright. We had to be.

"What are you going to do with all these kids, Pop? It looks like you opened a daycare center for the weird and insane."

Goof. Even with that thought, his being a goof, all I had in me was a weak smile. Because I'd missed hearing my boy call me Pop. It had always preceded him being a goof and saying something off kilter. Like now.

At least it kept me from focusing on how the mission had gone too smoothly. Nothing was ever THIS easy.

Even with Macchio running point due to the last minute change of plans that had me attending. Macchio had run point a lot when we were overseas together. He was the best man to have in your ear and at a keyboard. The best to have watching your back if you wanted to have an in and out, quick and clean successful mission. And with Balboa working the strategy; Minute on the inside and informed about all the meds, medical data and procedures; and KC, Boogey and Nina on grunt (taking out guards, creating distractions and blinding tech) we had the perfect team for a clean, in and out with no collateral damage. So why didn't I FEEL like it was clean?

"Seriously Dad. These kids? Did you know that some of them were in state custody? Some were runaways, kids that people wouldn't miss. They don't have parents to go home to. Grandparents, aunts or uncles for that matter. Some of these kids had found a place where they could eat decent and not think about tomorrow. I'm thinking those are the kids that are going to wake up wanting to know where their new home went."

I made a mental note to advise Macchio on that new development. It looked like we were going to be hacking some state and local databases in order to adjust or remove some records. That wouldn't be too difficult for him.

In the meantime, I wanted to give my son the answer that he was looking for. I wanted to tell him that I at least HAD an answer to that question. But the truth is I didn't. We hadn't thought that far ahead. And we hadn't expected to find this many kids. Over 20 mats were scattered around the site. If we hadn't safely constructed the foundation, three underground levels and the two levels above ground in the time since we'd started this job, I wouldn't have had even a clue about where we would put these kids. Luckily we were that good when it came to construction. Apparently not smart enough to map out a plan that included this scenario though.

I didn't realize that I was doing it. Ma had been adamant that her kids knew that prayer, no matter how short, was all you needed to remember who was in charge. She even taught us that one word prayers, she called them breath prayers (because they were said that quickly, in one breath or a heart beat) were more necessary for us. We needed to remember who He was... and that He knew what we needed long before we did. And so when we prayed "Help" or "Please" or "you promised,"... when we said that it was a reminder to us that He hears us.

So while I didn't realize that I WAS doing it, I wasn't shocked either. I could see my son's brow furrow and his head tilt in question, which wasn't strange since I'd just prayed "show me", out loud. It was just a quick, quiet comment said in the time it would have taken me to breathe. But I hoped it was enough. It had to be. Because as of right now, I had no answers. Not a one.

Chapter Twenty-Seven

Balboa's right cross was always so quick it was difficult to dodge. That didn't mean I couldn't do it, it just meant that nine times out of ten, I was going to be a bit off balance for a counter strike. Which usually left me open to either a knee or a round house. And since I was off my game today, even though I knew it was coming, I still found myself kissing matt from the round house-from-hades. Because she'd stopped pulling her punches and kicks a long time ago. I stayed there on the floor, cheek to the cool matt with my eyes closed, sweating like a pig and breathing like I had just sprinted five miles. But I'd been here before during our training. And I usually had no problem hopping right back up to get some punches and kicks in of my own.

Today, however, it was hard to move. Because it had been 3 days since the night of the party. Three days since I found out that hope could be powerful enough to strengthen you, or when dismantled, bring you crashing down and gutting you in one fell swoop. I was trying so hard not to stop hoping, but the effort of holding on was draining. I only had four days left to find a solution. It was more like 90 hours 45 minutes and 11 seconds... or something like that. I needed a fix and I needed one fast. I wasn't one for last minute miracles. And since the Doll makers were ready to play with their new toy, I don't think they would honor my request to extend the deadline.

I heard Balboa asking me if I was alright. And since I didn't have a good answer for that, because I was SO NOT alright, I chose to say nothing at all. Instead I wished that I could go back in time to prevent myself from letting go of Enoch. I let him go, pulled out of that hug that had been keeping me from losing it and said, "Going to the ladies to freshen up."

Man. Seven words. If I could have one miracle from God, I'd ask him to not allow those words to leave me mouth. To not allow me to leave Enoch's side. To not allow them to get me alone. Because when they got to me, they had GOT ME. And I didn't know how to fix that. Still didn't. And I was running out of time.

I'd walked into that bathroom pretty confident. Assured, even. God had things all covered, we had the kids safe and all we had left to do was kiss this whole ordeal goodbye.

Finishing my business and fixing my dress, I'd exited the stall in what had to be the plushest women's bathroom I'd ever seen. I headed over to the gorgeous marble counter and stainless steel basins to wash and dry my hands. It was the next two seconds that cost me. Admiring myself in that dress, I smiled at my reflection and thought, girl you are a FOX!

Because I was. The weight loss from my training hadn't been a goal, but it had brought out my best features. My hair, eyes and legs had always been a draw for guys. Some loved the curves while others didn't. But my curves hadn't gone away, they'd just gotten curvier even though I'd slimmed down. My waist was smaller, my face more defined which called even more attention to my eyes and the power of my Bare Escentials lip gloss was not to be denied. It defined and glistened, sparkled and shone; giving me that just been kissed look that Enoch couldn't keep his eyes off of.

And while I'd been standing there admiring myself and primping, just a little, in walks Delilah.

She didn't look happy to see me. It wasn't an, "I hate the fact that you draw breath," unhappy to see me either. It was more like an, "I wish you had run like I told you," kind of unhappy to see me. I could tell she was dragging her feet on the approach, but that she was approaching non-the-less. And that was not good. My little editor started bracing before I even realized that I'd crossed my arms over my chest, kicked my hip out and started tapping my foot. My stance said it all. BRING IT. Because I just knew that whatever she felt she had, whatever she wanted to dish out, I could take it and serve it right back to her in spades.

Only I couldn't. Because she wasn't serving the dish. She wasn't even cooking it.

Her hands had been behind her back when she'd walked up to me. Her head lifted slowly as she brought what she'd been holding behind her to the front. A tablet computer it looked like.

My foot stopped tapping. LEAVE NOW. This was the first time I'd ever heard the little editor scream at me... so real it was almost audible. I heard those words clearly in my head, as if my whole soul was invested in my immediate obedience to the command. But something else held me there. Not fear necessarily. More like a sick sense of dread that wanted to prove my earlier notions correct... because it really *had* been too easy.

The tablet powered on and there they were.

Sitting in some kind of room with a large mahogany desk, a couch and book cases, were the Doll Makers. It looked like they were in an old fashioned study or very small library. It was all class, down to the fibers in that beautiful carpet and the sleek matching drapes. While a part of me admired everything that was in that room with a passion that would send me into a catalogue fit later, I barely managed to deep breathe and avoid the freak-out that I was desperate to hold at bay.

Because how could they be sitting there in that beautiful, beautiful room... if they were wining and dining just 200 yards away in the other room at the same time?

"Is the camera on?" Doll Maker number one grinned and rolled his eyes. Doll Maker number two rubbed his hands together like he was anticipating his favorite treat.

What weirded me out the most is, at that moment, I wasn't thinking about how uber-creepy and disgusting those two had been just an hour or so ago with their double mint twin Barbie doll dates. Instead I thought about, if I saw them on the street, how adorable they would be to me.

Not pug or cute dog adorable, but little old people kind of adorable. There was a reason that I worked in the hospice health care industry. While I had an affinity to kids, it was difficult to fight the same affinity with an almost equal pull, toward senior citizens. It wasn't just the kids that appreciated my inherent silliness and strange sense of humor. Visiting nursing homes in costume on holidays wearing various objects that mysteriously "lit up" on my person had become something residents at homes on my roster had loved and eventually anticipated.

So while I stood there, arrested about how adorable and almost juvenile in their giddiness over whatever was about to happen was, they slaughtered me, with no remorse, right there on the spot.

After being assured that the camera was recording (thus my realization at that moment that this was actually a pre-recorded message, as if my night didn't have enough going on in it to win the freaky beyond measure award) Doll Maker number one also known as Lewis, began the gutting process.

"Hello Celine. May we call you Celine? Yes, we will call you Celine. No need to stand on ceremony here is there?"

My snort was poorly hidden. At the time I didn't care. What I should have realized is, it didn't matter. I should have remembered that arrogance goes before a fall and pride goes before destruction. I'd been enjoying throwing attitude and arrogance around all night. Who knew that I'd be getting an attitude adjustment in a big way during my brief visit to a plush (and very public) women's bathroom?

"You do realize that all of your strategies and plans are not a surprise to us, yes? We know what you have been planning, have known it for a very long time my dear. So your escapades staged this evening have gained you absolutely nothing."

"But we did enjoy making you think for just a moment that it did, however." This was said by Doll Maker number two also known as Cypher. I guess I deserved the snicker he delivered due to my earlier one. But old man snickers weren't cute by a long shot. It looked more like he was trying to stop a sneeze followed by a mini seizure, instead of the jaded amused look I'm sure he was going for.

"Yes, yes we will Cye. Celine, we are aware of your little faction; the doctor you've planted amongst our staff as well as the identity of every single person you have embroiled in this little plot of yours. Would you like for me to name them my dear? Let's see... we have Denise Ferry, oh now there's a pretty one. Too bad she's brunette. She would make an excellent mistress slash body guard. And then there is that Richard McDonald fellow. My, what a tiny one he is. If I hadn't read his dossier, I would have been quite unimpressed."

While my foot had stopped tapping a while back, the rest of my body had missed the memo by refusing to brace for impact. And, while it was hard not to react, I remained motionless and made it a point to take slow even breaths. My nails were digging into my palms however as I forced myself to wait them out. Once I heard what I'd needed to hear, then I would be better equipped to deal. Right before I whipped their old, crusty behinds. Or so I thought.

"Should we list the names of the entire crew Lewis?"

"Not at all Cye, I think she gets the point."

"Speaking of which, get to the point lad! I can't wait to see her expression when you tell her."

"Right, right. Well do be quiet Cye so I can get there, Shall I?"

See my expression? Wait... this WAS a recording right?

At that thought my eyes narrowed as I saw Delilah flick her gaze up to the ceiling before looking back at me. Apparently they were somehow watching me as I watched their recording. With a camera. In a ladies' bathroom... where women adjusted their clothing and some of everything else. Ugh. I forced myself to focus on the tablet as I vomited in my mouth a little. Only to go from disgust to near hilarity in the blink of an eye.

Because the sight of those wrinkled lips bitten together from within by what had to be a fabulous set of false teeth was definitely hilarious. And if Mags had been there it would have been all over. Nothing and I mean NOTHING would have been able to stop me from collapsing into a fit of giggles. But common sense held fast since there was no Mags in sight. I had one goal. To get to the end of this foolishness so I could get back to my man and get our kids and crew safe.

"Where was I? Oh yes, dear girl. You and your people have been on our radar since day one. After a bit of discussion, we determined that you would make quite the specimen for our upgraded Brainwaiver implant."

I could feel my nails nearly drawing blood, they were digging in so deep. Because this wasn't a threat or a "bring the kids back or else," message... this was something worse. So much worse I felt my throat close and my breath hitch. My silent prayer of "please no," went unheeded as his next words proved that my unmitigated horror was totally warranted.

"So here is your next mission dear Celine. You have seven days, seven days exactly..."

"Not a day more you see, we are anxious to get started really...," Cye blurted, cutting Lewis off.

"Don't interrupt Cye, it's rude and didn't you want me to get to the point?"

Cye buttoned his wrinkled lips again, his gnarled hand going to his mouth to make a twisting motion followed by a throwing motion.

Were these guys serious? They seemed more like an old comedy team, like Laurel and Hardy, than the old perverts they were.

"Thank you Old man. Now, back to what I was saying Celine, You have seven days to report back here to prepare for the procedure. You will either do so, and really my dear, punctuality ensures that collateral damage is nonexistent, or you will watch as we eliminate them all. Eliminate every single member of your team. Every person that you have grown to care about. Everyone that you love. Starting with your Balboa."

I didn't know whether I choked a little then because of what Lewis had just said or because of the creepy childlike giggle noises that Cypher was making.

"Quite right, My Dear. First your team. Then every member of your young man's family. What would you say Lewis? Heart attack for the Father? His current heart condition won't make it too difficult to believe eh? And the mother, poor dear. Grief is a harbinger of death as well you know, especially when a couple has been together for over 40 years."

"Exactly Old Boy. Who next? Cye, Oh I've got it. The daughter, Cassiopeia was it? So young, so full of life. So sad to be cut off so abruptly by... what Cye, what is it?"

"I'm thinking rape, Old man. It's such a tragic and horrid thing isn't it? Oh! So much worse if it is perpetuated by her own kin... her brother yes? Well no wonder the young girl commits suicide right after? How could she live, when her brother has attacked her which of course results in his murder by his own father? And what can you expect from a man Lewis, who has lost his wife to cancer and now his poor daughter to suicide. How could he NOT kill his own son in a rage? And then himself? What else could the man do but that exactly?"

My heart had seized the moment Enoch's father was mentioned. And every word after that was like a burn... a cigar burn being twisted into my exposed, aching flesh one word at a time. The pain was so deep, so engrossing, that by the time they'd arrived to the end of their tag-teamed presentation of crazy, I'd gone numb. I didn't have to worry about trying not to give them a reaction to their cruel games because I couldn't.

I was frozen. Frozen and perhaps perplexed in the face of what I considered true evil. To hear these men plot the visiting of such horrors on actual people, to speak of taking their lives as if we were in a horror movie or a video game, was more than surreal – it was, for lack of a better word, unbelievable. Could this really happen? I mean, could there be people that existed in this world that were really THAT heartless?

I desperately wanted to move, to scream... to understand. To yell at them while throwing things. To get my hands around their wrinkled, bird-like throats and twist until I couldn't twist anymore. But mostly I wanted to know why? Why do this? Why play with people's lives as if this was checkers or a chess game? And why me? Why was I the perfect specimen for this insane crap?

"Oh, and you're probably wondering My Dear, why you? Why have we chosen you? It's simple really, isn't it Cye? Yes, you my dear are a challenge."

"Exactly right," Cypher's continuation of the tag team game was wearing on my nerves. If this moment hadn't been so horrifying I probably would have rushed into the next room to chop him in the throat... sadly it wouldn't have mattered any way since this was a recording, thus he would be able to continue unhindered.

"A challenge is something we long for these days. People have become just too easy to subjugate. Like sheep really. They have become so needy, so desperate, so... just easy to buy. Everyone has a price my dear. For some its fortune and for others its fame. There is something that everyone out there wants, notoriety being chief of all desires. But someone with standards.... with character? Ahhhhh.... There is nothing as sweet as the surrender of a Believer, right Lewis?

"Just so, Cye. Believers that will stand in the midst of a Roman arena, praying as they are being ripped to shreds. Or a Believer kneeling before a young gunman, refusing to recant her faith.... Those moments are so delicious, my dear. Because whether a Believer yields and becomes a slave or is destroyed in the making... the very challenge of it all gets the blood going like nothing else! And Dear, Dear girl... I cannot wait to taste your surrender... or watch you die, impotently suffering, knowing that your hope brings you naught in the end."

It was silent for a moment in the room. The Doll Makers had ceased their diatribe, probably for a few seconds, though it seemed like hours. I guess they wanted to give it a moment for their big reveal to sink in.

And had I had anything in me, they probably would have gotten a double middle finger which good Christian girls never EVER even DREAMED of flashing, right at their stupid camera... but I had nothing.

A lone tear slid down Delilah's cheek though. And I saw all of the despair, all of the pain... all of the frustration that I should have been feeling, reflected at me from her shining, stricken eyes.

"Seven Days My Dear. You must choose. It's either them.... Or you. Because honestly, what we have disclosed thus far is just us having a bit of fun. You don't want to even know what we have planned for your sister or your parents..."

"Or your daughter."

Lewis' delivering that last line, with a sneer and such ugly cruelty dancing in his eyes, was just the activator I needed.

The words that came to me then, came to me now as I trained for the inevitable.

The words weren't mine. But I'd spoken them nonetheless. Just as I did now. I shook myself, braced my weight on my hands and pushed up strong my body in full plank position with my arm muscles clenched in defiance of gravity...

"No weapon."

I'd been such a geek as a kid it seemed, able to remember bible verses almost at a glance. And I loved the sound of them rolling off of my tongue while I sang them, said them or hummed them. That was until I realized that people found it annoying. They thought I was a fanatic... felt I was too preachy. They saw me as weird. And so I'd stopped.

I'd stopped singing them, saying them, humming them or even writing them. But I never stopped believing them. So when the words, "No weapon formed against you shall prosper. Every tongue that rises against you shall be shown to be made in the wrong for this is your heritage as a servant of the Lord, and your righteousness is of me, saith the Lord..." came to mind, it was on. Those words had played in my head over and over again while Delilah shut down the power, shaking her head in what seemed like silent apology... I could do nothing else but repeat those words to the camera that had been, at that very moment delivering my reaction...

NO WEAPON.

Jumping to my feet now, I took my fighting stance. I had four days. Let them take their best shot. And they had better too... Because if I knew anything about My God... I knew that when it came to man giving his best, God always gave better.

Feeling that right then as in FEELING THAT, It was no wonder that I took an old Bruce Lee fighting stance against Balboa and wiggled my fingers in the universal "BRING IT" signal before tapping my nose with each thumb.

I was nuts to bait her like that. Because the woman was a power house. And when she came at me, she was coming fast and she was coming hard. But that was just what I needed... because I was a power house too. And even though dread tried to take over and freeze me into a catatonic state, God wouldn't let it. Because straight up... He was the biggest power house of them all.

Chapter Twenty-Eight

"**Babe**... you with me?"

My rapid fire blinking probably hinted that I was NOT with my man... well, that wasn't completely true. I was with him, as in physically with him. But mentally I was miles away. Because tonight might be the last time I would see him as ME. And I was not really coming to terms with that fact very well.

The week had flown by, because that's the way life usually works. When you want time to slow down so that you can savor every single moment and squeeze everything you can into every second, time speeds by with the swiftness of a race car. My time had run out, the race was about over and I had absolutely nothing left.

No bright ideas, no answers and no quick fixes. And worse, the man I had come to lean on so heavily lately to give me what I needed when I needed it (like said answers, quick fixes or solutions) had no idea that I was about to turn our big win into a huge loss.

Plus I hadn't told him I loved him yet. I had it all planned, the big reveal of all that was me and how I felt about him just in case things went bad. Which was kind of messed up in a way. Because how do you tell someone that, besides the beauty that was your kid, he was everything to you one day; then disappear the very next?

Flat out, it was not cool, not on any level. Yet how would I ever forgive myself if I didn't come back or didn't come back *the same*, if he never got that from me? So I was spacing a little which I hated. I tried not to because I needed to somehow fit an eternity of loving him and telling him so, into the few hours that we had left.

"Yeah honey... I'm here."

I said it as I squeezed in deep, my position half on him and half on the couch making that an easy thing to do.

My head was resting on his chest and my ear had a front row seat to his heart beating a staccato rhythm. And if I had my way, it would keep on beating that rhythm. My goal had become clear.

I didn't have to win in the end. But he did. And the kids did. Which meant I'd spent this week preparing for the fight of my life. Because I didn't plan to just go down for the Doll Makers' amusement. I was that new type of Christian. The one born to be like David was – with the heart of a lion. If I went down, I planned on taking RLS down with me. Even if it meant leveling the whole building.

"So are you going to answer my question or what?"

Sam's deep sigh, which I felt more than I heard since it pushed my head up a few inches before slowly bringing it back down, was my clue that he'd said something I'd missed. And since he wasn't stupid there was no point pretending that I'd heard him so...

"Sorry I missed it baby. Ask me again...," The rumble under my ear annoyed me. I know he was chuckling because I'd spaced again for what must have been the hundredth time tonight...

But so what? I had a lot on my mind...even if he didn't know that. Thus the attitude when I said, "You know what? Never mind since it must not have been that important." I put a little snark on the THAT IMPORTANT part and pushed up to finish my hissy fit somewhere *not* on his person. But that was sort of hard to do since I could only push up to a point. His arms had tightened around me, halting my progress. Which only annoyed me more. I'd been working out so much I felt like I could bench press the WORLD... but not enough to get out of his hold apparently. *Ugh.*

"Don't get all huffy babe." More, rumbles sounded under my ear again since not only did he NOT let me up, but he pulled me back down to my former position. Like I said, annoying.

"And since you asked so nicely, I don't mind repeating the question. I asked you for the name of the song we're listening to?"

Ah. Okay. Well since he put it that way...

"It's called COURAGEOUS by Casting Crowns."

"Hmmm."

My head only rose a little bit with his chest that time. I waited for more to follow because that sounded pretty deep. But I should have known better. To men, that hmm was communication enough. For us women, hmmm could mean various things from, "Oh! I love this dress, " to "Should I tell my coworker that she smells like cheese?"

After what felt like hours but was probably only a few seconds I was still waiting. As such, I had to ask because me and curiosity... we didn't mesh well together. Like, for example, french fries and shakes. A truth I've repeated constantly to Sammie. It didn't stop her from being gross and dipping said fries into said shakes anyway.

"You like that? The song I mean?"

"Yeah... it's nice."

I pushed up a little so that I could look him in the eye. I needed to get a bead on what he was thinking. I'd learned early on that Enoch was not a huge music buff. He could pretty much take or leave any kind of music you wanted to play. He had no problem with me being the radio commando in his truck or my car, that's how much it didn't matter. Which meant, when he took notice of a particular song, there was definitely a reason for that notice. And I was an inquiring mind that needed to know that reason.

"Just nice?"

"Babe."

I felt my eyebrows go so high that they were probably touching my hair line. Nothing got my hackles up as much as when he "Babed" me like that. Babe said in that tone could mean just about anything, but mostly it meant "let it go."

"Sa-am." Yeah, spoken like that with my lips pursed in a way that he couldn't miss clearly indicated that I was not going to let this rest. Plus I'd called him Sam. I NEVER called him Sam unless I was in trouble... or he was about to be.

"What's the big deal? It's a song. I heard it. I liked it. I asked you about it. That's it."

I should have known it would be something that simple. But I'm thorough like that. To some it makes me a pain in the butt. To me it's a skill. Po-tay-to, Po-tah-to.

Grabbing the remote off of the table, I hit the back button to replay the song. I then assumed my former position on his chest and allowed myself to be lulled while focusing on the lyrics.

And realized that God was at it... *again*.

Because the song was, at that moment, speaking to me in a way that was so spooky it was crazy! Not a creepy kind of spooky. A good, God-ordained kind of spooky.

The lyrics were so on target for what I was going through, from the very first words even, that my chest hitched. It felt as if all of the oxygen had been sucked from my lungs leaving them to fend for themselves. I was so engrossed by how this song was speaking to me, preparing me even, that I didn't realize (until Enoch's arms had tightened around me as he rolled and shifted me, reversing our positions) that I was silently sobbing my relief.

We were MADE to be courageous. The song was the perfect catalyst. A: Because it was awesome all by itself and B: Because it aligned perfectly with what Danny had said to me two days ago.

"Celine. Babe," spoken in Enoch's, *Do what I say woman,* tone should have been enough to calm me down.

But it wasn't. I just burrowed further into his chest and gripped him harder, soaking the front of his shirt.

I'd just received my marching orders. And I was going in alone with none of my team at my back. I would be fighting this battle on all fronts – mentally, emotionally AND physically... alone.

But for my family, for his family... I would do it. Because I had just found my battle cry. And I needed one as powerful as that if I wanted to even entertain the hope of coming out alive.

***

Sam

"Celine, talk to me." I heard how rough my voice was and I didn't even try to soften it. My woman was crying like the world was ending right in front of us; and I was oblivious as to the why behind that.

"Talk to me Babe. You have to give this to me so I can fix it." I grunted before ab-curling up and taking her with me into a sitting position. She was still wrapped around me tight. Like I was the only thing keeping her breathing. And I gave her that because I had to give her something. But it wasn't enough, not to me.

Taking the remote out of her hand I turned the music off and scooted backward until I was up against the arm rest; Celine tucked into me. The crying and hiccupping had given way to heavy breathing and an occasional cough.

I had to give her this moment to compose so I did. Wasn't happy about it. But I did it. And while I did so I mentally ticked off the events of the past few days to find something, anything, that could explain this. But beyond the bad vibe that I couldn't shake since last week's throw down I had nothing.

So much had gone down this week that just about anything could be the trigger. Case in point, the Same girls had been picked up by their grandparents just two days ago. That had been hard for Celine. You could tell that she'd wanted to keep them here where she could keep an eye, but we all knew that, not only was that not feasible, it wasn't cost effective.

The mission was over and the grandparents were done fitting the bill for it. Besides, we all knew that we had no play to make when it came to those girls. It was their grandparents or back to their parents in Alton. We'd have to let the grandparents fight it out in court for custody of the girls and hope for the best.

But Celine had managed to get her time in with them before they left. And, while she'd been a bit distracted after that last bit of quality time with Anabelle before the girls were picked up, I couldn't draw a bead on how *that* could be fueling *this*... whatever *this* was.

Resolving the rest of the kids' living situations hadn't been as cut and dried. Prayers had been prayed and answered in a way that left me stunned. Because I had never seen anything like it before. Strategies, end games, objectives, that was our thing. Finding relatives and housing for kids we didn't know when we had no idea where to start looking, not so much. The entire team had been at a loss, a fact that was not missed by my girl. It had been her idea to enlist our families. One I wasn't all that big a supporter of... at first.

Tremendous. My family. Specifically, my mom. She'd been amazing me for almost all my life. So this was no exception. Mom had swooped in with all of the power of a super-ninja-Christian-Grandma and taken over. Apparently her church already partnered with a shelter nearby along with a children's charity that specialized in locating missing children and reuniting them with their families. Between those two and some other entities she was able to enlist via her "connections," half of the kids had been reunited with their families while others had been taken on as fosters by families, many that attended Mom's church.

And when I'd asked Ma how they managed the monumental feat of bypassing state agencies and their bureaucratic-red-tape guerrilla tactics, her response? *Your Mama knows people Son, let's just leave it at that.* Even at the end of all of that, three toddlers (Cameron, Sidney and Jaime) two girls and a boy were taken on by none other than Ma herself.

So to say it had been a busy week was more than an understatement. Which meant that, when I finally got the chance to get Celine alone, I took it. And not to do the typical date night thing. I'd had enough of people and being around them to last me a life time. So bringing my lady back to her place where she could be herself had been the priority. That and dinner. Plus I still had to give her the words.

Being a guy raised by a woman that could somehow pull off being God-fearing while managing to put the fear-of-Mom into her brood of children without fail, I was taught truth. One truth being, women did not get that the actions of their men did all the talking. They needed the words. Which I did not get; I just accepted it as the truth it was. And because I knew this, I made it a point to add that to tonight's agenda.

So why I hadn't seen to that yet, I do not know. I was task avoiding. And I was nervous. It wasn't just the words that I planned on serving up. I had a ring in my pocket that I wanted to present as an addendum to my confession. Another truth? I was an action kind of guy. While the words would probably be all she needed to hear, the act of claiming her as mine by putting my ring on her finger, to me, said it better and was something I needed.

But before I could get to any of that, I had to straighten out this madness with the tears. Plus between the hiccupping and the crying, my wet shirt was not getting any dryer. It was time to nix the mental process and get on with it.

I palmed her chin to give me those gorgeous blue eyes, now wet and hazy.

Gorgeous. My girl was all of that. Even in the midst of a monumental crisis that my being a guy meant I was completely clueless about, I still wanted to loose myself in all that beauty.

Holding her chin steady, my forehead meeting hers, I closed my eyes. Feeling her lips touch mine I made another promise to myself. That I would enjoy tonight with my girl. That I would live in the now and just marinate in all that we were right here on this couch. And that wasn't such a bad deal since I could give her the words tomorrow. And the ring. In fact, why was I rushing anyway when we had the rest of our lives to look forward to moments just like this?

I couldn't help but take over the kiss as full on desire swept through me. I knew that Celine and I had boundaries. I would respect that and not push, but I needed her to know how mine she was, and I could give that to her better than with just words.

My hand slid from her chin into her hair and tightened so I could tilt her more, give her more of me in that. I repeated the promise to myself and took the time to explore, taking more of her. I'd give her the words tomorrow. That was definitely a promise I knew that I could keep.

Chapter Twenty-Nine

"**Tell** him. Tell him now Cee before it's too late!" Balboa gritted, her left hook barely missing my chin as I faded back.

I'd kept my head as we battled the entire day away. I had to stay on my game since tonight, in three hours to be exact, there was no turning back.

Jab, jab, right cross, jab, knee, right cross, left hook. It was almost like a ballet, our moves fluid with both of us at the top of our game. I'd kept my head the whole time even though I was scared out of my mind.

"Can't. You know I can't!" I couldn't tell if she understood my grunt through the mouth guard and my exhaustion. I just knew I couldn't... and did it matter? Not at all! Because she was a flipping robot. She never got tired or winded. Which made me want to land another punch all the more.

I spun into a back fist that barely skimmed the top of her head as she ducked then flowed right into a right upper cut that I smoothly blocked (yay me!), using it to push her off.

We cornered off again, both of us scanning for a weakness. Sweat and sheer butt-kickery flowed out of her pores. She danced a little to the left and chuffed at me, trying to get me to respond. But she taught me better than that. Besides, I was too busy dwelling on what she'd said to even be fooled by that crap.

Because I hadn't lied to her. And she knew I hadn't. There was no way I could tell him; nor could she – which was probably why all kinds of piss-tivity and fire bled from her eyes when she chuffed again.

Enoch was all Alpha. And there was no way he'd let me go. If I'd given in and told him everything last night (like I *SO* wanted to do) he would have gone straight Godzilla on me. And not Godzilla in a way that, Hey I'll protect the poor Asian weaklings by going straight monster on whatever the monster I happen to be fighting was this week.

Nope. Woulda been Godzilla in a way that there would have been no one safe from the fall out. With most of the team preparing to disband and head home and the kids getting settled, It would have been uncool for me to spill at the last minute – all, "Oh My, Mr. Manly Man hero! Save me from my own stupidity!"

Heh.... I wish. First off, my southern belle accent was deplorable. And second – after waiting so long to ante up, and having known all this time... that would have been worse than uncool, it would have been cowardly. So I did what any tough chick (or Balboa) would do.

I gave my man his night. We made out. I cried. We laughed. We argued and then made out some more. We talked about the song after I'd finished my fit. And we held tight. He'd had no clue that it was me grabbing hold to all the good that I could before letting go when the time came.

And while I know he'd been gearing up to say the three words that every woman needed to hear, I did everything I could to keep that from happening (despite my earlier conviction to make sure we'd said those words before the night was done). Because I might not be coming back.

Besides, his actions were loud and clear – I knew exactly how much he was into me. And in guy speak, that pretty much said it all. Truthfully, I had to give him an out. If he happened to see me a month from now and noticed that I had nothing for him - when I so want to give him everything - without those words being said, it wouldn't kill (as much). It would maim and it would hurt like all get out. But it wouldn't kill. And my man was ALL man, meaning he would recover. And that recovery would go much easier if he'd never given me the words in the first place.

So while I gave my guy his night, I gave everyone else I loved my day. Sammie learned that she still dug her mama who had not stopped being goofy, even after all that had gone down. So our time of snacking on s'mores for breakfast in front of cartoons this morning was not wasted. My girl knew that she was loved. Treasured. Adored even. And that no matter what tomorrow brought, no matter what happened, her mama would always love her some Sammie.

Mags and I spent the afternoon giggling together on a small bench at their tiny neighborhood pond. Because duck watching had become a much loved comedic routine of ours, it was a fun filled afternoon of guffaws, chuckles, crackers and deep exhalations in order to bring our hilarity under control. And before our time was up I said exactly what I needed to say. Giving her the letters I'd written to her, Mom and Dad and Sammie, I laid it out. If for some reason I left and never came back, those letters got opened immediately. It was easy, getting past her worried why's and what's going on's because tomorrow wasn't promised to anyone. Period. A big goof my sister was, absolutely, but a logical one. Preparing for the unknown made sense to her, so the letters made sense.

The parents weren't as easy, but I'd made it through. Loving on mom had never been a hardship, but loving on Dad required some maneuvering. So I maneuvered. I played around in the kitchen with mom then went out into the garage for some Dad time. I'd talked, I'd listened and I'd laughed. Doing all of that at the same time savoring every second. Much like the country song that inspired its listener's to live like they were dying, I took full advantage of that last 24 hours with my family. And last but very far from least came the time spent with the woman that was, at this very moment attempting to sweep my legs out from under me.

A woman who'd just learned, at the very last minute that all we had together was, indeed, this last minute.

"You cannot be serious!" Balboa muttered through her own mouth guard (which I somehow understood – maybe we were becoming clairvoyant...) as she danced to the side again and cornered off against me. Having been taught since day one that you never squared off against your opponent I did the same, coming at her from an angle. I'd attacked with another series of jabs, crosses, a knee then a push before dancing away to get my bearings.

"Dead serious." Oops. Weakness exposed again. I'd wheezed that.

Not at all surprised that I was unable to completely avoid the gut shot from her left uppercut. It glanced off of my ribs as I danced to my left (ouch! *Heifer!*), then I adjusted my guard before angling off again to her left.

Dropping her guard was her signal to me to pause, which I did by dropping mine. The air seemed electric and I could almost feel the weight of her anger as it buzzed around. I would have freaked out because I could feel her mad in a way that almost made my hair stand on end. But I was too tired to care. Instead I focused on deep breathing to slow my heart rate and catch a second wind since it was obvious she was about to vent. And because she wasn't one to mince words I didn't even get to start the countdown (in my head) until her imminent explosion.

"So you're just going to walk in there and let them kill you, then?"

Oy. The calm voice. I knew the calm voice. That meant that she was way beyond angry. She was royally teed off. Welp! In for a penny...

"So you're saying you are THAT horrible a trainer that I'm not prepared, then?" I probably shouldn't have copied her calm, sarcastic tone. But when you give me tone, you get it back in spades. Which was something she knew. But I still should have anticipated the roundhouse that knocked me on my butt... ugh!

Is that tweety birds? Or flashing lights? Possibly future events?

"Huh. I guess so" Her snort after that was not pretty. I would have laughed with her if the little editor in my head hadn't started packing his bags apparently hoping to get out while the getting was good.

Her grunt of satisfaction that followed probably should have ticked me off. But inappropriate hilarity was an inherited trait in my family which again, she knew. So I'm sure she wasn't shocked after a few minutes when I dropped back on the matt while holding my belly and rolled from side to side, giggling my tail off.

"You know I can't let you die right? That just can't happen Cee. Not on my watch."

Her quietly spoken seriousness in the face of my humor sobered me much faster than her yelling in anger would have. I knew it couldn't happen. I just had no idea how I was going to make it NOT happen.

I sat up crossing my legs Indian style, resting my arms on my knees. I had nothing to say that would bring her comfort, except maybe to tell her I was ready. She'd prepared me better than I could have ever hoped.

Instead I allowed yesterday's conversation with Danny to play back in my mind. Because while I didn't have an eidetic or photographic memory; for some reason, I could hear every nuance of what was spoken. I could also see – freeze frame style- mental snapshots of the entire scene. Everything – audio and visual – was just *that* clear.

He'd managed to freak me out a little with just two words. Enoch had gone to pick up Sammie and Cass from the dollar show in St. Charles while Danny and I chose to hang back and chat. We had plenty to talk about. From our favorite conversational pastime – basketball to oh yeah – girls, heh (and by girls I mean his obviously embarrassing- yet cute- crush on Cheryl).

Since Enoch and I had the night planned for just us, I'd been grateful to get that time in with Danny. No matter how many ways I imagined that our conversation would go, I'd never guessed I would hear those two words...

"It hurts."

I'd blinked because – *what*? But before I asked he continued in a more subdued way.

"You'd think it hurts so much that you must be dying. You wanna die in fact, to get away from it."

"Dan," my voice broke on his name because until now he hadn't spoken to me or Enoch about what he'd gone through. We'd wanted to give him time to come to terms with it and find out how best to cope rather than push him; be that via therapy or forcing our own ideas on him. The hardest thing for a parent to do is to stand by and watch their kid come to terms with something horrible – and choose how to deal.

And though I knew I wouldn't be there to help Danny through the process, I agreed whole heartedly with this approach. Which is why I never expected to hear about it. So, of course I wasn't even a little bit prepared for the words that followed.

In the short time I'd known him, he'd become mine. Not like Sammie was, but mine nonetheless. Just as his sister had clicked into my heart like a well made puzzle piece, so had he. So hearing him speak of the pain he'd suffered was akin to... I didn't know what. The best way to describe it was how I felt when Balboa worked me like a dog. That feeling of a slow steady burn in my lungs that built when I was forced to keep running despite exhaustion. Suffice it to say, not a good feeling.

Thus I'd said his name intent on stopping him because hearing it already hurt too much, but his voice carried over mine...

"But the pain wasn't the worst part. It was the pressure that killed. It killed Cee. In a way that nothing in my life has ever prepared me for. I wanted to give up. To give in to what it was asking me for. What it was telling me. It would have let me die if I had. But not die in a way where I would have had peace – in a way where I would have turned my back on everything I was, and everything I was raised to be. You understand though right? Why I couldn't let that happen?"

What was the "it"? That was the question I'd wanted to ask. But my mouth chose to answer his question instead...

"Your dad?" Ragged and rough, the words tore out of me so precisely that they should have cut me in half.

Dan nodded and swallowed. It had been so hard to sit there and watch him hurt like that. But he'd needed it, to get it out. And maybe I'd needed to hear it just as much.

"My dad. He was like, the ultimate you know? When he wasn't home, he still touched base with me, one on one. He taught me how to keep our girls safe, Cass and Mom, when he wasn't around. He showed me how to help people and to be the best me I could be. Everything my dad ever taught me, ever showed me... all of that was at stake. I am who I am because my dad is who he is. And I could NOT turn my back on that. He would always have my back, no matter what. I knew this. No doubt. So I had to have his, even if that meant that I would die trying. "

Swallowing hard I tried my best to keep the wet that was all over my eyes from spilling over. But it was a struggle... especially when he continued.

"He used to tell me that my worst enemy was IN me. You know, that my mind was where I won and fought every battle. He would tell this old corny story about the Indians and the parable of the two wolves inside – evil and good – and that, when the grandson asked which one wins, the answer was the one you feed the most... so corny right? But I think it was that story along with the other stuff he said that prepared me for that fight. Cause I wasn't fighting this thing physically. It was all in my head, you know? This thing knew my weaknesses, it knew the stuff that I wanted most in life – and it played me like Cass is constantly playing those bongos. I gotta say this Cee because it is the honest truth – if my dad hadn't taught me how to overcome myself first, there is no way I would have been able to get through that. He used to say, 'it's all mental son. You can't be telling yourself what you see... you gotta rehearse in your mind what you WANT to see. And if you WANT to see that shot going in – you gotta see it and SAY it to yourself, one step at a time.' That's how I got through the pain... and that's how you have to do it. You gotta look to everything you know about God, everything you've been taught – I don't know much about you and your Dad, but I do know you love God like, a LOT. So you gotta hold on to that through the pain. It's the only way you'll make it. The only way you'll come back to us."

There was no controlling the wet then. It blinded me right before it overflowed into all kinds of mess. None of which I'd noticed much. Because I hadn't told anyone anything about what would happen today. Until Balboa... like, just now. Speaking of which...

"If you die, I WILL kill you. You do know this?"

"Yada yada yada. Help me up Special," I said it through my grin. Because when we were at "the threats that made no sense" stage, we'd already made a left turn past anger thus completely avoiding "tattle tale" road.

"Call me Special again and my next right cross will dot your eye in a way that your eyeball will never forgive you."

"Heh... you forgot to say, 'and cross your teeth'." I snickered that because yeah... I'd heard it way too much in the last few weeks to not have memorized THAT psycho pun on correct grammar-turned-violent.

"No I didn't. I'm not predictable, unlike your roundhouse kick. Which *IS* predictable... and sad." Again, I should have seen that push kick coming by the way she gritted her teeth on that last part. And if I could have spoken through the wheeze as my lungs shouted to my brain, "WHAT THE FREAKING HECK!!!" I would have called her many *many* things... but predictable definitely wasn't one.

Chapter Thirty

Okay. So I loved movies. Many movies. And I had many favorites that ranged from *Fried Green Tomatoes* to *The Bourne Identity*. That said, why Ana chose to quote The Green Mile to me the day she left, I still have no idea. "He kill them wi' their love. Wi' their love fo' each other. That's how it is, every day, all over the world."

Yet, at the moment, it was those words on rewind, play and repeat in my head, which was blissfully blank otherwise.

I guess I figured my mind was blank because A: There was no little editor there, shaking his cigar at me (with work-stained hands – the guy really worked too hard for his own good) about the latest rudeness I'd uttered and B: There was nothing but white all around me.

And when I say white, I mean it was THE whitest white you could imagine. Like how movies try to depict heaven, only whiter than that and SO not what I knew heaven would be like.

There was nothing around me. Just stillness... like I was in a vat of air with no oxygen... air that was counterpoint to its very purpose. It felt more like what I envisioned hell to be than heaven.

So there was all that white, me... and those lines from The Green Mile. Which still made no sense. And served no purpose to me right then... other than to make me wish I had a strong cup of coffee... "Spelled Coffey, not like the drink but different..." Heh.

I was not wrong when I said that my sense of humor reared its ugly head during the most inappropriate of times. Feeling like I was standing in the midst of hell while recapping lines from a movie definitely ranked in the top five of these occurrences.

That said, no one could blame me for being caught off guard by the change of scenery.

Because one moment I was in this void of hot, dead, empty whiteness, and the next, I was standing on the bluffs... The bluffs above Piasa Park... The bluffs, near which, we'd found Johnny's dead body.

Did I say it felt more like hell? I was pretty sure that it WAS hell. And that being the case, there *had* to be a geographical error recorded on where I should spend eternity. Up! Not down people!!! I would have demanded to speak to the management (that would be God Almighty) but if there was one thing I knew about God, it was that you didn't get to tell HIM what you were gonna do or where you were supposed to be. I saw a magnet once that read, "God sits back as he hears our plans... then laughs." Totally fitting. Because the utter craziness that ran through my brain on constant replay would have cracked me up too if I were Him.

"Thinking you should have left the red pill alone are you?"

Oy! My freak-out was difficult to perpetrate since I couldn't really breathe to speak, yet being an overachiever, I somehow managed.

And just like I was not wrong when I said my humor reared its ugly head during inappropriate moments, I was NOT wrong when I said that I was a goof.

Of course, pointing out the obvious, it would be difficult to NOT believe I had fallen into a comedic nightmare that had combined movies I loved (and hated) from *The Matrix* to *Alice in Wonderland* with a sprinkle of *The Green Mile*. Because what would any person with any sense of logic have thought... when faced with the Piasa beast of legend... that spoke with an English accent... and sounded like Sean Connery? Yep... exactly.

And was it me, or did it look like the thing was actually OFFENDED as I doubled over and laughed just a little bit harder? And snorted (only a few times cause otherwise it would have been just rude) at ALL of that?

"Really? You're laughing now? And your sister isn't here to blame, by the way."

While I'd dialed it down to just chuckles, the threat of ramping back up to full, gut wrenching guffaws loomed. I had to do something to derail that and quick. Because the thing was right... now if it would just stop talking. I MIGHT make it out alive. Unless it was planning on killing me with hilarity. If that *was* its goal, it was TOTALLY working.

"Are you done?"

Chuckle, chuckle. "Yeah." Snort

"Seriously?"

Snicker, giggle, snort. "Okay. Seriously. Totally done now."

"Good."

Snicker. "Well, I'm sorry! But every time you talk... I mean really? Sean Connery?" Chuckle, snort.

"Fine. You have a problem with my current persona? How about this?"

And double oy! Because while NO one could take the cultured tones of James Bond coming out of a mouth riddled with fangs seriously... the image of a Vin Deisel, Dwayne "The Rock" Johnson look alike with a bit of Billy Zane thrown in for good measure... yeah. I didn't quite feel so much like laughing right then.

"Better?"

My wordless nod was an automatic reaction, though I probably didn't even need it to communicate the "better". Without the little editor present to make sure I wasn't gawking or drooling, I'm pretty sure my total fascination was obvious.

"Good. Let's get started shall we? I figured I'd give you a heads up on how this is going to go. I've found that this is the best approach with those of your temperament. Because once you realize how correct my assessment is, your surrender is imminent."

If I hadn't stopped giggling and snorting by then, no matter his appearance, THAT would have definitely put my humor to rest.

"Ah, I see you are finally ready to be serious now? I'm glad. While I rather enjoyed your unique reaction to my presence, I must say, it was a bit off-putting. I'm used to terror you see. But then again, those are children. I find this new persona and adult version of myself rather refreshing."

It didn't take a computer geek to realize that I'd been implanted. Nor did it take one to realize that the "upgrade" that the Doll Makers were referring to was a more adaptable version of the software that could take on the image of the beast of horror stories or... something else.

Lucky me. I got the something else.

War of the mind.

With that thought, everything came flooding back to me with razor sharp clarity. It was like going from an analog broadcast to a High Definition Digital transmission within a fraction of a second.

And while I marveled on how all of that just happened, the beast – because no matter what face he took on he was still a soul devouring monster – continued on in an "I'm talking to a three year old with small words," tone.

"The implant allows me to interact with your ID as it were... your base personality, as well as your Ego and Super Ego. Your being a Christian...,"

*Were the air quotes around Christian really necessary? I mean,
since when did we become the dingos that ate people's babies?
Why in movies, literature and just about everything else these days
were we painted as "the bad guy"? You get a few sicko's in a church
acting crazy when, let's face it, there were sickos EVERYWHERE, and
suddenly Christians are ALL hypocritical monsters with antiquated
beliefs? That was one parade of stupid that I couldn't understand
anybody marching in. That's right... I said it... PARADE OF STUPID!
There's your air quotes buddy! You can...*

"Are you paying attention?"

The condescension dripping from those words put a stop to my
mental mini-rant. It was then that I wondered how I could possibly
win a *War of the Mind* if I couldn't keep said mind focused.
Because, no. BIG FAT STINKING NO. I was SO not paying attention
that I forgot to be freaked. And I should have been, especially with
what it said next.

"As I was saying before being rudely interrupted by your soap box
moment, which is still rude by the way, even if you didn't say any of
that out loud... Christian's would better recognize and align with
Watchman Nee's assertion of the human soul – the mind, will and
emotions. My job is simple. I take control of all of that by attacking
your emotions first. A simple process really. I dig around in your
psyche until I can find what generates that emotion most useful for
my purposes. Fear. "

It was not lost on me that this program was danged intuitive.
Because just those words alone pretty much accomplished his goal.
Which is why I remembered just how much I hated upgrades.

* * *

Sam

"Since when are you so clumsy that you can't see the wall right in
front of you?"

Balboa's wince was not surprising. I would have winced too. And rubbed my head exactly like she was. I could have told her that she could rub that thing till it caught fire and it still wasn't going to stop that lump from growing.

I would have told her that too, had she not just run into a wall at my mention of Celine. It did not need mentioning that the two had become thick as thieves. Coupled with the fact that I'd sent two texts, left three voicemails and stopped by with no one answering the door, one could say that I was getting suspicious.

"Talk to me."

I didn't have to be listening to know that my tone had gone stone cold. Because I had gone stone cold in just that instant.

That "bad feeling" that had been niggling me for days blared all types of warnings into my head. And I did not ignore warnings – a promise I made to myself long ago was never to do that. So I didn't. And that instinct never failed to pay off.

"Oh no you did NOT just go all Commando on me."

All attitude and swelling up like a chicken in a fit, she turned with her hands on her hips and started tapping her foot.

I felt my eyebrow go up as I crossed my arms over my chest, my feet spreading to give me a more solid base. I was settling in for the long haul. Because Balboa pissed meant a chop to the throat, a spinning back fist or a knee to the groin. It did NOT mean attitude and foot tapping. Which meant that this was a show. And I was NOT buying a ticket to catch the matinee. The niggling eeriness increased and I tried not to grind my teeth. Because not only was this a friend, this was my family. My team. There is no way she would allow Celine to go into a situation knowing that she was in danger and not have her back. Or not tell me. Would she?

It was when she bit her lip, for the first time EVER since I have known her, looking indecisive that I knew.

My girl was in trouble. Real trouble. Which meant I had been right before. All hell was about to break loose and I would personally be responsible for bringing the burn.

***

Danny

"So Gram. How do you pray for someone that you know is in trouble?"

My grandma was not one of those old, wrinkly grandma's that smelled like moth balls or baby oil.

She was a real cool old chick. Somehow she managed to stay down with how my generation communicates and still be real about her Faith.

Before I'd met Minute or Doc as the kids and I called her (also known as my future wife) my grandma had been the epitome of all the things I would want in the woman I married once I decided to settle down – except the old part.

She loved God for real. Not just like, at church and around people or whenever she wanted to make somebody feel bad. But through and through. And it wasn't because of what she said really, just in everything she did. You know that she would get an attitude or sometimes grumble about punching somebody in the head – but in all that, she still was all about God. She was herself. And loving God was a part of who she was.

Even my mom, before she passed, struggled with being who she was verses who other people thought she should be. My Gram was the only woman I'd ever seen that did that and was cool with herself doing that. Until Celine.

I kind of asked Celine about it before we got into the heavy stuff the other night – about how she was so confident about herself and who God was. She had just looked at me real calm, not wide eyed and a little freaked (like some adults I asked at a bible study I went to once – man did they hate questions) before smiling real wide.

I expected something goofy to come out, cause my dad called her a goof all the time and my dad did not lie, she was a total goof, when she shocked me by leaning forward like she had a secret before she said, "Because God started this hot mess I call self – and he is faithful to complete the good work he began. So I have like, no pressure you know? I'm me. He made me the ME I'm supposed to be. So I can be free to be goofy, have fun and enjoy my life. He's on His job, teaching me and training me to be the best version of me, the one he had in mind when he made me. Whether it's a trial by fire or a lesson in patience because I'm stuck in traffic, every day He's on His job. And since He is good at what He does, I let Him do that and worry about the other stuff that I actually CAN do something about... like help the kids that ask for my help. Taking Duke's cupcakes to my neighbor next door who LOVES Duke's cupcakes. He told me to worry about the easy stuff – because when I do that I show people how cool God is, and let him worry about the hard stuff, i.e. the shaping up and shipping right of the hot-mess-ness that is moi."

So I'd decided it then, at that moment. That if I couldn't marry Doc, my future wife would be a woman that looked and sounded like her, had faith like Celine and Grams, but was a total goof about it. In other words, I was definitely my father's son.

"Why you ask baby boy?"

Gram was wiping down the sink when she said it, like she was distracted. But I knew that she would not miss anything I said. She was sharp. And she was smart. So while I was mixing up in my mind the woman I'd one day marry, I decided to throw those features in the pot too.

"Because I remember the Lord's prayer Gram. They made us do that in bible study when I was a kid. But I know someone that's going through something. A dark place, you know? So how do you pray for that?"

I don't know how I missed her moving from the kitchen counter, to the family room and then back again but, it felt like I had just blinked and she was suddenly right there... I mean like, *there*. And she had the family bible in front of me. The thing was huge. It was old, ratty-looking and *a book*... and my Gram still used it despite the Kindle Fire Dad had gotten her for her birthday last year.

Underlined and highlighted was the chapter titled, Psalms 23. I glanced up to see that Gram had already left the kitchen, but I didn't need her to explain why she turned the bible to that page.

And that was because it started off with, "Yea though I walk through the valley of the shadow of death, I will fear no evil. For Thou art with me..."

Yep. That sounded about right.

∗∗∗

Celine

"Welcome to the second stage of Project Fear – I do adore that title by the way, so descriptive. How do you like my demonstration so far Ms. Baltimore? Please say you'll join with me. While I will rather enjoy what comes next, I can assure you, that you won't."

I gritted and grunted and twisted on what felt like ground, tangled in a web of air that wouldn't move and held no oxygen for me to breathe. I had heard the word agony used a few times in my life. From cartoons where the word was used with humor to hospice care where seniors or cancer patients suffered through it before their passing. But never, not even when giving birth, would I say I had ever experienced it. Until now.

The pain that gripped me was excruciating. While I would hazard a guess to say that the point of origin was my head – only because I knew where the implant was located – the feeling of muscle, nerves, tendon and bones being shredded, was everywhere. I didn't scream. I refused to give that thing the pleasure. But I wanted to so bad. Because no matter how bad FEARING what was to come had been, nothing was more painful than this.

And to me, that meant he'd lost his edge. Even through the pain I sensed that he knew this. So he threatened the next phase and "something worse." But what could possibly be worse?

"That is an easy question to answer My Dear. Watching your beautiful daughter Sammie, suffer the same fate."

And true to its word, the beast somehow caused the pain to dull – slightly- while at the same time, I was arrested in midair – where I was incapacitated in front of four jar like structures. Only they were human sized.

"And your MAN... Enoch is it? His children? And what about the Same girls... oh yes, their suffering shall be delightful."

War of the mind.

The words reverberated through me even as each person that the Beast spoke of appeared in each jar like structure. My Baby. Sammie!!!

I would rather have had my heart ripped from me than to see what I saw – invisible hands ripping at this image of my child. And a part of me recognized this truth; that it was just an image... but my heart didn't know the difference.

"He kill them wi' their love. Wi' their love fo' each other. That's how it is, every day, all over the world."

Sammmiiieeeeee!!!!! My soul screamed louder, even with Ana's sing song voice trying to override it.

"He used to say, 'it's all mental son. You can't be telling yourself what you see... you gotta rehearse in your mind what you WANT to see. And if you WANT to see that shot going in – you gotta see it

*and SAY it to yourself, one step at a time.' That's how I got through
the pain Cee... and that's how you have to do it. You gotta look to
everything you know about God, everything you've been taught..."*

At that thought I opened my eyes. And, instead of screaming at
what I saw... I quietly spoke what was real, what was true. Sammie
was safe. All of them were. I had no reason to worry. And I spoke
this over and over as I felt my focus dim. Because while I saw what
was before me, I didn't see it. I saw what I knew to be true.

Suddenly, peace. I have never experienced anything like it. It was
like God had shut out the noise, just for a second so that I could
hear. Everything dulled... the Beast, the sounds of screaming from
my tortured loved ones... even my own inner screams... all quiet.
And Danny's words.

While Danny's doppelganger was right before me, screaming in pain
and horror as scorpions and snakes bit stung and scoured him... His
words spoken to me in hushed tones echoed through my mind.

I alone had the power to govern what I wanted to see. The beast
could not take that away from me. It was a gift. From God... He
made me an "imager" just like Him. And because we were created
in HIS image, I too had the power to "IMAGE" what stood before
me... to see what I wanted to see – more importantly – what I
NEEDED to see. God had taught me that a long time ago. And it
had been a long time since I'd done it. But before I watched my
baby being ripped to shreds in front of me, I'd been more than
willing to give it a try... I'd had to succeed.

I don't remember saying the words per se. Because to me I couldn't
breathe, let alone speak. All I remembered was KNOWING them. I
didn't just understand and bear the knowledge I'd read in a book
somewhere about what I was saying. I KNEW it. With everything
that was me – knew them to be safe.

I didn't have to believe it. Because what I said was a PART of me.
And no sooner could I say to my arm, you don't exist, would it
disappear – in the same way, no matter what went on in front of

me (it was so NOT true) nothing it said or I said could make it true. Because the TRUTH was that ingrained... while I'd read that "the truth shall make you free," someone once told me that, it's the truth YOU KNOW that sets you free.

And they were right on the money. So on the money that I cried in relief as each image before me (though barely there by now) faded into nothing. It had to. It didn't exist.

Nor did the still, airless quality of the atmosphere. I knew that because suddenly I could also breathe. And just like I could breathe, I could move.

And just like I could move, I could thumb my nose at the beast that was, as I thought that, frowning so ferociously at me that I would have been more afraid if I had any sense. But I didn't thumb my nose. Because I didn't need to. I had just found out that he was on MY turf. In MY mind. And while I wanted to channel an old cartoon, He-Man, I once saw on cartoon network and say – I HAVE THE POWERRRRR... I didn't have to. Because I knew it. And I knew that the beast knew it.

Which meant that it was about to go down!

Chapter Thirty-One

Sam

I had just finished my weapons check. I was now simultaneously strapping the throwing knives to my arm while holstering one of my side arms when I felt it.

I knew she was behind me but I didn't care. I didn't care because she'd withheld on me. I didn't care because Celine was in trouble. I also didn't care because I had nothing good to say to her. And because nothing else needed to be said. So I kept strapping on my weapons before grabbing the brass for my fists and the leather gloves that gave me grip.

The rest of the team was already on stand-by. To me, it was more than luck that had them still hanging around. Minute had decided that she wanted to move her practice close. St. Louis University Hospital had an opening that they were dying for her to fill. And since she'd wanted to stay awhile to monitor the kids and the effects of the implant, she was seriously considering that. Which meant she hadn't headed home to New York just yet. And because she was staying, so was Boogie. A pain in my butt before, his unrequited crush was now a happy circumstance since it meant I had more men at the ready. Macchio was content to hang as long as I needed him, though I sensed that something was going on with him and Balboa. Max didn't kiss and tell. And I didn't bother asking. Whatever it was, it was their business; at least, it was until I filleted her for not coming clean. Nina u-turned from wherever-the-hell I had no idea, heading back this way when I called her this morning after I couldn't reach Celine. And Matt was hanging. But Not like Max... we weren't that tight. In fact, I had no idea why Matt was hanging. I just knew he was. And that was fine by me, especially now.

"We roll out in ten."

That would put our arrival at RLS at about midnight. And I had a feeling that this time extraction wouldn't run as smoothly. Because I'd dismissed the intel that John had supplied initially once Minute had verified where the kids were held. Intel about the caves and caverns that ran under RLS... the caves that exited nearby – at Piasa Park. I had a feeling our op was going subterranean in a way that we were not prepared for. But as I heard the click of the chambered round into my sidearm I felt that cold click inside of me resonate.   And that click pretty much said it all. My woman was coming home. That wasn't a promise either... it was just plain truth.

***

Danny

"Gram, what's the prayer of agreement mean?"

It was past dinner time and getting late. I'd helped Gram clean up the dishes. I complained that it was Cassie's turn but that was just to hide the fact that I liked helping Gram out. Something I'd always done as a kid, whether at the table stirring something or at the sink washing, it was just Gram and me time.   J had always made me feel bad about that so I hid it by complaining whenever he was around. And wouldn't you know it, he'd been around. Which sorta gave me the creeps ever since I'd gotten to Grams. I hadn't forgotten his role in all this. I couldn't help but breathe a sigh of relief when I heard him telling grandpa that he was going out to hang with friends.

What was weird was, I think Gram knew something was up with me and J. But she never said anything.

"It's when two or more people get together and pray about something. You know, now that you ask me, I used to wonder why you needed two or more people to ask for something from God. I guess, if you think about it – he's always been partial to people overcoming their own self interest to work together as a team."

Funny. "So does that mean that God was the first Coach like, ever?"

Gram chuckled. I loved her laugh too. Because it wasn't one of those old lady titter kind of laughs. It was a real, in her belly, kind of laugh. Her eyes sparkled with it and her shoulders shook. It was obvious that when she laughed, she *laughed*. Like I said, another trait for the future Mrs. Daniel Sampson.

"I guess so. I mean, think about it. He sent the apostles out in twos. He created marriage and blessed the sanction of it by giving them a wedding gift – the power to subdue and have dominion over the whole earth... and He always called Himself the God of generations... He wasn't just the God of Abraham. He was the God of Abraham, Isaac AND Jacob. So that right there lets you know that he was all about numbers – the more the merrier I'd say."

I thought on that a minute. Because it hadn't been just Ana in that place. It had been Robert, Me and Ana. That was three.

That meant something. I just didn't know what. After asking Gram to make me a list of everything that came in "threes" in the bible that she could think of, I sat and thought more about this agreement stuff. It wasn't like I was familiar with that term. While I'd gone to bible study I wasn't necessarily a regular church attendee... It just wouldn't leave me alone though. Because in a way it didn't make sense. God was supposed to hear ALL prayer right? The fact that prayer, particularly this type of prayer, was stuck in my brain like baseball stats should have worried me. But I was too confused to be worried.

"So say if I prayed for someone right now to win and you agreed with me. God will hear it?"

"God always hears you baby boy. But look at it like this. If you say Gram, I'm hungry... is it time for dinner? I might tell you to wait a minute because no one else is hungry. I will still feed you... it just might take a minute. But if you and all of your cousins were bugging me about fixing sandwiches because you were all hungry, I might decide to get on that a little sooner. Does that make sense?"

I thought on that too. It made sense. But God knew everything right? Wouldn't He know that we were all going to be hungry and have it all ready when we needed it?

"And if you were thinking God should know that already and have it ready when you are all hungry, my answer would be, where's the fun in that? If you didn't help me out in the kitchen, when would we have our time to talk? If you didn't have to ask for anything, when would you appreciate my giving it? Or sometimes, having it after not having it? And when would I feel like I was doing something special for my grand-children if they never asked. How would we appreciate each other? And sometimes baby boy, there may be a delay, even when I know you need it. Because to appreciate the good, sometimes we have to know what bad feels like."

And now I'm getting tired of thinking. Which was okay since my cell phone rang with perfect timing.

"You got Dan." I saw Gram smirk at my greeting as she slid her list of threes my way. Her smirking made me smile on the inside because I liked making her smile. And my sounding just like Granddad and Dad when I answered my phone always made her smile.

"It's Rob, man." *Uh oh.*

"What's up? You alright?"

It got quiet. And quiet was something my boy Rob was not well acquainted with... he was the talker in our friendship. He asked all the questions and had all of the charisma. So his quiet threw me off. I honestly don't remember a time in EVER when that happened. I opened my mouth to tell him to speak up or hang up when I heard him say real quiet...

"That little girl Ana just called me."

Uh. Okay...

"Yeah?"

"And um. Yeah. Okay man. She's on the line, I conferenced her in."

"Dude!" I squeaked....

"DANIEL WILLIAM SAMPSON!"

Pulling the phone away from my ear I rolled my eyes up into my head so far I could swear I saw my medulla oblongata. It was either that or my groan of horror that sent Gram into another fit of chuckles. And I wasn't sure if I should sit there and enjoy the fact that I just made her laugh again or ask her to pray the prayer of agreement that my phone suddenly died despite the fully charged battery.

***

Celine

And now I knew what it felt like to be Neo from the Matrix. Everything Beast boy (because of course I had to give him a less threatening, humorous name. While he in no way resembled the Teen Titan character that was all kinds of adorable to me, I knew that it yanked his chain) threw at me got fielded and tossed back like so much confetti.

No matter the torture, no matter the visual, no matter his words – for everything he did, I had a comeback. It was like playing tennis with the world's most psychic bully. He could read me like an open book, knew all my fears and my desires. But God's thoughts were bigger than mine and so were His desires. In other words, it was two against one "up in here". And I was all over kicking beast boys behind with the truth as GOD saw it.

I guess that's why I blinked like a gazillion times, almost blinded by the weak fluorescent lights buzzing over me. I was so used to the startling white of wherever I'd been that reality seemed more like a dream as my vision was full of haze and gray shadows. Everything, despite the lights, was shadowed, the air dank with the tangy smell of mold and moisture. I struggled to get my bearings, my attempts at restoring my vision became a challenge. Which means I fought to do so all the more.

Adaptability meant survival. If I learned nothing else during Boogey's weapons and field training, I learned that I had to get a grip and get a grip fast when in unfamiliar territory. Because the seconds it took to do so could be the difference between life and death. And I didn't just fight the world's biggest toddler-slash-bully in my head and win only to come out of it and lose because I couldn't adapt.

I guess I failed at that because what finally swam into focus couldn't possibly be what was actually hanging over me.

It had to be another version of that stupid alternate mental state because why else would the person I liked only slightly less than my ex husband be waving their hand over my face, stage whispering, "Yoo hoo," no less?

Yet as much as I willed the visage to go away, it didn't. It was dawning on me that this just might be real which made my freak-out only slightly less apparent when it continued to speak and confirm what I'd dreaded...

"Hey Mrs. B. Your baby sitters back. I hope you saved my spot."

Really? Was the sing-song voice really necessary?

Uuuugggghhhhh. Brittany. Brittany the gum chewing, rug defiling, all around crappy baby sitter – was standing over me blowing another bubble in her gum and popping it over my face. Since I'd thought she'd gone missing, I had no problem with my next thought – which would have turned that misconception into reality. It would be kind of like turning a frown upside down... only better.

***

Sam

"Radio silence the moment we reach the perimeter. I need two by two formation based on the schematics we discussed. Nobody goes solo. You buddy up and you stay low. Macchio and I will take the north entrance. We go through the building once he's disabled their tech. Balboa, you and K.C. take the south hidden entrance through the exterior building that looks like a shed. Minute and Boogey have already entered through the caves entrance and are waiting on the signal. After that, all radios go dead. First team to Celine, grab her, clear out, set your charges and get to safety. Blow that whole area. That's our signal to make for all exits. Celine is our ONLY mission, do you understand? No one else is extracted. At this point if they are there, they wanna be, got me?"

Silent nods all around. They all recognized the sound of my voice. I was a man that was done.

D-O-N-E. And either they would back my play or they'd be left behind. Having verified that they were all in, I faced forward again and started the ignition. In half a second our surveillance van was on its way to the target.

I felt like a piece of me was missing. There was no cold sleet in my head, raining at me or freezing who I was and locking me up in my mind. There was only a cold assurance. I had no doubts about my team or the fact that they had my back. Irritated at Balboa did not equate disloyalty. We'd all been ticked before. We'd all gotten over it. This would be no different.

It was just going to take a minute. Getting Celine back safe would definitely kick start healing that breach. No other outcome was acceptable.

We were about a hundred yards outside the perimeter when I pulled over and killed the engine. It was go time.

I didn't have to turn around to see that everyone was preparing and on their mark. I heard weapons clicking, being shuffled and secured. When the noise of preparedness died down I raised my right hand and two-finger saluted us into motion. We exited the van and crab ran, staying low and in the shadows, hurrying towards our appointed positions.

Hold on baby. I'm on my way.

I hoped she heard me. Because honestly I didn't know whether to choke her or hug her first when I got to her. Never doubting that I would have the opportunity to do one of those, for the first time I decided not to plan my action – I'd go with the flow. Let go and let God. Funny how that was a lot easier than I thought it would be.

***

Danny

"I know you're a girl Ana. Dude is just an expression."

I tried not to yell it into the phone. But my body language couldn't hide my frustration. My hand was gripped over my eyes as I practiced the deep breathing technique dad taught me to use on the free throw line.

And it wasn't hard to tell that Gram was eavesdropping since she was cracking up in the background.

"DANIEL WILLIAM SAMPSON! DUDE IS NOT ON MY FACE!"

Another deep sigh. And since Rob was laughing so hard he all but busted my ear drum, I figured that this conversation had already gone ninety seconds past my patience. The time counter on my phone was at two minutes. Yeah. Thirty seconds was pushing it. Therefore my mind was set and my finger was inching its way toward the end call light when Ana got to the point.

"WE HAVE TO DO IT. AND DO IT TOGETHER. TWO WOULD WORK. BUT THREE WORKS BETTER."

In the words of Ms. Celine, Oy! We had to get past this Dr. Suess rhyming thing. I don't know what that was all about but if it hadn't been for my earlier thoughts about numbers, agreement and what not, I would have hung up on them and not given it a second thought.

It was at that point that Rob decided to chime in with his Burton Guster from the tv show *Psych* voice.

"Dude. Seriously. I know this is weird but I had this chill walking up my spine right before Ana called me. And don't ask how she got my number. You don't want to know. Because I don't want to know. All I know is I got that creepy back chill, she called and now you're quiet. Which tells me that either you know something about what she's talking about or you're over there catching z's on me. And since you snore and I don't hear that, you know something."

I wasn't ignoring him. I mean, I wanted to answer him. I just couldn't. Because I'd glanced down at Gram's list of threes. Father, Son and Holy Spirit. Faith, Hope and Love. Outer Court, Inner Court and Holiest of Holies. These three agree – the blood, the water and the spirit.

Aw man. I hadn't said it in a while but truer words had never been spoken. *Makes total sense.*

***

Celine

"You miss me?"

I was done blinking. And I was beyond done with the Barbie from purgatory popping bubble yum in my face.

So I'd found the strength to move. Sitting up wasn't hard. But standing up without falling on my face? Yep, that one was a bit more difficult to manage.

But I managed it. So well in fact that I was facing off with my teenaged nemesis (not really, but, you know – if I had a *nemesis*) with my arms crossed, secretly trying to determine if a breeze was hitting my naked butt or not. I was in a hospital gown (which was not cool) in a dank room that looked like I was underground (which was really not cool) attached to an IV with my head wrapped like I was in a world war two battle scene (which was beyond not cool since my hair must have looked jacked!).

My true answer, somewhere along the lines of, "have you lost your freaking mind," got lost in my throat as I noticed the people standing inside the huge curved entrance.

There was that guy who'd come to my place that day to pick up Brittany. Which explained a lot. But he wasn't alone. Delilah stood slightly behind him to the left, her focus on the floor. Those standing off to her right were the reason my throat decided to stop working. I'd somehow expected to encounter the Doll Makers (though their current garb of Indiana Jones like apparel was quite the shocker) what I did not expect to see was Lance the creep with his uber-creepy hands on the shoulders of *MY* Sammie and *MY* Cassie.

The Doll Makers didn't seem to mind that I didn't have any words. Their creepy old guy grins and Lance's little side smirk told me that.

They were glad that I had nothing to say. It meant that I was at a loss. Because dealing with my girls being hurt in my mind was one thing. Seeing that up front and in living color could NOT happen.

"You might want to get dressed and follow us Mrs. B. And can I say that it's so AWESOME to have my old babysitting job back. I totally missed my Sammie girl."

 I swallowed the scream that scratched at my throat and instead, turned to look at the small enclave behind me where Brittany-the-demented had pointed to. There was a small natural shelf there with clothes folded on it. I focused on that and that alone.

Removing the IV (um... *OW!*), I yielded to the autopilot activity that would lead to my getting dressed.

And I refused to think. I refused to dwell on what I just saw. Just because I wasn't in the land of make believe anymore didn't mean that the game (therefore the strategies) had changed. However, even if I'd tried to think about escape, I knew I'd be drawing a blank.

I had not ONE idea of how I was going to get my girls out of there alive. I had no plan B, no exit strategy and no game plan that included keeping them safe. We were trapped.

Staunching the bleeding in my arm from where I'd pulled out the IV, I grabbed the yoga pants and turned with my back again to the wall before putting them on. I secured the ties around my waist up under my gown. Okay. That's done.

I reached for the sports bra and tee shirt then stood straight, cocking an eyebrow at my audience. That's when, as if on cue, I saw everyone turn away (but not leave) to give me some sense of privacy. Which (even though I'd silently demanded it) surprised me seeing as they were sick perverts and all.

My hands moved but held no feeling. I could hear the clothing sliding into place but not feel the semi soft slide of the fabric on my body. Because for the first time, since I'd shown up all bold, brazen and full of attitude in the fake heaven foyer of RLS did I know true, unrelenting fear (sans my Piasa experience).

On bare feet I followed as they led me from the cavern to some unknown place. My head was bowed. My shoulders sagged as my plodding steps echoed off of the cave walls. I tried hard to communicate brokenness and failure with my posture, letting them think that I'd given up. All while praying I wouldn't fail, especially not now.

I had been so sure… but I should have known that they wouldn't keep their word. Because Ana, in her way, had spoken the truth about how evil operated and manipulated others. It kills us with our love. Our love for each other. Every day, all over the world. It uses what we hold dearest against us to try to take our power. By hook or crook, by fright or fight. It's the only way evil can win. Because what else was there, besides our love for each other and God, worth dying for?

Chapter Thirty-Two

Celine

Battle *of the Heart...*

"Oh look at you. So whipped. So subjugated. I think I'm in love."

A maniacal gleam danced in Lance's eyes, eyes that were still too small and way too far apart. If I hadn't been shivering with numbness and cold (which I assumed were signs of shock…. Yeah, I watched way too many cop shows) I might have been offended by that last part. However I'd made it a practice of not being offended by idiots. And that first part was dead on what I wanted them to believe. That I *was* whipped. That I *was* subjugated.

I knew that he was prodding me for a reaction. Any reaction. Because that was the kind of sicko that he was. He wanted his prey to go down fighting. And I didn't have enough in me to give him that kind of satisfaction. But I had to find something in me to somehow get my girls out of here.

One glance out of the corner of my eye at Sammie's shaking, terrified frame held in Cassie's arms was all I needed to commit to that action. Because Cassie stood tall. She was freaked all the way out, true. I could see sparks of fear flashing in her eyes. But she stood tall anyway. She was her father's daughter, definitely a fighter. And like Enoch and Danny, she would go down fighting. But not today. This one was on me.

Because I had the tools to do this. God didn't bring me this far only to leave me hanging.

I knew this because I'd heard it. I'd ignored it for a second when terror had spread and tried to take over. But those words were planted in me. No way would they die, not the words OR the song.

This was the battle of the heart. But I was MADE to be courageous...

"I bet you have so many questions Ms. Baltimore. Why don't we dispense with that part of tonight's activities so we can get on to the more entertaining events we have planned shall we? Go on, don't be shy."

I buried my scorn along with the smart aleck response I wanted to give the Doll Maker, whichever one that had just spoken. I didn't remember which one was which. But I did know – that on a different day, in a different time, I would have been howling at their outfits. Their creepy Indiana Jones get up with wide brimmed hats, khaki scarves, khaki shirts AND khaki shorts made my inner clown grab his red nose and shoes, ready to put on a show. But since I did have a question and lives were at stake... I cleared my throat instead of laughing (or crying) and spoke my mind.

"How long have I been here?" I croaked the words. But the question was relevant. Because it had taken those kids weeks to recover from their surgeries. Not days... weeks.

"Only a bit over 48 hours." Doll Maker number one responded with a little hop and clap. It was like talking to the world's oldest, creepiest kid EVER.

"Then how...?"

"Are you up and moving? Cogitating? Speaking complete sentences? Oh please Ms. Baltimore, if you're going to infringe upon our precious time with questions the least that you could do is make them difficult. You have been implanted with the upgrade my dear. A much simpler process with an implant no larger than this," At those words he held up what looked like a small wire with a circular bulb on the end no bigger that a tear drop. He then twirled the wire between his finger and thumb as he continued, "A remarkable process really. No cranial surgery needed. The implanted is simply transferred to the subject through the naval cavity. After which it follows its programming, navigating to the brain stem where it attaches itself and upon command, " a snap of his fingers brought out several little wires that had been attached to the larger (but still small) wire. The little wires waved back and forth and *GOOD GLORY THIS CRAP WAS IN MY HEAD AS WE SPOKE!*

"and voila! That's it. Minimal recovery time, costly surgical procedures eliminated... the perfect little slave maker. Fantastic yes?"

My mouth opened and closed. A couple of times. But I shook my head to clear the terrible image away. I couldn't let the horror of the creepiest mechanical silver fish known to man derail me. I had to get my girls out of here. So it was time to figure out why they were here at all. But before all of that I had to ask because I really couldn't resist...

"Then why am I wearing a head wrap? Did you push me off of the table after the procedure or something?"

Everyone, well, all of the certifiably insane and evil people anyway, chuckled at that. Which tee'd me off! I didn't have time for their games. And from the looks of people moving equipment around us as if they were packing up and rolling things out, we didn't have much time at all.

While I waited for an answer to my sensible and, to me, simple question, I took a moment to unravel the head wrap and get a bead on my surroundings.

They'd brought us to a wide open space within the caverns. The floors had been sanded smooth somehow to almost resemble concrete. The size of the wide open space was as large as two basketball courts situated side by side. Above the space you could see little enclave-like arches where it was obvious smaller caves and caverns funneled into this larger one. There were hewn paths that had poles with halogen lights attached somehow embedded in the stone all around us.

Having checked out the surroundings, I could see why Heckle and Jeckle –or was it Jeckle and Hyde – dressed the way they did. Didn't mean that they weren't idiots, though. I wasn't sure which set of insults best fit since both references were really dated – one being an old cartoon that my grandma used to watch and the other a scary book. Either way, the moniker "Doll Makers" was too refined a term for them. These guys were clowns. And they belonged in a looney bin, not at the top of the food chain running one of the top technology corporations in the world.

Realizing that they still hadn't answered my question I immediately shelved those thoughts and assessed my situation as I'd been taught. The guy that had partnered with my ex-baby sitter had attempted to move stealthily behind me; something I quickly positioned to prevent. Circling backward and angling off while subconsciously dropping into a defense stance I held my ground.

So what was this about? It really had been a simple question. That said...

"So is this how you answer a simple question before we move on? Because I'd hate to see what you creeps do when I get to the more challenging ones."

The Doll Makers had wound down from their little chuckle fit and, from the looks of their expressions (that being their narrowed eyes and chins going up a notch) they no longer found me so amusing.

Interesting. *Let's play poke the bear.*

"Lance? No response? You can't possibly tell me that my simple question stumped *you*? You're the big man on campus right? The one who's running things behind the scenes?" I chanced a quick glance and a wink his way before focusing again on the college boy and grinned before I taunted, "Or are Heckle and Jeckle over there pulling your strings too?"

Yeah. I went with the dated references. I figured since those two were as old as Methuselah, they'd get that. The indignant humphs and foot stomps I heard plus the scrawny arms I saw crossing over their chests — synchronized no less (all of which I'd caught out of the corner of my eye) — told me that I *was* not wrong.

College boy decided to use that moment to make his move. He lunged. It was a good thing that his strategy was probably to incapacitate verses to damage because this kid was built. Even so, I was fast. Throwing my head-rag in his face, I made my move; with him stumbling past me as I sidestepped him, I grabbed hold of his left arm and gave it a twist. It was an elementary move. But it worked nonetheless, sending him flying.

The easiest thing for a woman to do against an attacker is to use their own force against them. And had he been a mugger or rapist, I would have had exactly the time I needed to get away after executing such a move. But he wasn't. And I had nowhere to go. So I angled off instead while putting some distance between us. Speed was my asset, but strength was his. Meaning, I couldn't allow him to get those huge mitts he called hands near me.

Which I'm sure he wanted to do since after he'd slammed into the cavern wall and crumpled to the ground, he'd jumped back up with a lip curl and a curse. I could see the intent to rush me in the way his eyes narrowed. He bent forward like a bull about to charge. I could almost see the smoke rising from his nostrils. But the command, "HOLD," stopped him.

And that's when weird took a left turn into insanity town. Because at that word, his entire body locked, despite his momentum. I could see him struggle and not gain the slightest inch. The fear, strain and anxiety in his eyes as his body refused his own will was both incredible and devastating to watch. He was like a pit bull, caught in mid lunge by an unbreakable chain. Again, it was his eyes that told the story. In his eyes I saw the anger give way to resignation then acceptance. I could literally see the fight go out of

him. And I wasn't sure what was worse at the moment. Being me...
or being him.

"A little demonstration of what we are capable of. And of your
future."

Lance had crossed his arms and smirked, mimicking the stance of
the Doll Makers. And while he gloated – and from the looks of that
kid he had every reason to gloat – something was still off. Because
they *still* hadn't answered my question.

"So will my future include oh... I don't know... possibly an answer to
a fairly simple question? Which I notice you are STILL avoiding?"

I tried my hardest to dial down the "tude". But Lance irked me like
nobody's business.   And when I got irked I either got goofy or
mouthy. Guess which one I felt this crack pot deserved.

Arrogance does not hide anger well. This truth was proven fact
because Lance-of-the-hot-temper tribe went from calm to vibrating
with menace in point five seconds flat.

And then I blinked. He'd moved. I know it was just a blink but in that
half of a millisecond, Lance went from standing yards away and
scowling at me like I'd kicked all of his dogs and his neighbors, to
being right in my face. As in IN MY FACE –so close that I could count
the fillings in his teeth.

But I didn't have time to be freaked, shocked or impressed. Quick
on the draw with my tongue, I wasn't quick enough. Because before
I could shape words to even come close to what I wanted to say, he
got there first.

With his lip raised on one side in a sneer he leaned forward until he
was speaking directly into my right ear and whispered, "So you
think you can take me little girl? Because I recall the last time you
tried, you failed." His hot breath on me was enough to tee me off.
That little reminder? Oh, this was about to get nasty...

Moving, I'm sure, quicker than he expected, I brought my right elbow up executing a perfect blow to his chin with a quick follow up of grabbing his head and slamming him into my knee (by this I mean slamming my knee into his chin, hitting it *again*... because it was ugly... and I hated it) only to finish with a spinning back fist.

And during all of that, I realized that something was different. I was a little stronger than before. Well, actually a lot stronger. Because the back fist would have been just powerful enough to turn his head, possibly even stagger someone his size if I'd put all of my weight behind it. But I'd felt the inside of his jaw cave. And heard at least three of his teeth crack. And I'd felt and heard all of this as if it were in playback mode in slow motion. Which couldn't have been possible. Except when he straightened up after staggering a bit I watched him spit out one... two ... three teeth.

And then he grinned a bloody, evil grin at me. Because I'd just given him the fight he apparently wanted. Oy Freaking Vey!!!

***

Sam

My eyes bugged right out of my head at Macchio. Because I knew that my baby was good. She had been working hard to become so. She was driven and she was committed. What I did NOT know was that she was that strong. Pride and something else I didn't care to name gripped my insides, at least until I happened to catch the glare on that guy.

And saw the reason why my girl started backing up. Because he was excited... in more ways than one. Therefore the disgusted look my girl gave him, her nose curled like she smelled rotten eggs? Definitely warranted. Which put him on the top of my hit list. Especially since I owed him from that last time.

Disabling the tech and finding our way down hadn't been difficult. Most of the floors, including the main floor had been empty. These people were cleaning house and preparing for an evacuation *STAT*.

So no one checked for I.D. when we picked up boxes and followed a couple of guys down to storage. Knocking them unconscious and dragging them behind the crates had taken no time at all.

We'd followed the specs that lead us in a zig zag pattern using a series of elevators into the caverns. While we hadn't run into our other two teams yet, we knew that they were here because this place was the center of an entire network of caves. What I didn't get is the lack of security. It was like they didn't expect us to come at all… like they expected us to just lie down and take whatever kicks and punches they doled out, not even trying to get in our own in return. And I was okay with all of that.

Macchio's chin lifted to my left directed my attention to the other side of the cavern. I glanced that way hurriedly wanting to keep my eye on the prize, but instinct forced my attention back for a second look. A second look that registered what the first one had refused to believe. My girls. Both of them. Standing, hugged close and terrified. That Delilah chick was apparently their guard. But she wasn't paying much attention to them at the moment, busy watching Celine back away from a stalking Lance. I didn't have time to analyze the expression on her face because we had to rewrite our exit strategy and quick. None of my girls were getting left behind. End of story.

***

Danny

"Dude. Did you see that? Did that just happen?"

I spun in a circle, more than a little freaked at the white surrounding me. I hadn't seen anything like this since that night at RLS where I'd faced off against the Piasa. And why I was all of sudden there, I had no clue.

"Yeah man, that absolutely just happened." I mumbled.

"Whoah man! Who's the hottie?"

Okay. Only Rob could scope out a hottie in what I considered my own personal hades. But since I *am* a dude, I could not ignore the presence of an unconfirmed hottie, so I owed it to myself to cast a cursory glance in the direction that he was pointing toward. And my jaw dropped.

Because that was definitely a hottie walking toward us. But it was something familiar about her... something that made it feel almost wrong to call her that. It was those eyes. I knew those eyes...

"Hey guys."

Gorgeous with blond hair hanging down to her waist in curly waves, her blue eyes sparkled and shimmered with obvious amusement. Not the mocking kind though... more like, I don't know... I couldn't put my finger on it. It was like a well of happiness was locked up within her, threatening to spill over.

Her voice was music though. It had a cadence to it, almost like Cass when she's softly trying out different rhythms on her bongos. I'd never heard that voice before, but at the same time I had. I knew this girl. I just couldn't put my finger on exactly how I knew her.

Rob had muttered the same "hey" in response as me and looked just as uncomfortable as I did. And since Mr. Magic-with-words had obviously run out of them, it was me who had to ask the uncomfortable questions. No point in delaying it so...

"Uh. Who are you?" Not eloquent, I know. Meh. Not beating myself up about it either.

"Come on guys, it's me!"

Rob looked at me and I looked at Rob. We both had our hands in our pockets and stood the exact same way. He shook his head from side to side. And I did the same. So, on to question number two...

"and by 'it's me' you mean?"

She laughed another one of those cadence type laughs before tilting her head to the side. Recognition nibbled at the corner of my mind. I knew that head tilt. I'd seen it before and... Oh no... uh uh...

"No. No way."

"Yeah. Yeah way."

Did she have to laughingly say everything she said?

"Ana?"

"That's me!"

Robs jaw dropped like mine did earlier. Because there were several reasons why ALL of this was impossible. Such as: Ana was a whole country away in Washington – as in the STATE of Washington, Rob was just over the river but I'm pretty sure he wasn't currently standing in my bedroom pranking me with white space and a blond I'd never met, and there was absolutely nothing around us – no houses, no rooms, no grass, no trees... nothing. All of that meaning I was giving myself permission for a full on freak out; when Ana decided to cut that short.

"We have to get to work guys. There isn't much time."

Which meant we had no time to ask the important questions like, why do you look like a 20 year old model and why aren't you yelling every word like normal. Rob had finally found his voice because I heard him asking, "Much time for what? What's going on and how did we get here?"

It was instant. I now know what folks mean when they say something happened "in an instant". Because as quick as Rob asked it, we had all of the answers. Frea-Ky. One minute I was wondering how we ended up back here and then I knew everything. Because this wasn't the same place I'd faced off against Piasa. It was white... but it wasn't false. And for some reason that fact seemed really important. But that wasn't all...

I knew that Celine had the implant. The upgrade. I knew that my cousin Jeff or as we call him J, who'd gotten me implanted in the first place had somehow convinced Cass to leave with him by pretending that he was meeting up with dad. Once he had Cass, it had been easy for him to get to Sammie. Having stolen the girls right out of their grandparents' homes, my own blood – Jeff AND Britt (who was also a cousin) had taken them both into that place.

I knew three things after that. First, that I had never known such rage in my life because Jeff and Britt were family – but they'd turned their backs on us, handing our girls over like so much trash. Second, that the questions I thought were important like how did we get here and how much time have we been here, were irrelevant. And last, that if I ever saw Jeff and Britt again, they would deal with a part of me that they would NOT like.

But I shelved all of that because little Ana was right. There wasn't much time. And I was here... WE were here... because we had a job to do.

Chapter Thirty-Three

Celine

Brittany and the college guy along with Lance formed a triad around me. Which creeped me out since for some reason I'd always hated triangles. I don't know if it was the three sides or the three corners thing. All I knew was, not a fan. I was a circle girl all the way.

I kept Lance at my front after quickly assessing that he was the greater threat. I assumed that because he had physical control via voice command of the other two (I figured this was a safe assumption since he'd controlled the jock earlier. And also because Brittany had bubble yum for brains so yeah, not a feat of strength to control *that*). Keeping him at an angle, I kept watch on the other two using my peripheral vision. A more confident fighter would have attacked first. But I had to think strategy. Balboa would strangle me if I didn't. And if I were Balboa, I'd feel them out, judge their strengths and weaknesses all while preserving my own strength since Lance would be most likely trying to get me to face off with them to tire me out before finishing me off.

If my focus had not been mostly directed at him, I would have almost missed the eye flick and head motion directed toward Brittany. Finally. Something I could work with.

She came at me with an attempt to put me in a headlock. Amateur. A step back, twist of her body, snap kick to her calf causing her knee to buckle, I wrapped my hand in her hair for two quick power punches to the face. She was out like a light. I dropped her quickly and took a step back. I'd accomplished my first goal which was to thin the herd. One down. Two to go.

Had I had a moment to be freaked I would have taken it when I heard Lance's jaw bone snapping back into place. A quick glance at his mouth affirmed that guess. But I didn't have time to consider what that meant because college boy had decided enough was enough. And it didn't look like Lance would be intervening this time around.

I saw the lunge coming and was ready. What I was not ready for was the body of a guy, a guy I knew in detail etched on my brain, flying between us to intercept him. I wanted to watch what I heard happening, the punching, the body shots and grunts of two men going at it no holds barred, but I couldn't.

Because Lance cackled the creepiest laugh like, EVER before he moved in quicker than I anticipated. It was like watching a Vampire on steroids, the guy was that fast...

Battle of the hand...

And with that song again, playing in my head, I knew... just KNEW that I was just as fast as he was. So while chaos, explosions and shouting sounded all around me, I was still somehow able to slow him down in my mind and see his punch coming at me in slow motion.

Which was when I realized why they didn't answer my question. Like Danny and Ana, I'd resisted the programming in the software. So I must have hemorrhaged from my ears or nose (most likely ears because my head was wrapped). Which explained so much.

One major detail that had fascinated Minute about the kids was that those who'd resisted the programming had developed faster. Grown quicker, stronger... more powerful. The possibilities were limitless because the implant gave them access to parts of their brain that they'd never used before.

And now I had an implant... the upgrade... but free of all their controls.

All of which to make my stand. They'd wanted to make me their slave. But instead they'd made me a weapon for God.

It was SO on.

Moving right before Lance's fist connected, I landed a punch of my own. I no longer had to think and strategize the combinations, they just came to me. And blow after blow, kick after kick, I dealt out damage. Damage that he deserved.

For all of the pain he'd caused. For all of the families he'd harmed. For all of the people he'd hurt. I landed blow after blow after blow. My fists were moving so fast, nothing could be seen but blurs until Lance lie before me unmoving.

So I stood there, after all of that, shaking with relief.

Then I turned.

I turned to let the person that had been standing there watching for a good long while do what he'd been waiting to do. I was so proud of him for not interfering. It had been my fight, my battle. I knew that, in the future, he would probably fight other battles for me. He was a man's man and that was what men's men did. But today he'd let me have mine to myself and stood back, watching me and God kick serious butt.

However the true victory was feeling him wrap his arms around me and hold me tight. I didn't have to see him to know it was him. I could smell him. I could feel him on the slight breeze in the cavern. I didn't hesitate to wrap my arms around the man that was holding me. It felt good to give him my weight; to lean into the chest of the man that always, always, ALWAYS had my back.

So I didn't hesitate one second to say what I had to say.

"Love you honey. I knew you had my six."

I didn't complain about the squeeze that nearly forced the breath out of me. I was tired. I was bruised and I had been through a war of the mind, battle of the heart and a battle of the hand, all in one night. Directly after a medical procedure that caused massive hemorrhaging. But I didn't complain. Because he gave me the words right back. Well, in his way anyway.

"And I love you baby. I'll always have your six. Which is probably the only reason I'm not choking you out right now."

Me being me, I giggled. And I snorted, but only twice. Which was all I managed to get out before I was pulled back so fast I was dizzy, then kissed within an inch my life.

And that was cool. I was so okay with that. My little editor was too, nodding his head as he smiled big and wide for me. Apparently he'd been on vacation or something and was back now that the trouble had passed. Which was totally fine. Because burrowing into the chest and arms of my man just before both of my girls grabbed hold of us, I was content in this perfect, beautiful truth: I could love without fear of losing. Which meant I could let go. And let God. So I did.

***

6 months 3 weeks later

Danny

"So did you decide? We sign the letters tomorrow man."

Laying back in my bed, passing the basketball from hand to hand I searched for the best way to answer Rob's question.

He was my boy. We had been through a lot. But I wasn't sure we were supposed to keep doing everything together as a team.

Over the last 6 months of our senior year we'd won trophies, conferences and divisions together. Gone to church together. Prayed together. Took our girls to the prom together. And now, we were deciding on our respective basketball scholarship acceptance... together.

St. Louis University was calling his name. And I knew why too. Because Amanda Same would be in the vicinity, having committed to the Mass Communications program at UMSL - the University of Missouri in St. Louis, after her senior year. I knew this because he'd already broken it off with his now ex-girl, Michelle Farmer. She was a sweet girl. But that was it. The truth was, she had no depth. My boy had been to the mouth of the beast and back. Michelle had barely left her front yard. She was sweet but Rob could not do sweet long term. He needed edge. He craved it. His near stalking of my cousin Nina was my first clue. His desire to follow Balboa around like a lost puppy was my second. So it didn't surprise me when we found out via Ana in what we now called "the white room" that Mandy was heading back in our direction after she graduated. Rob had been committed to that path ever since. And I wished him the best with it.

But that didn't mean it was mine. For some reason I was really feeling Mizzou. I didn't know why since their basketball program had been subpar lately. But something was calling me to Columbia, Missouri. And that call was getting harder to resist, despite my temptation to stay with what I knew.

"Come on man. You can't be seriously thinking about Mizzou?"

Rob had been grumbling a lot lately. So his grumble just now? Not shocking.

I grunted my answer because what was the point? This was what I hated about that stupid implant. It made us all closer than close. We could almost read each other's minds, we were that close. Me, Ana, Rob and a few of what we now termed "the kids" could somehow have a "meeting of the minds" in the white room, no matter where we were or what we were doing in the world. All while going about our business outside of our heads, like our bodies were on autopilot or something.

I learned this from Gram the night of the Big Bang. We called it that because Dad and Cee had blown RLS sky high. After beating the crud out of, like, everybody. Balboa gave us the highlights when she got back. I hated that we'd missed it.

But we'd done our part. We discovered a lot of things in the white room that night. Like how we were linked somehow. Not like witches and that power of three mumbo jumbo. But like, we were free there. Free from our own doubts and fears... there it was like we were actually how we were meant to be. And God was there, right in the midst. We were His and He was ours. And that, through Him and the power of Christ that dwelt in us, literally anything was possible; including the complete and utter shutdown of all emergency systems at the exact moment that RLS went up in flames. Initially there had been no police response and no emergency response whatsoever. Our people had gotten away clean and there was absolutely no record of who'd been at the site. By that I mean no record and no witnesses. Even to this day, it was like our families were shielded somehow. Realistically, we knew that these people were major players. Major players that had all types of power and surveillance at their back. From what Cee had mentioned about them knowing everything about everybody, there was no doubt that they'd try to find us. That they wouldn't be letting this go. We'd even heard rumors from the old neighborhood about men in suits asking around about us. But we were not to be touched. God just wouldn't allow it.

And so basically, with the quieting of all doubt, fears, anger and eventually, un-forgiveness – in this place we'd come into closer contact with God and his presence.

It was indescribable. So we didn't bother to describe it to people. We just did our thing.

In the meantime, I'd learned a few things like how to let things go. Which was actually something I needed since Jeff lives with Gram now, working and helping Dad with construction. While I'm glad that Macchio and Doc did their thing on his implant, he was still family... A part of me had still wanted a piece of him. Even though Dad and I knew in the beginning that he wasn't right in the head. Which was why, after Dad had beat him into the ground at RLS, he hadn't mentioned it since. It didn't changed the fact that I'd wanted to bust his kneecaps for putting my sisters in danger. Knowing that helped me let it go later... much later.

And Britt? Gone. The team had managed to extract everyone out of there, including Jeff – except Britt. One minute she'd been unconscious and the next minute she was gone. Of course, that might have had something to do with those really old dudes that disappeared too. Dad had freaked when he'd found out they'd gotten away with all of that crap. That's when Cee pointed out that the police and military were in these dudes pockets. No point in trying to have them investigated when that would only result in wasted time and energy. From my time in the white room I knew she'd been right.

Like I'd mentioned, those old dudes were major players, in cahoots with some serious evil. Not only that, they had the same types of set up all over the world. The more people they got to take the implant, the closer they felt they were to reaching their goal – subjugation of the masses. But they hadn't counted on something important. God always reserved a remnant unto Himself. No matter how evil times get – God still got this. Which meant that we spent a lot of time in the white room recruiting minds that wanted to be free of the controls. And we were good at it.

So we were confident that we were safe for now – one big weird and happy family. While Doc, Macchio and Balboa had stuck around, Boogey and KC had headed home.

I guess what shocked me the most is that, KC had taken that Delilah lady with him when he'd left. I had absolutely no clue why he'd done that. And since the white room gave no answers on it, I asked no questions. There were some things I just didn't need to know.

Rolling over I grabbed the remote. Rob was pouting. He wanted me at SLU with him in a big way. But I was satisfied for now with my choice. Who knows what would happen there? I just might even meet the future Mrs. Danny Sampson there. Because Dad and Cee's wedding had been all kinds of awesome. Which is how I pictured mine would be one day.

It would be outside, just like theirs had been, maybe even close by at Hawk Point. And all of our family would be there too. Except my future wife didn't have a sister (also known as the matron of honor) like Cee's. Cee, all by herself was goofy as all get out but still cute with it. You throw that sister of hers, Mrs. Maggie in the mix and hello nuclear explosion. They laughed so hard they'd nearly fallen in the punch bowl! What could women possibly find drop down, roll on the ground funny about a punch bowl?

Since all of the mayhem had died down, I'd tweaked my list of traits belonging to my future bride loads of times. So much so, I was pretty sure about the type of woman I was looking for. So she shouldn't be too difficult to find. The final trait was going to be the deciding factor though– because whoever she was, she had to have a high threshold for crazy–if she couldn't handle the white room or my relationship with God, she couldn't handle me. And that, to me, made total sense.

Epilogue...

Amanda paged through Anabella's diary, the part she'd considered "her section," again, searching for more clues.

Because she needed answers. Anabella had gone to sleep a pre-teen that first night they'd arrived in Seattle and awoken with a visage more mature than Amanda.

Not only that, but her behavior had started changing, her voice fluctuating from loud and sing-songy like it always had been to soft and melodious, and back again.

Amanda had tried asking Ana about these sudden changes, but Ana would just nod and smile, revealing nothing.

Yet Amanda had refused to let it go. She was the older sister. And despite how Ana had matured physically, it was her job to take care of them. Her grandma, her little sister and her Mom's future depended on her.

Amanda re-read the dog-eared page again knowing somehow that it was written just for her.

In the gateway where there is no key
In the midst of the Scot you will find ME
Your journey isn't your own, it is mine to chart
He will meet you there while I heal your heart
The soundwaves seduce, the lies openly hide
The voice of this evil and your call will collide
In time, daughter Moses, your draw, your voice
Will interrupt the lies and give my
Children a choice.

Go back little one, retrieve what was lost
With your call comes great burden, it comes

at high cost.
But your bearer needs you, do not leave her
in the dark.
To help her and your sisters you must be
pure in heart.

Seek me. In the place of Joy and 9's
I wait for you to know me, to truly be mine.
Together we shall expose them and
Make plain their lies, give their victims
hope
Against their *Waivering Eyes.*

Right away she'd known three things after reading that passage. That it was a message to her, that God wanted her back in the Midwest and that she had to go back for her Mom.

Unfortunately that's where her clarity had ended. And she was getting desperate.

Having finished school early she'd graduated in a hurry, ready to return and retrieve her mom. But two weeks ago, right when she was about to leave, her grandmother had fallen ill with the flu. A flu that was still going strong. And at her grandmother's age that was a dangerous thing.

Amanda had prayed. She'd cried. She'd tried friends and family of her grandparents, hoping to find someone that would help out. But in the end, she knew what she'd always known. She had to stay. They were all her responsibility, her grandpa having passed away months ago.

So, though it had grated, she'd enrolled into the community college in downtown Seattle to start on her General Education courses.

She'd applied for and gotten a job at the Elementary School nearby helping out with the before and after care program. But she still wasn't ready to give up on what she knew to be true: that she was going back home to Alton.

"It's not time yet, he's not ready."

Amanda tried to hide the fact that Ana had just scared the heck out of her but she wasn't very successful at it. Having jumped at least a foot out of her chair, she heard the diary she'd dropped clunk to the floor. Clearly her assumption that Ana was napping on the couch had been wrong.

Ana's grin indicated that the little sneak knew what she'd done. But Amanda was too busy trying to slow her rapidly beating heart to dwell on that. In fact she was more interested in what Ana had been saying.

"Who's not ready?" Yeah, her voice was a little shaky but that didn't matter near as much as Ana's answer.

Ana giggled.

Amanda raised an eyebrow and crossed her arms over her chest. Ana probably couldn't see her tapping foot, but it didn't take that to recognize this as Amanda's signature, "Big sister pulling rank," pose.

Which never worked by the way. Hence Ana's giggling transformation into outright laughter.

Amanda started popping her knuckles, one by one, after that.

Ana hated that. The utterly DESPISED type of hate, hated that.

So she wasn't surprised at what came next.

"SISSY!"

Amanda grinned. Because it was good to be the big sister. The perks just kept coming.

Ana rolled her eyes and pouted like Amanda had just kicked her puppy... a puppy she didn't have and never would have, not as long as Amanda had anything to say about it. Because her little sister was so full of love, she'd love a pet to death, literally. However it was time to get to the bottom of what Ana had been about to say.

Because one thing about her sister, she ALWAYS had something interesting to say.

"Spit it out squirt."

Ana's frown gave way to a huge grin, nearly blinding Amanda with the beauty of it. Her little sis was flat out breath taking. And the thought of leaving her suddenly scared Amanda more than her fifth grade bully, Jimmy had. Just the thought of him broke her out in hives ever since the day he'd broken her nose. She was almost grateful when Ana's next words yanked her train of thought off of the tracks on memory lane and onto the present.

"You're going on a Cruise."

What the what?

"Ana..."

"SHHHHH! DON'T INTERRUPT!"

Amanda choked back her laughter, hoping the cough covered it sufficiently. Ana wasn't trying to be funny so laughing would really hurt her feelings. But the big eyes, pointing finger and yelling... something about all of that AND her little sister got to Amanda every time. All she could do at this point was clench her fists and hold desperately to some semblance of control. She couldn't stop her eyes from tearing up from that effort, but she would try.

"So sorry," Amanda choked out after calming a bit, "please continue."

Ana nodded her head regally, apparently pleased that her big sister recognized the gravity of the moment.

"You are going on a cruise. Where houses and clothes and pretty things you'll see. But that ship can't sail, the cruise isn't quite ready. Four is the number of seasons that pass. So you need to get ready and take a class: Motorcycles, guns and martial arts. Those are some classes you need to start. Change your name. Go back to your roots. And don't forget Rocky, this tale is her tale too."

Amanda cleared her throat after the silence stretched into the realm of uncomfortable. She searched hard for something to say but could find no words.

Instead, she bent to grab the journal and quickly paged to a clean one near the end. She didn't know what most of that meant. But she knew it was for her, which was all she needed to know for now.

Amanda had learned from past experience to record these tiny limericks. Some helped people they knew, some spoke on world events but rarely had one been directed at her precisely... not like this.

Despite the mumbo jumbo, Amanda jotted it using her amazing talent of eidetic recall. It wasn't something she'd always known how to do. It was a skill that had steadily grown within her after that horrible night.

And writing it down brought even more clarity. Because in all of that confusing mess of a message, there was one truth that stood out.

Her journey wasn't hers alone. But Balboa's as well.

Pulling up the contact list on her phone, Amanda shot out a quick text message to Cassie about Balboa.

She wasn't surprised when Cass texted back that Balboa was consulting with Emerson Electric and Boeing, having relocated her firm from Miami to St. Louis.

It had been easy to put two and two together. Celine had loved movies and sometimes they'd watched them during sessions. One of them had been the movie Rocky. The fighter's name had been Rocky Balboa.

Dropping her phone on the desk next to Ana's diary, Amanda walked across the room to the rainy view before her. She didn't have any idea how long she'd stood there, only that light had become much darker and her head was starting to hurt.

But in that time she'd considered every angle and every outcome. Until only one choice stood out, so obvious and in your face that had it been a snake it would have bit her.

Walking back to her desk, Amanda powered her laptop back up and typed in the web address of her community college. Paging right to the continuing education section, she clicked on the link that would take her to the class, Motorcycle Riding for Beginners.

Because apparently she had four seasons to plan, to plot and to prepare. It looked like *Waivering Eyes* were awaiting her arrival in St. Louis. And it'd be a shame to make them wait any longer than they had to.

Acknowledgments

There are so many people that deserve to be acknowledged for their support in bringing the vision of Waivering Minds to pass.

While Jesus Christ was my Rock, my rod AND my staff (as in He used them ON me… frequently heh) my daughter Micante' James, my bestie Denise Johnson, my prior boss Debra Carter, and my Beta readers all pitched in to keep me going, keep me confident and most of all, to keep me from going off of the deep end!

And then there are those who just supported me in this wicked game called life – like the parents of my Middle School Girls Basketball Team – particularly the Callihans, the Lancasters and the Gombases… writing up a storm during the heart of basketball season isn't a walk in the park, but thank you for taking on some of the load.

And then there are my parents. Cloyd and Eunice Evans. Without you there would be no book. Without you there would be no me. And I guess that pretty much says it all now doesn't it?

Thank you all for being there. Especially you, Jay. Amazing how God turns things around for our good, isn't it?

More than anything, I give thanks, honor and glory to my God in the name of my Lord and Savior, Jesus Christ – the Messiah, King of Kings and Lord of Lords…. Because without you I could have all of this and more, and none of it would matter.

About the Author

Chantay James, winner of the Praize writing contest in 2005 published her very first novel and has been writing ever since. A jack of many trades - all centering around educating and assisting children - she has also served in many areas of ministry. Combining her passions of serving Christ and writing, Chantay strives to help others and to be a voice and influence to any and all that can use the encouragement to be all that they were intended to be. A devoted mother of one, she lives in St. Louis, Missouri, coaches Middle School Basketball and loves a good romance, a good laugh... and cartoons.

Made in the USA
Monee, IL
17 March 2022